DELIRIOUS

QUANTUM SERIES, BOOK 6

MARIE FORCE

D1598706

Delirious
Quantum Series, Book 6
By: Marie Force
Published by HTJB, Inc.
Copyright 2017. HTJB, Inc.
Cover Design by Ashley Lopez
Layout: E-book Formatting Fairies
ISBN: 978-1946136237

The Quantum Series

Book 1: Virtuous *(Flynn & Natalie)*
Book 2: Valorous *(Flynn & Natalie)*
Book 3: Victorious *(Flynn & Natalie)*
Book 4: Rapturous *(Addie & Hayden)*
Book 5: Ravenous *(Jasper & Ellie)*
Book 6: Delirious *(Kristian & Aileen)*
Book 7: Outrageous *(Emmett & Leah)*
Book 8: Famous *(Marlowe & Sebastian)*

CHAPTER 1

Kristian

I counted the days. I can't remember the last time I was so excited for something to happen that I counted the fucking days. I did that leading up to today, the day Aileen and her kids, Logan and Maddie, officially move to LA. I first met them in January when they came for Flynn and Natalie's wedding. Before Natalie's life blew up after she got together with Flynn, she was Logan's teacher. Aileen was sick with breast cancer then, and Natalie was a good friend to her and her kids.

The first time I saw Aileen at the wedding, she was painfully thin with deep, dark circles under her eyes and the shortest hair I'd ever seen on a woman. I found out later that was because she'd lost her hair during chemo, and it had started to grow back. I remember wondering about the odd haircut and then feeling guilty when I found out why her hair was so short.

But the signs of her illness aren't what I remember most about my friend's wedding day. No, it was Aileen's joyfulness that stood out. I'd never met a woman who had such incandescent light about her, even during what had to be some of the darkest and most difficult days of her life. She was, even in the throes of illness, so beautifully *alive*.

I was drawn to her like the proverbial moth to flame, and like a moth that doesn't know enough not to fly directly into the heat, I was unable to resist talking to her, getting to know her and nurturing an immediate and unprecedented attraction. The heat of that attraction swallowed me whole, and I was powerless to walk away. I let the attraction grow and flourish into friendship over subsequent visits, including the one in which I helped to convince her that she and the kids ought to move from New York to LA to live near us. Hayden offered her a job at Quantum, and we all encouraged her to take the leap.

And then I counted the fucking days.

So, what am I doing sitting on the floor of the game room closet in my Hollywood penthouse apartment, ignoring one call after another from my business partners, who are also my closest friends and the only family I've ever had? They want to know where I am, if I'm all right and why I'm out of touch on a day we've all been looking forward to.

We have plans. Flynn and Nat are picking up Aileen and the kids at LAX while the rest of us—Jasper, Ellie, Hayden, Addie, Leah, Emmett, Marlowe, Sebastian and I are supposed to be waiting for them at the house Ellie used to call home in Venice Beach. Since she's moved in with Jasper, Ellie is renting the house to Aileen. I'm sure the others are already there as the airport contingent is due home within the hour. Everyone is excited for them to get here.

We have surprises waiting for them. Two days ago, Natalie, Marlowe, Addie and Leah accepted the shipment from the company that moved Aileen's stuff from New York. Flynn, Hayden and I spent an entire evening putting beds together while the women unpacked their kitchen stuff. Aileen thinks she has all that to contend with when she arrives, but when they walk into the house today, their things will be waiting for them along with a black Audi sedan in the driveway.

I check my watch to confirm the car is being delivered right about now. The car will be in the company's name, but I bought it for her. I knew she'd never accept such an extravagant gift unless I billed it as a company car. I'm not sure why I felt the need to do such a thing, but I was at the dealership finalizing the purchase when it occurred to me that buying her a car might be too much too soon. By then it was too late to take it back, and besides, I didn't want to. She needs a car, so I got her one.

Natalie stocked the kitchen with groceries and filled the house with vases full of Aileen's favorite white hydrangeas.

Imagining her reaction to everything we've done has me yearning for something I simply have no right to. If she is an angel sent straight from heaven, I'm the devil himself in comparison.

I grew up mostly on the streets in the meanest part of Los Angeles, clawed my way into the film business, catching a couple of lucky breaks that brought me to where I am today. I'm one of Hollywood's most influential and powerful producers, a partner in the Quantum Production Company with some of the biggest names in the business. I'm on top of the world—literally—in my penthouse apartment right in the heart of Hollywood, which is suddenly trendy again.

Despite my many successes, despite the Oscar and Golden Globe that sit on a shelf in my office at work, and despite the fortune I've accumulated through hard work and determination, I'm still the homeless, rootless boy I once was. Crippled by fear, I'm sitting in the corner of a closet, ignoring calls and texts from the people closest to me and telling myself it's the right thing to do.

I'm a piece of shit compared to her. The things I've done to survive and thrive in this harsh world would horrify her. I'm wealthy beyond my wildest dreams—and I had some fairly wild dreams as a kid running the wicked streets of LA—but all the money in the world can't scrub the darkness from my soul.

I shudder in revulsion when I think about the things I did to stay alive. I don't believe in regrets as a matter of principle. You can't change the past, so why waste the present with regrets, or at least that's always been my philosophy. But for the first time in my life, I wallow in a vast sea of regret. I wish I were someone different so I'd be good enough for a beautiful, unspoiled angel like her. Bile stings my throat, bringing tears to my eyes. I have to stay away from her and her precious children, even if everything inside me calls out for her, wishing I could let her fix what's wrong with me, wishing she could be the one to chase away the darkness and fill me with her light.

She's finally here. I could see her *right now*. All I've got to do is get up off the fucking floor, get in the car and point it toward Venice Beach. Everyone I care about is there. They're looking for me, wondering where I am.

Moaning, I drop my head into my hands and rock back and forth as my phone rings again.

I can't. I just can't.

Aileen

I've never been this excited about anything, except my babies, who are now nine and five and out of their minds with excitement. I couldn't believe it when Flynn insisted on sending the Quantum jet to pick us up.

The Flynn Godfrey, who is now my *friend*. I still can't believe that!

Even though he's now happily married to one of my best friends, I have the biggest celebrity crush on him. I've seen every movie he's ever been in at least five times. I've watched *Camouflage* a dozen or more times. He won the Oscar and every other major acting award for that film this year, and having met and spent time with him, I know firsthand that he's as good of a person as he is an actor.

I'll never forget the first day Natalie brought him to my apartment. That was last winter when I was so frightfully ill and fearful of what was going to become of me and my children. Then Flynn made a humongous donation to the fund that the kids' school started for us, alleviating so many of my worries. Then he went a step further, hiring a housekeeper and nanny to help me with the kids. He single-handedly saved my life in every possible way, especially by getting me in to see the top breast cancer doctor in the city, who took over my care and made a few tweaks to my treatment program. Within weeks,

I was feeling better than I had in a miserable year of surgery, chemo and radiation.

I'm not out of the woods yet. It'll be years before I can consider myself "cured," but I'm doing much better than I was, and I have Flynn to thank for that, too.

The entire Quantum team has become like family to the kids and me during our trips to LA for Flynn and Nat's wedding and later for school vacation. They took us in and made us part of their tribe, and when they teasingly suggested we relocate, the kids begged me to do it. They love California and the people we've come to know there. With nothing much holding us in New York, they prevailed, and I agreed to the move, but only after they finished the school year.

School ended yesterday, and today we're on the Quantum jet about to land in Los Angeles, our new home. If there's one person among our new friends I'm looking forward to seeing more than anyone else, well, that's my little secret.

I don't know what you'd call the flirtation or whatever it is between Kristian and me, but it's *something*, and I can't wait to find out if it might turn into something *more*. It's been years since I've dated anyone or been interested in a man, and I've never been attracted to anyone the way I am to him. He makes me feel so special by listening to every word I say like they're the most important words he's ever heard. The last time we were in LA, when we all stayed at his place in the city to avoid the reporters who'd swarmed around a scandal in Jasper's family, Kristian and I sat on his patio and talked until four in the morning while everyone else was asleep.

With wavy dark hair, intense cobalt-blue eyes and sexy dimples that appear only when he's truly happy or amused, he's so gorgeous that I often find myself staring at him like a lovesick puppy.

I'm *dying* to see him again, to find out if the attraction is still there and to see what might come of it. I'll never admit that he was one of the primary reasons I wanted to move here, but I'd be lying if I tried to deny it.

"How much longer, Mom?" Logan's question interrupts my delightful thoughts of Kristian Bowen.

I check the time on my phone. "About twenty minutes."

The kids are so excited to see our new home, to get settled and to spend the summer in LA. I'm starting my job at Quantum in two weeks, part-time for the summer while the kids attend camp and then full-time when they go back to school. I can't believe I'm going to work for the company that produced *Camouflage* and counts among its partners Flynn Godfrey, Hayden Roth and Marlowe Sloane. Talk about being starstruck! And I haven't even mentioned the other two Quantum partners, Jasper Autry and Kristian Bowen.

Kristian Bowen.

His name makes me want to sigh in anticipation, knowing I'm going to see him again *today*. If I were to let out my inner high school girl, I'd be writing his name next to mine on the cocktail napkin the steward gave me with the glass of wine I ordered and then drawing hearts around our names. But I'm not a high school girl. I'm a mature woman of thirty-two with two incredible kids who are my whole world and a brand-new life in a dynamic city to look forward to.

With maybe a brand-new man, too. *God, I hope so.* He's so beautiful and sexy and intense, and I haven't had sex since the dinosaurs were roaming the earth, or at least that's how it seems. The last time was when I was pregnant with Maddie, who just finished kindergarten. There are dry spells and then there's my life, a barren sexless wasteland. I'm ready to get my groove on again, and Kristian Bowen is the one I want.

He's the *only* one I want.

But does he want me like that? Or are we stuck firmly in the dreaded friend zone? Why in the world would a man like him who could have—*literally*—any woman in the world want to be with one who's fighting an ongoing battle with breast cancer while raising two young kids alone? There's baggage and then there's my two-ton trunk, a heavy load for me, let alone a man who can have any woman he wants.

Ugh. Do yourself a big favor, girlfriend, and don't put the proverbial cart in front of the sexy horse. He's apt to run for his life away from you and all your luggage.

Before I can let that depressing thought derail my excitement, a crackling sound comes from the speaker system ahead of the pilot's voice. "Hello from the cockpit, Gifford family."

The kids bounce in their seats, their excitement palpable.

"We've begun our final descent into LAX, and we'll have you on the ground in about ten minutes. We ask you to fasten your seat belts and prepare for arrival. Welcome home, folks."

The pilot's sweet words of welcome bring tears to my eyes. After what I've been through, I'm so grateful for every day and determined to make this move the best thing that's ever happened to my little family. My primary concern is making sure the kids are happy and healthy. They will miss their friends in New York, but they're excited about moving to California, especially Logan, who missed Natalie terribly after she left in the middle of the school year.

A few minutes later, the plane descends through the clouds to reveal the sprawling city of Los Angeles below. "Look, guys." I point to the window. "There it is."

"Move your head," Logan says to his sister. "I want to see, too." She insisted he sit with her, and she allowed him to have the window seat, even though he wanted it for himself. He's so good to Maddie and often stepped up to help with her when I was too sick to care for them. He's far too mature for his nine years, and I hope this move will allow him to be a kid again and not a kid with a sick mother and a little sister who needs him more than she should.

They cheer when the plane touches down with a thud and the roar of the thrusters, which they're used to from our earlier flights to LA.

After taxiing for quite a few minutes, the plane finally comes to a stop.

I supervise the kids, making sure they have everything and ushering them to the door, which opens right onto a tarmac where Natalie waits with her movie star husband, who is now our friend. Pinch me, please. *Flynn Godfrey* is *my friend!* It's taken some practice to get used to saying that sentence, but he's made it easy by being so amazing from the first time I met him. He's done so much to help make this move happen, and I'll never be able to repay him for his astonishing generosity. It's easy to forget just how beautiful they both are until I'm with them, and then it hits me all over again that my lovely, wonderful friend Natalie hit the husband jackpot with her gorgeous, generous husband. They both have dark hair, and while her eyes are green, his are brown. I can't imagine how stunning their future children will be. It'll be unfair to the rest of the average-looking world.

Logan and Maddie run to Natalie, who embraces them both at the same time while Flynn looks on, grinning widely. He and Natalie are so in love that being around them gives me hope for myself. Maybe someday I'll find someone who looks at me the way he looks at her. I'm mildly disappointed to realize that Kristian didn't come to the airport, but then I check myself. *Why* would he come to the airport? I'm Natalie's friend, after all.

Flynn hugs and kisses me. "Welcome to LA."

"Thank you so much for everything. The plane, the movers, all of it."

"Anything for you."

He'll do anything for Natalie—and her friends—and has proven that many times in the months since we met.

They load us and our suitcases into a silver Mercedes SUV, one of sixty cars that Flynn owns. Natalie mentioned that once, and I thought she was kidding until she told me she was dead serious. *Sixty* cars! It boggles the mind. But like he says, he could be addicted to worse things than cars.

On the way to our new home in Venice Beach, Natalie and Flynn point out landmarks and other points of interest, none of it registering with me because all I can think about is whether Kristian will be there when we get to the house. Now that I'm finally here, I want to get to know him better. I want to find out if the attraction that burned so brightly between us is still there or if it will fade now that we're going to see each other more often.

I hope that doesn't happen. I'll be so disappointed. I've allowed my crush on him to get totally out of control, blowing it up in my mind into a romance with epic potential. In reality, he was probably being nice to me because he feels sorry for the single mom with cancer.

I'm appalled by the tears that fill my eyes. I stare out the window at the passing scenery as I try to get myself under control. With everything else I've got to deal with, including a new home, a new job and two kids who've been uprooted from the only life they've ever known, I simply don't have time to obsess about a man.

But then we arrive in Venice Beach and pull up to the bungalow that now belongs to us, thanks to Flynn's sister Ellie. The street is lined with some of the nicest cars I've ever seen, including a black Range Rover, a gray Jaguar, a Porsche and something else I don't recognize, but it looks expensive. I begin to feel hopeful again. Does one of those fancy cars belong to Kristian? I have no idea what he drives, but it's probably something amazing.

In the driveway is a black Audi sedan that looks new. The porch is decked out in balloons, and the yard is full of friends waiting to greet us. My heart pounds with excitement as I take in the familiar faces— Marlowe, Leah, Emmett, Sebastian, Addie, Hayden, Ellie and Jasper.

Everyone is here. Everyone, except Kristian.

CHAPTER 2

Aileen

*M*y friends are simply unbelievable. I start crying the minute I step out of the car, and I don't stop for what feels like an hour as they hug me and the kids, show me what they've already done to make the house our home and present me with keys to the car in the driveway, a company car being made available to me to use as I see fit.

It's too much—and not enough, because Kristian isn't here, and that makes what should be one of the best days of my life a little less than it would've been if he'd been part of it. I want to ask about him, but I don't dare show my hand where he's concerned. If it were just me and Nat, I might ask her, but I can't ask about him with his closest friends and business partners all around me.

Ellie left me the grill on the back deck, and Hayden fires it up to cook burgers under Addie's supervision. We eat on the deck, enjoying the warm Southern California sunshine, sitting on the gorgeous teak furniture that Ellie has also left for me after moving in with Jasper.

"I have palm trees in my backyard," I proclaim during a quiet moment, making them laugh. "Sorry, but it's the little things."

"You have lemon and orange trees, too," Ellie says, pointing them out to me.

"Do you eat the fruit?"

"Absolutely."

"That is *amazing*—and don't laugh at me. I'm still getting used to the fact that I have a yard, let alone trees bearing fruit that I can actually eat."

"It's a big culture shock to move here from New York," Natalie said. "It took me a while to get used to having a yard, too."

"So where's Kris?" Flynn asks the others.

The question has me sitting up straighter, hardly breathing as I wait to hear what they say.

"No fucking clue," Hayden says. "He hasn't been answering calls or texts."

"Do we know he's okay?" Flynn asks, seeming alarmed.

"We assume he is," Hayden says, "until we hear otherwise."

Now I'm worried that something has happened to him. Was he in an accident or... *No, stop.* He's a grown man with a life of his own. Maybe he had other plans.

"It's weird because he said he would be here today," Marlowe says.

Okay, well... What does that mean? Did he think it over and decide he didn't want to be part of my welcoming committee after all? That would totally suck. I feel like a balloon that's been hit by a pin. Deflated.

"I'll track him down later," Jasper says, seeming unconcerned.

From what I've observed in the past, Jasper is Kristian's closest friend. If anyone would know whether we should be worried or where to look for him, it's Jasper.

"He probably left his phone somewhere again," Addie says.

I want to ask if he loses his phone frequently, but again, I can't bring myself to voice the question because I don't feel I have a right to ask about him. I want to know everything about him, and that isn't creepy or anything. Needing a moment to get myself together, I check on the kids, who are running around in their new yard, and stand to begin cleaning the paper plates from the table.

"Let me help," Natalie says, gathering bowls of potato chips and tossed salad and following me inside.

"Do I have you to thank for fully outfitting my kitchen with things like plastic wrap?" I ask her as I use the wrap to cover the bowls.

"I might've had something to do with that."

I can tell I take her by surprise with a tight hug. "You have to be the best friend anyone has ever had. Thank you for all you and Flynn did. I love it all, especially the white hydrangeas."

She hugs me back. "We're so glad you're finally here. I couldn't wait for today."

"What you all have done here... You've made everything so easy for me and the kids."

"We love you," she says, her sweet, simple words moving me to tears.

"I love you, too. All of you. I can't believe I'm hosting a cookout for Flynn Godfrey, Hayden Roth, Marlowe Sloane and their closest friends." I laugh as I wipe tears from my cheeks.

"In a few months, you'll forget they're celebrities, and every time you see them, they'll just be your friends."

"How is this my life now?"

"We have Fluff to thank for all of it," she says, referring to her four-teen-year-old dog, who broke free of her on a walk last winter and ended up biting Flynn. The rest, as they say, became the stuff of Hollywood films when Flynn the movie star fell for Natalie the school teacher.

"Thank goodness for Fluff."

"Leah and I say that every day." Natalie's former New York room-mate has also relocated to LA to work as Marlowe's assistant.

"How is Fluff getting along with Flynn these days?"

"They're BFFs. He calls her his daughter, and she hasn't bitten him in months. I think they've turned the corner."

"That's so cute."

"She's a holy terror, but she's our holy terror."

I glance at the deck, where everyone else is enjoying drinks and the sun. "Could I ask you something?"

"Of course."

"Is it weird that Kristian didn't come today? I sort of thought, you know..." I'm so embarrassed and anxious that my body feels like it's been plugged into a heater.

"That he had a thing for you?"

Her blunt comment makes me even more uncomfortably warm. "I wouldn't go that far."

"Why not? We all saw it. He could barely take his eyes off you from the minute you met at my wedding and every time you've seen each other since."

"I've seen him exactly four times."

"Okay... All four times, he was obviously into you. So where is he today? As far as I know, he was looking forward to you getting here as much as I was."

"Why do you say that?"

"Because he confirmed the date with me—several times. The car in the driveway? He did that. And last weekend, when we were all at Hayden and Addie's, he asked if everyone was planning to be here today to help you get settled."

Hearing he did all that has me more confused than ever. "Maybe he changed his mind. About being interested." I glance at Natalie, feeling oddly vulnerable. "In me."

Natalie shakes her head. "No way. No one changes their mind that quickly. Something must've come up. I'm sure it's nothing. You'll see him soon."

"That would be nice. I've been looking forward to seeing him again."

"I have a good feeling about you two," she says with the big smile we've seen so much of since she fell for Flynn.

"Don't jinx me." The emotions of the day catch up to me all at once, and when I wobble ever so slightly, Natalie notices. I hate that I still haven't completely recovered my mojo after being ill. Among other things, I suffer from lingering fatigue that regularly creeps up on me, taste buds that don't work the way they used to, scars and anxiety over whether the cancer will come back. I've heard that last one lets up somewhat over time, but I still wake in the middle of the night in a cold sweat from the fear of dying and leaving my kids without a mother.

Natalie puts her arm around me and leads me to the sofa I sent from New York. It's old but still in decent shape even after two kids did their best to ruin it. "You need to take it easy, Aileen. You're still recovering."

"I know. We've had lots of excitement today and over the last couple of weeks. I thought the kids would spontaneously combust waiting for today to get here."

"Well, now you're here, and you're going to take it easy. Tomorrow you guys are coming over for lunch and a swim and then staying for the birthday party we're having for Mo."

"Oh. We are?" All I hear in her kind invite is another possible chance to see Kristian. He wouldn't blow off Marlowe's birthday party, would he?

"You are. If you want to, of course."

"We want to. Thanks for the invite." As I smooth a hand over my skirt, which is wrinkled after the long day of travel, I try not to think about how I wore this outfit with Kristian in mind, hoping it'd make me look young and healthy and appealing to him. Despite the wonderful outpouring from our new friends, I feel oddly let down.

"Is everything all right?"

"Yes! This has been such an incredible day." The last thing I want is for Natalie or any of my other new friends to think I'm disappointed after all they did to make us feel so welcome.

"It's okay to admit that you're bummed he's not here."

"Is it?"

"Sure, it is."

"I built it up in my mind to be something it's not. We've only seen each other a few times, talked a little." But those conversations were some of the most meaningful I've had with anyone. I've thought about that night on his balcony so many times over the last few months. That one night made me want to move here so I could live closer to him. Foolish, stupid, *ridiculous*. You'd think someone who's been so totally burned by a man in the past would be so much smarter and at least a tiny bit wary. "I feel silly."

Natalie takes my hand and gives it a squeeze. "Please don't. I'm sure there's a perfectly good explanation for why he didn't come today. We'll figure out what happened and go from there."

"You won't tell him—or Flynn—that I was disappointed, will you?"

"I won't say anything. Don't worry."

Ellie and Jasper come into the living room, smiling and laughing about something. They're so damned cute together, and Ellie's rounding baby bump has her glowing with happiness and excitement.

"I'm taking my baby mama home for her afternoon nap," Jasper announces.

"That's code for he wants to have sex," Ellie adds.

Natalie cracks up laughing. "Funny, Flynn uses that same code."

"Ew," Ellie says. "Don't tell me things like that about my brother. It's gross."

"There is *nothing* gross about it," Natalie assures her.

I cover my ears. "TMI, ladies." In fact, I'm wildly jealous of their obvious love for their partners and can only imagine what it might be like to have sex with guys like Kristian, Flynn, Jasper and Hayden. *Dear God...*

"Forget about TMI in this group," Ellie says. "There's no such thing as too much information."

"That's true," Natalie says.

"In fact," Jasper adds, in his delicious British accent, "we believe the more information, the better."

Natalie pats my leg. "Don't worry. You'll get used to us. Eventually."

Smiling at her, I say, "I remember when you used to be such a nice, sweet first-year elementary school teacher."

She laughs. "That feels like a million years ago."

"She's been thoroughly corrupted," Ellie says. "Listen, if you need anything or have any problems with the house, just give me a call."

She gave me her number weeks ago when she offered to rent her house to me.

I get up to hug her. "I can never thank you enough for this. I know you're giving me a sweet deal on the rent, and I so appreciate it."

"It's not that much of a deal," Ellie says, smiling.

"Yes, it is."

"My lady is very handy with a screwdriver if you need anything," Jasper says.

"Good to know." His sexy accent makes me want to swoon. How can she listen to that all day and get anything else done besides him?

"Darling," he says to Ellie, sliding his arm around her, "can we play the handy-lady game when we get home? You know the one where you wear the tool belt and nothing else?"

Ellie rolls her eyes at him. "Sorry about him." She nudges Jasper to move him in the direction of the door. "Hope you enjoy the house. I love where I live now, but this place…" She shakes her head when her eyes fill. "I loved it, and I hope you do, too."

"I'm sure we will. Thanks again for everything." I still want to pinch myself that the kids and I live within walking distance of an actual beach. We'll be there every day all summer. After glancing at the backyard to make sure the kids are still entertaining themselves, I return to the sofa. "They're adorable together."

"They really are. Flynn said he's never seen her so happy."

I fan my face. "That accent…"

"*Right?* It drives Flynn nuts when I get all swoony around Jasper, but I can't help it!"

"I was just wondering how she gets anything but him done every day."

Natalie loses it laughing. "That's a very good question."

Leah, Marlowe and Addie come in to find us a few minutes later, bringing a bottle of wine and glasses for all of us. We sit around my new living room and talk like old friends for an hour while the guys play horseshoes with the kids in the yard. By the time they all leave, it's after seven, and I have two very sleepy kids on my hands since it's three hours later in New York where we began our day.

The kids are sharing a bedroom, which they've assured me will be fine. For now. But as they get older, they'll want their own space, and we'll have to look for a bigger place to live. We have plenty of time before I'll need to worry about that.

I see them through baths and bedtime stories from the books each of them brought in their backpacks, and I tuck them into bed. Maddie can't believe her bed from New York is now in her room in Los Angeles. I worry that they're too excited to sleep, but when I look in on them fifteen minutes later, they're both out cold.

I go into the kitchen, my gaze drawn to the half bottle of red wine on the counter. Rooting through cabinets, I find the glasses I sent from New York and pour myself a glass of wine, taking it out to the deck to enjoy the warm evening. I sip the wine, grimacing at the metallic taste that's a carryover from chemo.

I hear it'll go away in time, but for now, it makes eating or drinking anything a chore. My doctor in New York has been urging me to start drinking protein shakes because he's concerned about how much weight I've lost. I've never been so bony or fragile, which has made me extremely self-conscious about my appearance for the first time in my life. And my weight isn't the only thing that's different. My stick-straight hair is growing back *curly!* It's the strangest thing. Sometimes when I look in the mirror, I barely recognize myself.

I'm determined to get healthy again this summer, to put on some weight and to lose the sickly looking pallor that has left me with deep dark circles under my eyes and overly prominent cheekbones. Hell, all my bones are overly prominent. The kids and I are going to take full advantage of the beach we can walk to from our new home, and I'm going to lie in the sun without a single worry about wrinkles. When you've battled a deadly disease, you don't worry about stupid things like wrinkles. That said, however, I'll still lather on the sunscreen because I never want to hear the word "cancer" again.

I take another sip of my wine, but the taste is so bad that I put it aside and hope my taste buds will eventually get back to normal. I've read it can take months for that to happen, and sometimes it never happens. That would truly suck, because back in the day before I got sick, I used to love to eat. I loved my cocktails, too.

My thoughts wander again to Kristian. I hope wherever he is, that he's okay. I suppose I shouldn't be surprised that he probably changed his mind about the flirtation or whatever it was with me. Why would he, who could have any woman in the universe, want to take on a skinny, half-bald, single mom who might still succumb to a fatal illness?

I start to laugh, and then I'm crying, tears leaving hot streaks on my cheeks as I try to accept that it's not going to happen with him.

Now I just have to find a way to live with the disappointment.

CHAPTER 3

Kristian

Someone is pounding on the door and ringing the doorbell. I raise my head off the closet floor, where I've apparently fallen asleep. Christ, how long have I been here? The apartment is totally dark now, so it's been hours.

More pounding. More doorbell.

Then someone is yelling for me. "Kris! Where are you?"

Jasper. He's let himself in. What the hell does he want at this hour? Doesn't he have better things to do now that he's engaged to Ellie and expecting a baby?

I drag myself off the floor and take a second to get my bearings after I'm hit with a dizzy spell. When was the last time I ate? Last night? No wonder I'm light-headed.

I head downstairs and turn on a light, my eyes protesting the brightness after so much darkness.

Jasper is standing in my living room. "Where the *hell* have you been all day?" my best friend asks.

"I was here."

"Why haven't you answered your phone or responded to the two thousand texts we sent you? We were worried."

"Oh, sorry. I've been down hard with the flu. I was asleep all day and never heard the phone."

"Aileen was disappointed you weren't there."

His words are like a knife to the gut. The thought of her disappointed because of me is crushing. But better now than later, when her disappointment would be so much more profound. I'm doing the right thing for her, or so I tell myself. It's agonizing to stay away from her, especially knowing she's so close now. "I'm... I'm sorry to hear that, and I was sorry to miss it."

"You sure you're all right?" Jasper eyes me with the kind of insight only a longtime friend would have. "You look weird around the eyes, mate."

"I'm fine." I will be. Eventually. "You've probably got better things to do than check on me. Where's Ellie?"

"In the car. We're on our way home."

"You were in Venice, and you live in Malibu. How is this on the way home?"

"Everyone was worried, Kris."

I feel bad about that. "Apologize for me."

"Will you be at Marlowe's birthday party tomorrow night at Flynn's?"

Oh God. Is that tomorrow? Everyone will be there, and they're sure to invite Aileen and the kids. *Fuck.* "I'll see how I feel."

Jasper gives me an odd look, filled with a million questions. But he only asks one of them. "If something were truly wrong, I hope you know you can talk to me about it. You know that, don't you?"

"Of course." This... This is too personal to share with anyone, even him.

"All right, then. I'll leave you be. Ring me if you need anything."

"I will." I walk him to the door. "Thanks for coming out of your way to check on me."

"No problem."

I appreciate what he's done. I'd do the same for him if the circumstances were reversed. I hate that people were worried and Aileen was disappointed.

And then I'm elated because she was disappointed. That means she wanted to see me as badly as I wanted to see her.

No! You're not elated! You can't have her. The voice inside my head reminds me of the understanding we reached earlier, when I decided to stay home rather than go to her. That voice has directed my entire life, and it's never steered me wrong. I'm counting on it now to lead me through the greatest dilemma I've ever faced.

I should eat something, but the thought of food makes me nauseated. Instead, I go upstairs to the master bedroom and lie down on my bed. Closing my eyes, I allow my mind to wander in Aileen's direction. After all, no one can be hurt if I *think* about her, right? But instead of her sweet, beautiful face, I see the parade of women with whom I've had superficial dealings, most of them sexual, over the years.

In our clubs here and in New York, I've worked out my aggressions on willing subs who allowed me to control their pleasure. I've bound them, controlled them, fucked them in every way a man can fuck a woman. In the past, my dominance has been all about the mind game, exerting my power to bring the ultimate pleasure.

But I've never felt a goddamned thing for any of them. Not one of them has ever stirred me the way Aileen did from the first time I saw her. I've never felt powerless around a woman until she came strolling into my life at Flynn's wedding. I may as well have been standing on a table that she upended, because she knocked me on my ass, and I've been there ever since.

I tell myself I was much better off before I knew she existed in this world. Before that day five months ago now, my life was under my control and everything was fine. Since then, nothing has been the same. Of course, I've heard about love-at-first-sight bullshit happening to other people. I *saw* it happen to Flynn after he met Natalie and went off the deep end over her. Hell, I'm a fucking film producer. I've seen the movies and read the books.

But I didn't honestly believe it was a real thing until it happened to me.

I think about the night a couple of months ago when we were

hunkered down in my apartment, dealing with the threat levied at Jasper and the rest of the Quantum partners. Aileen and her kids were on their way to LA to visit Natalie and Flynn for the kids' school vacation when the shit hit the fan. Natalie brought them here.

Aileen walked into my home, and the second I saw her, it was like someone had sucked all the oxygen from the room, proving that what happened at the wedding wasn't a one-off. No, it was the start of something so far outside my realm of understanding that I'm still trying to wrap my head around it all these months later.

Things like *that* don't happen to people like me. Someone as pure and perfect as Aileen doesn't belong with someone like me.

So, it doesn't matter if meeting her was like grabbing a lightning bolt with my bare hands. It doesn't matter that the hours I spent with her were the best of my entire life. It doesn't matter that I want to do everything I possibly can to make life easier for her and her two adorable kids.

No, the only thing that matters is staying the fuck away from her so she'll have the chance to meet a nice, normal guy who can give her the kind of life she deserves.

There is nothing normal about me.

I can't have her.

Somehow, I have to accept that and move on. Oh, and while I'm doing that, I also have to find a way to see her every fucking day at work and at the frequent gatherings with my friends without losing my fucking mind.

I'm trapped in a hell of my own making with no way out. I've got to get out of here before I lose my mind. I get up, grab my wallet and keys and head for the elevator.

CLUB QUANTUM IS ROCKING. EVER SINCE WE LET IN OUTSIDE MEMBERS, our revenue has skyrocketed. If anyone was surprised to find out the Quantum principals run a BDSM club, we haven't heard about it. People in the lifestyle tend to keep their mouths shut, especially those in our business. Members sign airtight nondisclosure agreements that ensure our privacy and theirs.

Sebastian says something to a guy at the crowded bar. He gets up, nods to me and moves along. Apparently, Seb told him to give his seat to me.

I take his place, sliding onto the barstool and mumbling my thanks to Seb for the Grey Goose and soda he puts in front of me.

"How you doing?" Sebastian asks.

"Good. You?"

"Busy."

"That's how we like it." When my partners started falling like dominoes and stepping away from the club somewhat, I suggested opening it to the public or shutting it down. No sense paying Sebastian and the rest of the staff to run a club that most of us had lost interest in. I'm glad it worked out, because I love coming here. In the fishbowl of Hollywood, I prefer the privacy of our club to the more public options for late-night entertainment.

Despite my high-profile business, I keep a low profile in my personal life and wouldn't have it any other way.

I nurse my drink and try not to dwell on the anxiety stirred up by Aileen's arrival. I came here for a break from that, and I'm determined to find a distraction to get my mind back where it belongs. A distraction such as the young woman who stands a few feet from me, watching the action on the floor, her expression an intriguing combination of curiosity and fear—my favorite qualities in a sub. Her shoulder-length curly blonde hair, big blue eyes, plump lips and curvy, sexy body make for an attractive package. If I have a "type," she's it.

Taking my drink with me, I get up and go over to her. "How's it going?"

My presence seems to startle her. "Umm, fine?"

"You're new."

She nods. "This is my first time here."

"What's your name?"

"Evelyn, but my friends call me Evie."

"Nice to meet you, Evie. I'm Kristian."

"I know who you are," she says, blushing. "Everyone knows who you are."

"That's what I get for having famous friends." Mindful of the million-dollar initiation fee we charge new members to keep the riffraff out, I wonder what she does. "Are you new in town?"

She laughs. "Hardly. I've been here ten years chasing the dream. So far, I've had quite a bit of success with modeling, but the acting career hasn't materialized."

I immediately wonder if she joined the club to gain access to us, but watching her watch the action on the floor, I begin to see that she's here for the right reasons. On the far left-hand stage, a Dom has his sub attached to a St. Andrew's cross. She's facing away from him, and her ass is bright red from the flogger he's been using on her. Two men are tag-teaming a woman on the middle stage. Her ass is plugged, her nipples and clit are clamped and her Doms are driving her wild with feathers.

The stage on the right features two men, one of them on his knees sucking the cock of the other.

"Have you had a tour of the club?" I ask Evie.

"Sebastian said he'd give me one when things die down at the bar."

"I could do it if you don't want to wait for him."

She glances back at the bar where Seb is up to his eyeballs in customers. "Sure, that'd be great."

"Right this way." I lead her through the big room, watching her take in what's happening on the various stages. "We allow everything but intercourse on the main floor." Curious, I ask her, "Have you belonged to other clubs?"

"Yes, but none as nice as this one."

"How long have you been a sub?"

"Always," she says. "But I only understood it for what it is about five years ago."

"Do you have a Dom?"

"Not now. I... I recently ended an unhealthy relationship."

I sense a much bigger story, but I don't ask her about it. I've got enough of my own problems without taking on hers, too. "Do you like to watch?" I ask, even though I already know the answer to my own question.

She nods.

We walk down a dark hallway lined by a series of doors. I gesture to the first door, and she opens it. I follow her into the observation room, where we encounter a scene in progress between a Domme and her sub. He's a big guy, easily six-foot-two or three, muscular and completely at the mercy of the much smaller woman who has him tied to the four-poster bed. She circles the bed, running the leather tip of a crop up his inner thigh.

His cock is so hard, it's purple against the pale skin of his belly.

I press a button on the wall so we can hear him moan. His every muscle is tight and tense as he tries to anticipate what she will do.

With a flip of her wrist, she flicks the crop against his balls.

He screams.

She does it again and again and again as he shrieks. "Don't you dare come. Do you hear me?"

"Y-yes, Mistress," he sobs.

Evie watches the scene, her fingers white from gripping the molding that frames the window.

"Do you like what you see?" I ask her.

She licks her lips. "Yes, Sir."

That word, so fraught with meaning in our community, has me moving closer to her, slipping an arm around her waist to bring her in tight against me.

She leans into me, and we stand like that to watch the scene progress to her sucking his cock while he begs for permission to come.

"Do you like to be bound?" I ask Evie.

"Under the right circumstances."

"Such as?"

"I have to trust my Dom completely. Trust has been an issue for me in the past."

I could easily win her trust and show her how it should be. I could take her to a private room and negotiate an agreement that would leave us both drunk with pleasure. With her leaning into me and expressing tacit interest, all I have to do is suggest it to make it happen. I'm about to say the words when an image of Aileen pops into my head. My arm drops from Evie's waist.

She looks up at me, her brows furrowed with confusion.

Sebastian comes into the room. "Ah, there you are," he says to Evie. "I wondered where you'd escaped to."

She blushes at the sight of Sebastian. He's a big, strapping, muscular dude with dark hair and eyes, sleeve tattoos, pierced ears, scars he doesn't talk about and a ten-inch cock that keeps him in hot demand with the female members of the club. He could have any woman he wants, but he's choosy. I've known him to go months without a woman. He told me once he'd rather wait for someone who does it for him than settle for someone who doesn't. I admire his restraint. I've been much less choosy in my dealings with women.

"Kristian was kind enough to offer to show me around since you were busy at the bar."

"I'll take it from here," Sebastian says to me.

I note the hungry, needy way he looks at Evie and take a step back. "It was nice to meet you, Evie."

"You, too."

I leave the room feeling shaken once again by the realization that Aileen has so totally taken over my body and soul that the thought of touching another woman intimately makes me feel sick. I haven't been able to bring myself to be with anyone else since the day I met her. I've never gone this long without sex. Turning down a willing sub is highly out of character for me and further proof that I've lost what's left of my mind.

I return to the bar, order another drink from the backup bartender covering for Sebastian and down half of it in one big gulp. About two seconds later, I remember I never did eat anything, which is why I'm more than a little drunk after one and a half drinks. "Can you order me a salad with grilled chicken?" I ask the bartender.

"Of course. I'll put it right in."

Out of the corner of my eye, I notice Marlowe coming toward me.

She slides onto the stool next to me and orders a glass of chardonnay. "There you are. You had us worried earlier."

"Sorry about that."

"What's up?"

"Nothing." *Everything.*

"Don't give me that shit, Kristian. I can tell just by looking at you that something's wrong. And where the hell were you today?"

"I was... I..."

Her hand lands on my arm. "Talk to me, Kris," she says gently. "Tell me what's going on."

I take another swallow of my drink, seeking the courage to say it out loud. "Aileen."

"What about her?"

I glance at my friend and partner, someone who has been there for me any time I needed support, encouragement, friendship. As much as I love her and know that she loves me, I can't say the words.

So naturally, she says it for me. "Aw, damn. You're in love with her."

"*What?* No, I'm not in love with her." *Really?* My own conscience calls bullshit. I want to tell my conscience to shut the fuck up and stay out of it.

"Would you even know love if you felt it?"

Marlowe is one of very few people who knows a little about how I grew up. No one knows the full story, and if I have my way, no one ever will. What does it matter to who I am now? Her question about love strikes at the heart of all my insecurities where Aileen is concerned. She's hit the nail squarely on the head. How would I know what true love feels like?

"This," I say gesturing to the club and all it entails, "is my life, my home. Can you see her here?"

"Not really, but I never expected to see Natalie or Addie or Ellie here either." Our partners' significant others have taken on our lifestyle after being introduced to it by the men they love.

"That doesn't mean Aileen will be like them. She's a mom and a cancer survivor. How does one go about sexually dominating a woman like her?" I take another deep gulp of my drink because thinking about sexually dominating her is all it takes to make me hard as concrete. *Motherfucker*.

"You're getting too far ahead of yourself. You haven't even talked to her about anything that truly matters. Perhaps she'll surprise you the same way Natalie surprised Flynn and Addie surprised Hayden and Ellie surprised Jasper. Maybe it'll all be fine."

"It's different with her."

"I understand."

I raise a brow in her direction. Marlowe is notorious for her avoidance of anything that smacks of romance or commitment. "Do you?"

"I've been in love before. I know how it feels and how difficult it can be to reconcile the emotion with the lifestyle."

"I'm *not* in love with her." I'm such a fucking liar.

"So you said, but something has you tied up in knots where she's concerned. Is that why you stayed away today?"

I shrug. I don't want to talk about why I stayed away. Everything about Aileen makes me feel raw and unprotected, the same way I felt after I witnessed my mother's murder. I hate that feeling, and part of me is angry with Aileen for resurrecting emotions I'd sooner live without than revisit.

I signal the bartender for another drink. We have a two-drink limit for members, but I'm not a member. I'm a fucking owner, and I'll have a third one if I want it.

The bartender delivers my drink, and I down half of it in one swallow. Across the bar, I make eye contact with a redhead, who raises her glass to me. Under normal circumstances, that's all it would take to start the ball rolling. I could be engrossed in a scene with her within thirty minutes if I so desire, but I don't desire her. I desire someone else, and the craving need I have for her is making me insane.

"I'm worried about you, Kris," Marlowe says softly. "I don't like seeing you this way."

"I don't like feeling this way. Why do you think I stayed home today?"

"Avoiding it won't make it go away," she says softly.

"Won't it?" I'm the king of avoidance when it suits my purposes.

She shakes her head. "If she's in your heart, you'll take her with you everywhere you go, no matter how far you run."

The truth of Marlowe's statement hits me like a rock to the head. I'm so totally fucked, it's not even funny.

CHAPTER 4

Aileen

The kids are up at four thirty in the morning, which is seven thirty New York time. How long will it take them to adjust to West Coast time, and will I survive waking up this early? Those are the burning questions on my mind as I drag myself out of bed to make coffee.

"What time can we go to the beach?" Maddie asks.

"We hafta wait till the sun comes up, dumbhead," Logan replies.

They're seated at the kitchen table eating cereal and drinking apple juice, like they do every day, only nothing about this day is routine. It's the first day of our new life, and even though it started *way* too early, I'm still excited. "Logan, don't call your sister names. She asked a perfectly reasonable question."

"Sorry," Logan mutters.

"So what time can we go?" Maddie asks, her golden eyes big with wonder and curiosity and excitement. I love seeing her so happy. My kids had to grow up far too fast, plagued with worries about me and what would become of them if anything ever happens to me. Which reminds me I need to talk to Natalie about whether she and Flynn would take them if the worst should happen.

The thought of that conversation takes my breath away. I don't need to think about that today, but I do need to do something about it soon. My friends love my kids and would do anything for them, but it's an awful lot to ask of anyone.

"How about nine?" I say.

"How many hours is that?"

"Four," Logan says.

"That's a *long* time," Maddie says, sounding whiny.

"You guys woke up really early, so we have to kill some time until the rest of the world wakes up, too."

"What does that mean? 'Kill time'?"

"It means find other stuff to do until it's time to go to the beach," Logan says.

"Exactly." I smile at my son, who is too smart for his own good—and mine. The first conversation I ever had with Natalie was about how bright he is. She saw it from the beginning and nurtured him during the months she was his teacher. "We can do some unpacking before we get ready for the beach."

That's met with groans and protests.

"No beach until everyone unpacks at least one box. And, we've been invited to swim at Natalie's house and for Marlowe's birthday party, but we're not going unless everyone has a thirty-minute rest after the beach." *Especially me.*

"I don't wanna unpack," Maddie says.

"It's one box," Logan replies. "Don't be a baby. The sooner we get it done, the sooner we can go to the beach."

"Will you help me with mine?" she asks him.

"Only if you help with mine."

"Let's go. This is gonna be the best day ever. The beach *and* a pool!"

They scamper off, leaving their bowls on the table. Usually I'd call them back to do their own dishes, but I don't want to get in the way of progress. Still smiling at their excitement, I clear their bowls and put them into the dishwasher and then take my coffee outside, where the first streaks of color crisscross the sky. Everything is covered in a thin layer of dew, and when I take a deep breath, I swear I can smell the beach.

That scent takes me back to my childhood summers on the Jersey Shore, to a time when everything seemed possible and life hadn't disappointed me yet. I met the kids' father there the summer after I graduated from college. I haven't thought about him in a long time, but the scent of the beach resurrects powerful memories.

"Mom, Maddie's not helping." Logan's voice interrupts my thoughts, which is just as well. I have too many good things happening in my life to bother revisiting the hard times. I head inside to supervise the unpacking, which keeps us busy for a couple of hours. We have much more space here than we had in our New York apartment, but it's still a challenge to find a place for everything. I reach my limit around the same time they do. "Who's ready to check out the beach?"

"*Me!*" they say in stereo.

While they change into bathing suits, I pack a lunch for us, making sandwiches from the turkey and rolls I find in the fridge. Nat thought of everything, even juice boxes and cookies for the kids. I dig towels out of a box, sand toys from yet another box, and retrieve sunscreen from my suitcase. "Give me one minute to change, and then we can go."

It takes all of five minutes to walk from our house to the beach. We're even closer than I thought, a fact that delights me as much as the kids.

"*It's so close!*" Logan says with a shriek as he runs ahead of me onto the sand, his little sister in hot pursuit.

I speed up so I won't lose track of them, calling out for them to wait for me.

They stop, let me catch up and walk with me to the water's edge. "Sunscreen first."

"Aw, Mom, come on," Logan says. "I want to swim."

"Sunscreen first."

We swim, we build a sandcastle, we eat lunch and then swim again. On the way home, we stop at the playground, where the kids run around with other kids for half an hour before I signal that it's time to go. At home, we use the outdoor shower to rinse off the sand. Both kids are yawning by the time we're back inside, and it doesn't take much convincing to get them to lie down for a short time.

They gave up napping years ago, but the time difference has their internal clocks out of whack. I can't take two ragged kids to Nat's or they'll be melting down by dinnertime, so I hope they'll sleep for a little while. I choke back a yawn as I unpack the beach bag and hang the towels outside to dry. Being here feels like being on vacation, only this is our home now. We can *walk* to the beach!

I go into my room to take a shower, and have I mentioned how much I love having my own bathroom? It's the third best thing about this house, after the proximity to the beach and the yard. Sharing a bathroom with two little kids is no fun, and it's a delight to step into the shower without first having to rid the tub of bath toys. I shower off the sand and sunscreen and wash my hair. If there's anything good about my hair being short and wild, it's that I don't have to spend lots of time tending to it. Nothing I do to it matters, so I let it have its way.

Wrapped up in a light robe, I stretch out on my bed and close my eyes, intending to take a quick twenty-minute nap.

The next time I open my eyes, it's after four o'clock and my cell phone is ringing with a call from Natalie. I can't believe the kids slept for two hours! That hasn't happened during the day in years.

"Hey," I say to Nat. "I'm so sorry. We were up at four thirty and crashed at two. If the invite still stands, we'll be over soon."

"Of course it still stands. We're here, and everyone else is coming for dinner around six. Come whenever you want."

"I might let the kids sleep for a little while longer so they don't melt down later."

"I can't believe they were up at four thirty!"

"That's seven thirty in New York, which is late for them. What can I bring?"

"Absolutely nothing. I have everything, and Marlowe insisted on no gifts."

"All right, then. I'll see you soon."

"You have our address, right?"

"I do."

"Just punch it into the GPS, and call me if you have any trouble finding it."

"I'm sure I'll be fine."

"Just remember, the later it gets, the worse the traffic will be."

"I haven't driven in so long, I've forgotten what it's like to be stuck in traffic."

"You're about to get an unpleasant refresher course. If there's one thing we have plenty of in LA, it's traffic. See you soon!"

I iron a cute dress and apply enough makeup to complement the healthy glow from the sun without appearing to have tried too hard, which is a fine line. I manage to cover the dark circles without looking like I'm overly made up. My heart beats fast and steady at the thought of seeing Kristian.

"Please let him be there," I whisper to my reflection in the mirror —as if she can somehow make it happen. "*Please.* I just want to see him. That'll be enough for now."

I smooth on scented lotion that makes my skin soft and shimmery and top off my look with lip gloss that makes me feel young and fresh and healthy. I'm none of those things, but you'd never know it to look at me. Satisfied with my appearance, I wake the kids and pack yet another bag with swimsuits and towels. Good thing I bought them several new suits before we left New York.

Armed with snacks and juice boxes and in good moods after their rest, the kids lead the way to the car.

"Mom," Logan says. "Check it out. There's a booster seat for Maddie already in the car."

I realize I hadn't even thought of that since it's been so long since we needed them living in the city. "Someone thought of everything."

"Probably Natalie," he says. "She's super nice that way."

I'd planned for the kids to call everyone Miss and Mister, but that was swiftly vetoed by our new friends who insisted the kids call them by their first names. Oh well, I tried, and as a single mom, I've learned to choose my battles. This is one I can't win with everyone else working against me.

The car is incredible! Sleek and gorgeous, I can't believe it's mine. However, the GPS is complicated, and it takes me a minute to enter Nat's address into my phone. I pull out of the driveway and drive like an old lady until I get a feel for the car.

"It's so fun here, Mommy," Maddie says. "We can go to the beach any time we want, and the playground and Natalie's house."

"Yes, baby, we can. It's going to be a lot of fun. But we have to work hard, too."

"Not in the summer we don't."

"You still have to do your summer worksheets, and Logan has to read."

"That's what July is for," Logan declares.

We talk about what we see on our way to Natalie and Flynn's home in the Hollywood Hills—fancy cars and palm trees and art deco buildings and signs. They're interested in everything about our new home, and their interest fuels mine. We pass a dance studio not far from our house that I make note of for the fall. Maddie took dance in New York, and I want her to be able to continue here. I want to try to get them both into a few activities this summer so they'll meet some new friends before school starts. I need to find a new pediatrician and dentist for them, register them for school and finalize the plans for their summer camps.

My to-do list is long, but like Logan said, I don't have to worry about any of that today.

I make a couple of wrong turns in the Hills and discover that when the GPS says, "Turn," it means *right now*. I pull up to the gate outside Natalie and Flynn's home around five thirty and press the button on the security panel.

"Hello?" Natalie says.

"It's Aileen."

"Come on in!" She buzzes me in, and the gates swing open. I drive in and park next to the usual group of drool-worthy cars. Mine looks rather nice next to them, if I do say so myself. Before the kids can bound out of the car, I stop them.

"Please remember your manners, and follow the rules in the pool."

"We know," Logan says impatiently. "No screaming, no running and no swimming unless an adult is with us. Can we go now?"

"Go ahead," I say, amused by him. It's not for nothing that I refer to him as my Little Man. He's been the man of our family since before Maddie was born. He barely remembers his father, which I tell myself is a good thing. But it won't be long before I'll have to answer tough questions that I know he has but hasn't articulated yet.

I'm retrieving the beach bag from the trunk when another car pulls into the driveway. Turning to see who it is, I lock eyes with Kristian, driving a silver sports car that roars when he accelerates into the spot next to mine.

As I wait for him to get out of the car, I can't move or breathe. I break out in goose bumps from head to toe, my body reduced to one big nerve ending on full alert.

He unfolds himself from the low-slung car, and when he stands, I recall how much taller than me he is. He's easily six-two or three. His hair has gotten long since I last saw him, and when he props a pair of aviators on his head, I can see that his eyes are every bit as blue as I recall. His jaw is covered in a light stubble, and he's wearing a T-shirt with swim trunks. Right away, I notice he seems troubled.

For a long, charged moment, we stand there and stare at each other. He doesn't say anything and neither do I. But so much is said without words. It's still there. The crazy attraction that's had so much of my attention since I met him in January is still alive and well and arcing between us now like a fully charged live wire.

The kids. I should go to them, but Natalie is there, and she'll watch them for a minute.

Finally, after what seems like an hour has passed when surely it's only been a minute or two, I clear my throat and force myself to look directly at him, which isn't all that different from looking directly into the sun. "It's nice to see you."

"You, too. Are you all settled in?"

"Not quite, but we're getting there."

What was once so easy and effortless between us is now awkward and stilted. I feel like I've lost something I never really had.

"Could I carry that for you?" He gestures to the beach bag that sits at my feet.

"Oh, um, sure. Thanks."

As he reaches for the bag, I do, too, and my hand brushes against his, sending a charge of electricity through my body. That's all it takes to make my nipples tighten and my sex clench with need. *Dear God.*

His sharp intake of air tells me the brief contact had a similar effect on him.

I know I shouldn't, but I have to ask. "Is everything all right, Kristian?"

He stares at me for another long moment, his expression unreadable. "Everything is fine. Come on, let's go in." Grabbing the bag, he waits for me to close the trunk of my car and gestures for me to go ahead of him into Flynn and Natalie's house. He said everything is fine, but it isn't. It's not fine at all.

I only wish I knew why.

Kristian

Seeing her again is like a punch to the gut delivered by a baseball bat. She looks *so* good. Her blonde hair has gotten longer since I last saw her, and she's gotten some sun that gives her a sweet, healthy glow. She looks at me with big brown eyes full of wonder. What is it about her that makes me want to wrap my arms around her and protect her always? I've never in my life had that kind of reaction to anyone, and I have no idea how to handle it.

I forced myself to come to Mo's party, knowing Aileen and the kids would be here. I couldn't disappoint one of my best friends. And after spending all day answering questions about where I was yesterday, I can either show my face or have everyone speculating about what the hell is wrong with me.

I don't want them speculating, so here I am.

As I follow Aileen into the house, it takes everything I have not to grab her hand and spin her around so I can kiss her senseless, the way I've wanted to since the first time I ever saw her. I want to kiss her and hold her and protect her—and her children. The only people I've ever felt protective toward in my life are my business partners, so feeling this way about a woman I barely know has upended my entire world.

I resist the urge to grab, spin and kiss. I'm reeling. I don't know what to do or say or how to act, and I always know what to do and say and how to act. This isn't me. I'm never out of control or uncertain, and I hate feeling this way. But I can't make it stop, and I'm not sure I want it to.

When we walk into the kitchen, Natalie hugs Aileen. "You found it!"

"I made a few wrong turns, but I figured it out."

Even her fucking *voice* turns me on, husky and sexy and sprinkled with infectious amusement that makes me want to lean in closer so I won't miss a word she says.

"Now that you know how to find us, you can come over all the time."

Flynn's wife is a doll. I'll admit to having had concerns about how fast they got together as well as his insistence on marrying her without a prenup only a few weeks after they met. But you can't be around them for long and not see that they're the real deal. I'm so happy for my friend, who deserves every good thing this world has to offer. He'd do anything for me, and the feeling is entirely mutual.

Flynn and his father are the reason for my extraordinary career. His dad gave me my first major break years ago and set me on a path toward a life that never would've happened without his guidance and influence. Max Godfrey is the closest thing to a father I've ever had, and there is literally nothing I wouldn't do for him—or his son.

That's one of many reasons I need to rein in this insanity with Aileen. She's the close friend of Flynn's wife, which puts her firmly under the protection of the Godfrey family. For me, that means hands off. I keep my hands to myself, but my eyes... They're drawn to her every move. I watch as she goes out to the pool deck to check on her kids, who are playing in the pool with Flynn's nephews, under the supervision of Flynn, his brother-in-law Hugh and our partner Hayden Roth.

Her kids are so damned cute. Logan has dark hair and a serious demeanor that tugs at my heart. The poor kid has been through a lot, and it's so nice to see him laughing and having fun. His sister has the same color hair, but hers is curly. She has golden-brown eyes, the cutest dimples and an impish way about her that I find completely irresistible. Maddie doesn't seem to have been as affected by the trauma of her mother's illness, probably because she's too young to understand the possible implications. But Logan... He knows. He watches over his mother and sister like the man of the family that he is, with far more awareness than any child his age should have.

Flynn takes Logan by surprise when he lifts him up high and sends him flying.

For a second, my heart stops as I wonder if Logan swims well enough to be dropped into the deep end of the pool. Then Logan pops up, his face alight with laughter as he swims back to the shallow end, looking for more of the same from Flynn.

I release the breath, reminding myself that the safety of Aileen's children isn't my responsibility.

I wish it was.

I no sooner have the thought than I'm again asking myself *what the fuck* is wrong with me. Whatever it is, I need a drink and I need it now. I head to the bar that's been set up next to the pool and pour myself a vodka and soda—emphasis on the vodka—with a twist of lemon. I prefer whiskey, but I only drink it on vacation when I can get rip-roaring drunk and not have to function the next day.

Mo comes over to say hello and kisses my cheek. "You feeling better?"

"Yeah, I'm good. Happy birthday."

"Thanks." She gives me a look that makes me feel like she can see inside me. "You sure you're okay? You still look a little strange around the eyes."

That's our Marlowe. If she thinks it, she says it, and we wouldn't have her any other way. "I'm fine."

"I'm right here if you need me."

I kiss her cheek. "I know, and that means a lot." Taking my drink, I move to safer territory, joining Jasper, Ellie, Addie, Leah, Emmett and Sebastian at one of the tables next to the pool.

"There he is," Ellie says. "Are you feeling better?"

"I'm all good. Sorry to concern you guys." I tell them what they want to hear, but Jasper looks me over the same way Marlowe did, and I'm sure he sees that I'm anything but fine. But unlike Mo, he won't push the issue. Not now anyway.

I spent most of my life wishing for a family. Now I have one, and for the first time ever, I wish they cared a little less than they do. I want desperately to keep my unusual feelings for Aileen to myself. The thought of sharing them, even with the people I'm closest to, makes me panicky.

Thankfully, the party kicks into high gear with steaks and drinks and cake and laughs, and no one pays much attention to the fact that I'm quieter than usual, less engaged and thoroughly distracted by Aileen.

She catches me staring at her a couple of times, which is embarrassing. But I can't seem to help it. If she's in sight, I want to look at her.

We're sitting around the fire pit after dinner, enjoying the warm evening and the company of our favorite people. Before I had my Quantum family, I'd never loved anyone in my life. But I love them. I love them all so much. I love nights like this when we're all together, Addie on Hayden's lap, Natalie on Flynn's, Ellie on Jasper's, the rest of us happily unencumbered. Wrapped up in a towel, Logan is on his mom's lap, his eyes heavy as he snuggles up to her. And I find myself jealous of a nine-year-old because he has her arms around him.

I'm such a fool.

But then I catch her looking at me, our eyes crashing into each other, attraction arcing between us so fiercely, I can't ignore it, even if I know I should.

Maddie comes out of the house, dragging a towel behind her. She runs toward her mom, and I watch in horror as the towel gets wrapped around her feet, sending her hurtling toward the pool deck.

I'm out of my chair and bolting for her before I'm aware of what I'm doing, but I can't get to her in time to stop disaster.

Time stands still for a second as she crashes down, her forehead taking the brunt of the fall since her hands are wrapped up in the towel. She lets out an unholy scream that gets everyone's attention.

I get to her first and recoil in horror at the sight of blood pouring down her sweet face from an open wound in her forehead. Grabbing the towel, I press it to her head as I wrap my arm around her, trying to keep her still so I can apply pressure to the wound.

Aileen is right there, comforting her injured child, but I can see the wild panic in her eyes at the sight of so much blood.

Maddie is inconsolable.

"Let's get her inside," Flynn says, taking control.

I gather her into my arms and stand to carry her in, my gaze meeting Aileen's. "She's okay. It looks worse than it is." As I say the words, I hope I'm right. I carry the sobbing, screaming child inside to the kitchen where the light is better and we can see that she has a deep gash right at her hairline. "We need to get her to the ER."

"I agree," Flynn says.

Aileen fights a losing battle with her emotions, and tears slide down her cheeks as she wipes blood from her baby's face.

All my protective instincts kick in. "I'll take them."

Natalie produces towels and an ice bag that she forces on Aileen. "Go. We'll keep Logan for the night. Everything is fine."

Aileen nods, but as she takes the items from Natalie, I can see that her hands are shaking violently. She turns to her son. "Will you be okay with Flynn and Nat?"

He nods, his face solemn and his eyes big with shock. "Let me know how she is."

"I will." Aileen kisses her son and goes ahead of me to get the doors as I carry Maddie to the car.

CHAPTER 5

Kristian

We agree that she's better off in her mother's arms for the short trip to the ER than strapped into a car seat. I settle them in the other seat in my car because it's behind hers and moving cars would take time I don't want to waste. Reaching under the dashboard, I shut off the airbag.

As I start the car and head out of the driveway, I realize my hands are shaking, too. I try to remember what's closest to where we are, and then I decide to go straight to Cedars-Sinai because I know how to get there. I drive fast, faster than I should with such precious cargo on board.

Maddie continues to whimper and sob.

Aileen speaks softly to her, offering words of comfort, but I can hear the panic she's trying so hard to keep hidden from her child.

I glance at her, and her gaze connects with mine. Even in the middle of a crisis, I feel the connection to her. I'm forced to tear my eyes off her to focus on the road when I'd much rather look at her.

The hospital is close and I'm driving fast, so we get there in about ten minutes. I pull up to the emergency entrance and run inside, asking for help. A nurse accompanies me to the car.

"Let me take her, honey," I say to Aileen, who hands over her injured child. The front of Aileen's dress is covered with blood, and her face is pale, like it was the first time I met her. I'm as worried about her as I am about Maddie. "Come on," I say to her when I realize she's frozen in place. "Maddie needs you."

That seems to spur her to move, and we hustle inside, following the direction of the nurse, who leads us straight to an exam room. I'm thankful that we won't have to wait hours. I leave them only to move my car to an actual parking space and return in under a minute. I'm running on pure adrenaline.

"What happened?" the nurse asks as she settles Maddie into a bed that makes her seem so tiny.

"She tripped on a towel and fell on a pool deck," I say. "Landed face-first."

"Aww, poor baby." The nurse gives Aileen some medicated wipes so she can clean the blood off Maddie's face. "We need to get her checked in. Can you come with me for a minute?" she asks Aileen.

She glances at me.

"Go ahead. I'll be right here."

She doesn't want to go, but she kisses Maddie's cheek. "I'll be right back. Mr. Kristian will be here with you."

"Don't go, Mommy," Maddie says, sobs hiccupping through her tiny body.

"Is there any way you can check her in right here?" I ask the nurse.

"I'll see what I can do."

She leaves the room, and Aileen sends me a grateful smile. "Thank you."

"Whatever you need. Both of you." *Forever*, I want to add, but this doesn't seem like the right time. I hold back a laugh that would be wildly inappropriate under the circumstances. I'm seriously losing my fucking mind.

Another nurse comes into the cubicle, pushing a mobile computer station. She goes through the steps of checking Maddie into the ER. "Insurance?" she asks.

"We're between plans at the moment," Aileen says, her face flushing with embarrassment that infuriates me.

"I'll pay whatever charges there are," I say.

"That's not necessary," Aileen says. "I can pay for it." She hands over a credit card.

I decide we'll argue about that after the nurse leaves the room. She takes the rest of the information and lets us know the doctor will be in shortly.

"I'll get you enrolled in the Quantum plan on Monday," I tell her when we're alone.

"I don't start for another week."

"I don't care." The words come out harsher than intended. I soften my tone when I say, "You shouldn't be without insurance."

"I'm usually not, but the move and everything... I had a plan in New York that doesn't cover us here."

Now I'm afraid that she thinks I'm criticizing her, but before I can correct that, the doctor comes in to see Maddie. He determines she needs stitches and recommends they be done by a plastic surgeon. "I've paged her, and she'll be here within the hour." He also orders a CT scan to check for a concussion and to make sure she's not bleeding inside.

As new tears leak from the corners of her eyes, Aileen thanks the doctor while continuing to cling to her little girl's hand.

"I'll call Flynn and let them know she's okay," I say when we're alone again.

"That'd be good. Thank you for everything."

I'm standing next to her so it's easy enough to put my arm around her and kiss her forehead. "I didn't do anything."

She looks up at me, her heart in her eyes. "You're here, and that means everything."

Fuck me to hell and back again. When she looks at me like that and says such sweet words, all my resolve to keep my distance disappears like I never had it to begin with. I *want* her. I *burn* for her. I *need* her. I *crave* her. And then she leans her head on my chest, and I'm fucking lost.

I'm supposed to be calling the others, who've got to be worried as they wait to hear from us. But for as long as she wants to lean against me, I'm not letting go.

Aileen

I shouldn't be doing this. I shouldn't be letting him comfort me this way, but I can't seem to get the rest of me to cooperate with the message my brain is sending out. It feels so damned good to be close to him, to let his heat warm the chill that invaded my body the minute I saw the blood on my baby's face.

His hand slides up and down my arm. He's comforting me, but his touch is like a jolt of electricity waking up the rest of me to his nearness.

I'll never forget the way he reacted when Maddie fell. He saw her going down before I did and was out of his seat and running for her before she even landed. That makes him that much more appealing to me. I wonder how it's possible to be even *more* attracted to him than I was before.

Maddie is sucking her thumb and watching us, her face pale and her eyes big.

I take a deep breath, the first I've taken since she fell, and it makes me feel light-headed.

Kristian tightens his hold on me, and I find myself sobbing into his chest with both his arms around me. "It's okay. She's going to be fine and so are you."

He says exactly what I need to hear and makes me feel less alone with my fears than I would be without him here with me. This is the closest I've ever been to him, and I can't help but notice the way my body seems to fit so perfectly against his. I breathe in the warm, sexy scent I've found so appealing since the first time I met him.

I feel his lips brushing against my hair, and I shiver from the sensations that zing through my body, making me hyperaware of him. Suddenly, it feels wrong to be standing next to my daughter's hospital bed allowing myself to get carried away by a man who's just being nice and trying to comfort me. "I'm okay." I pull back from him even though that's the last thing I want to do.

He seems reluctant to let me go, but he does. Tipping his head toward the hallway, he says, "I should call Flynn."

I nod in agreement. "Thanks."

He leaves the room, and I focus on breathing. Deep breaths in and out. What the hell is happening to me? I've never wanted to crawl into a man the way I do him. The magnetic draw to him is the craziest thing I've ever experienced. It's like I can't help myself. If he's in the room or anywhere nearby, I want to be near him. I want to touch him and hold him and let him hold me and tell me it's going to be fine.

All of which goes against everything I believe in as an independent woman who has cared for two young children—by herself—for years while working and undergoing cancer treatment. I'm not a woman who needs a man to make things okay for her or her children. But *damn*, it felt good to let him comfort me, even for a few minutes.

I brush Maddie's hair back from the uninjured side of her forehead. The hair on the other side is caked with drying blood, and her face is paler than I've ever seen it. For the first time in a very long time, her thumb is in her mouth, and I'm not trying to get it out the way I normally would. Whatever she needs, she can have. I was so terrified by the sight of all that blood. I almost fainted when Kristian lifted her off the pool deck and I saw how bad it was.

A nurse comes into the room to take Maddie for the CT scan.

"Can I go with her?"

"It'd be better if you wait here. We'll be quick."

I lean in to kiss Maddie. "I'll be right here when you're done, okay?"

"Okay, Mommy." Her lower lip quivers.

I watch the nurse wheel the bed out of the room, and then take a seat. My legs feel like rubber. I finally look down to find the entire front of me covered in blood.

When Kristian returns a minute later, I notice the front of his shirt is also bloodstained. He comes over to sit next to me, once again putting his arm around me.

Like before, I lean into him because the pull is too strong to resist. "They took her for the CT. The nurse said it would be quick."

"I talked to Flynn. He was glad to hear she's okay. He said to call if you need anything."

"You don't have to stay if you want to go back to the party. I can get an Uber home."

"I'm not leaving."

Is it my imagination or does he sound annoyed that I suggested he might go?

"I feel badly that we ruined your evening."

"You didn't. I'm exactly where I want to be."

His statement hangs in the air between us, filled with significance. Or is that my imagination running away with me again? I don't know, and the not knowing makes me crazy. But then he pulls me even closer to him, and I begin to believe he means it when he says he's right where he wants to be.

Kristian

Watching Maddie get the stitches is complete agony. They give her shots to numb up the site, and her shrieks make me feel so fucking helpless. It takes fifteen stitches to close the wound, and by the time they're finished, we're all done in.

Since the scan was clear, they allow us to take her home to sleep in her own bed. They bring in a wheelchair for her, but I insist on carrying her, and she curls up to me like she's been doing it all her life. Even though sobs continue to jolt her little body, she's asleep before we reach the car.

I hand her in to Aileen, who holds her in her arms for the ride to Venice Beach. When we arrive, I again retrieve Maddie and carry her inside, following Aileen, who deals with locks, doors and lights.

"You can bring her into my room," she says.

I can hear the exhaustion in every word she says. There're boxes waiting to be unpacked in every room, but the house already looks like a home, and they've only been here two days. As I enter Aileen's bedroom, it's almost funny to me. If you asked me where was the last place I expected to be tonight, her bedroom would be right at the top of the list. But here I am with her and her little girl, and somehow it just feels right.

We settle Maddie in the middle of Aileen's queen-size bed.

"I should wash her hair," she says.

"The morning will be soon enough." I draw the covers up to cover her small chest, which is still hiccupping from the sobs at the hospital. Now that Maddie is settled in bed, I should go. I should get up, tell Aileen I'll check on them tomorrow and get the hell out of here. But my limbs don't agree with the orders from management.

"I can't thank you enough for everything tonight," she says, looking at me from her perch on the other side of Maddie.

"I didn't do anything."

"You did everything, and it meant a lot to me."

"It did to me, too." I can't stop myself from spilling my guts to her. "She's such a sweet little girl. I hate to see her hurt."

"I don't know about you, but I could use a drink."

"Yes, please. A really big drink would be great."

"Your friends left some good stuff here yesterday. Shall we see what we've got?"

"Lead the way."

I follow her into the kitchen, where we investigate the bottles sitting on her counter from the get-together I missed yesterday.

"You like vodka, right?"

"I do."

She hands me a bottle of Absolut Citron, and I pour a healthy amount into the glass of ice she provides. She pours wine for herself, and I touch my glass to hers.

"Cheers," she says.

"Bottoms up." I take a healthy drink, keeping my gaze fixed on her gorgeous face as she sips her wine. Everything she does, even drinking wine, is sexy to me. "We look like we just survived the apocalypse or something."

She laughs. "If you want, I can toss your shirt in the wash with my dress. We can probably save them if we get them in soon."

Every instinct I have tells me not to remove my shirt. But if I let her wash my shirt, that means I get to stay a little longer. The shirt is clearing my head before I have time to second-guess the wisdom of being half-naked in front of the woman I want so desperately.

At the sight of my chest, her mouth drops open and then slams shut, as if she realized she was gawking and thought better of it. I wish she hadn't.

She takes the shirt from me. "I'll, ah... I'll put the wash in and be right back."

"Okay." I love that she's as rattled as I am. I want to ask if I can help her out of her dress, but that's one impulse I manage to contain in an evening when my impulses are completely out of control. While she's in the other room, I send a text to the Quantum group chat.

Maddie is home and resting comfortably after 15 stitches. The plastic surgeon said she shouldn't have a scar. CT scan showed no sign of concussion. All's well that ends well.

The responses flood in, filled with relief and good wishes.

How's Aileen? Natalie asks.

Rattled but okay. We're having a drink, and then I'll let her get some sleep.

Tell her to sleep in. Logan is fine with us tomorrow.

Thanks, Nat. I'll tell her.

Aileen returns to the kitchen, having changed into a tank top and pajama pants, which are as sexy on her as lingerie would be on

Delirious   51

another woman. I wonder if she would find it weird that I want to hug her some more. Probably.

On many Saturday nights, I'd be at Club Quantum, a willing sub at my feet and hours of debauchery to look forward to. Tonight, I'm completely satisfied with a good strong drink and the company of a single mom who makes me yearn for things I've never wanted before.

"Let's go outside," she says.

"Will we be able to hear Maddie?"

She holds up a device I hadn't noticed she had in her hand. "I set up the baby monitor in there. I'm glad I decided to bring it. I came *this* close to getting rid of it before the move."

"Good thinking."

We go outside to the deck, where it's warm but not overly humid.

After she stretches out in one lounge chair while I take the one next to her, she takes a deep breath and a sip of her wine. "I love that I can smell the beach from here."

"You like the beach?"

"I *love* it. I always have. That we can walk to Venice Beach from here is such a huge treat. We were there earlier today. Or I guess it's yesterday now. What time is it anyway?"

"Just after one."

She moans, and that's all it takes to make me hard for her. "I'm going to be a zombie tomorrow."

"I texted the group to let them know Maddie is home, and Natalie said to sleep in. They're fine with Logan tomorrow."

"That's so nice of her. He'll be thrilled to have Ms. Natalie all to himself. He adored her as his teacher."

"He'll have to share her with her very territorial husband."

Aileen laughs, and the sound goes straight to my heart. "True. Flynn is nothing if not territorial. That lucky bitch."

Hearing her say that Natalie is lucky to have such a possessive husband sends me reeling. Is that what she wants for herself? If so, where do I sign up?

She looks over at me, her soft expression making my heart swell with affection for her. "You were really great tonight. Thank you so much for taking such good care of us."

I can barely swallow around the huge lump that settles in my throat. "Sure," I say gruffly. "It was no big deal."

"It was to me."

"I should probably go and let you get some sleep."

She reaches over to take my hand. "Don't go yet."

CHAPTER 6

Kristian

Her skin brushing against mine sends a charge of heat through me. Stunned all over again by my unprecedented reaction to her, I pull my hand back, though that's the last thing I want to do. "Aileen..."

"Did I do something wrong, Kristian?"

The question shocks me. "What? Why would you ask that?"

She takes a deep drink of her wine, as if seeking liquid courage. "I can't help but notice that you are, or you *were* before Maddie got hurt... different." She swallows hard. "Toward me. So I wondered if maybe I did something—"

"No." That she could think such a thing is unbearable to me. "*No*," I say again, more emphatically this time. "It's not you. It's me."

"Nothing good ever comes of that statement," she says with an ironic laugh that's followed by a sigh.

I'm making a goddamn mess of this, so I decide to level with her. "You could do so much better than me, Aileen."

She stares at me, her eyes big with shock. "*Why* would you say such a thing?"

I could give her so many reasons, but I decide to go with the most important one. "You deserve better."

"Do you know why I wanted to move here?"

Thrown off by the change in direction, I say, "Because Nat and the others talked you into it?"

She shakes her head. "It was primarily because you live here."

Closing my eyes, I rest my head back against the chair. I shouldn't be here. I don't deserve her sweetness, her honesty or her blatant desire. But God, I want it. I want it all so badly, I burn with the need for more of her.

"Should I not have said that?" she asks in a small voice.

I keep my eyes closed as I shake my head.

"Did I read this wrong?"

"Aileen..."

"I'm sorry. I'll get your shirt into the dryer so you can go." The rustling sound of her getting up has me opening my eyes and reacting.

Like before, when Maddie fell, I'm moving before I decide I should. I grasp Aileen's arm, catch her off balance and bring her down to my lap, my lips landing on hers before either of us can take the time to ponder the massive implications. I cup her face in my hand and try to remember to be gentle with her. My inner Dominant needs to stand the fuck down. There's no place for him here.

When I use my tongue to coax her lips apart, she whimpers, another sound that goes directly to my cock, which has been hard since she moaned about the time. I kiss her with months' worth of pent-up desire that's made all other women pale in comparison to her since the day I met her. I don't want anyone but her, and now that she's warm and soft in my arms, I want to show her what she's come to mean to me.

My heart is pounding and my palms are sweaty. I'm light-headed, off balance and out of whack. Everything about this is new to me, as is the craving desire that swamps me when her tongue brushes against mine for the first time. *Fuck. Fuck. Fuck!* I'm so screwed. One taste of her has me addicted. It's never going to be enough. In the scope of two seconds, everything I want to do with her and to her runs through my mind like the dirtiest movie I've ever seen.

That has me pulling back from her, gentling the kiss, putting a stop to this before it gets even more out of control. I stare at her swollen lips and the stunned expression on her face. "Does that answer your question?"

"I seem to have forgotten the question."

Smiling at her witty reply, I say, "You asked if you read this wrong." I kiss her again, tipping my head to better the angle. "You didn't. You read it exactly right." I force myself to keep my hands still when they would love to wander. I want to touch her everywhere, but her little girl is sleeping inside, and this is not the time for that. However, in the last five minutes, I've begun to accept that this, whatever it is, is going to happen, whether I think it should or not.

"Something is different, though," she says, her lips hovering near mine, her hand caressing my face as she gazes into my eyes. "*You* are different."

It is both upsetting and exhilarating to realize she already knows me well enough to see that I'm troubled. "I don't mean to be." Nuzzling her neck, I breathe in the fresh, clean scent of her. It's not perfume or anything other than *her*. "I couldn't wait to see you again."

"Then where were you yesterday?"

"I was..." I start to tell her I was sick, but I can't. I can't lie to her. "I had myself convinced that this couldn't happen. I still don't think it should."

"*Why?*" she asks imploringly. "Is it because I have kids? I wouldn't expect you to take them on or—"

And then I'm kissing her again, because I can't bear to hear any more about her being afraid I don't want her because of her kids. I kiss her voraciously, forgetting that I'm supposed to be gentle and soft with her. She makes me so fucking crazy. "Your kids are adorable, well-behaved and beautiful, like their mother."

She snorts with disdain. "I'm not beautiful. I'm scrawny and pale, and my hair is growing back curly, and I have no idea what to do with it."

Her description of herself enrages me. "*You* are *beautiful*."

"So are you," she says, her voice husky and sexy. "If you knew how much time I've spent thinking about you since the day we met, you'd run away from here and never look back."

"Aileen..." Filled with despair, I drop my head and try to find my resolve. "Sweetheart..."

"What is it? Please tell me what's wrong. I don't understand."

"I want you too much, and I'm all wrong for you—and your kids."

"Shouldn't that be up to me to decide?"

Before I can reply, a soft cry comes from the baby monitor.

Aileen is up and off my lap, gone in a flash to tend to her child.

I take deep breaths of the cool air, trying to find my balance after kissing and holding her. I never should've done that, but I can't wait to do it again. I hear her through the monitor and wallow in the sweet words of comfort she gives her daughter.

I never had that. I don't know how to be soft or sweet or any of the things they'd need me to be. I'm selfish and arrogant and focused on my career. I need dominant, kinky sex the way some people need caffeine to jump-start their day. It's not just what I like. *It's who I am.*

Listening to Aileen softly sing to her baby, I'm stunned when tears sting my eyes. Are you fucking kidding me? I don't *cry.* I haven't cried since the foster family I'd started to love kicked me out to make room for one of their sons who was coming home from college.

I should get up, tell her I'm leaving and get the hell out of there while I still can. But I don't move. I remain riveted by the sound of her voice and the sweet way in which she loves her child. For the little boy in me who never knew softness, sweetness or love from his mother, my emotions are all over the place, listening to her give everything she has to her baby.

I take a deep breath, as if that could slow the wild beat of my heart. Once again, I'm moving before I consciously decide to, drawn to her so powerfully, I can't stay away. I stand in the doorway to the bedroom, watching over them as Aileen soothes Maddie back to sleep.

She sees me there, bends to kiss Maddie and gets up to come to me, her arms sliding around my waist and her head returning to my bare chest. I'm powerless to do anything other than wrap my arms around her and hold her as close to me as I can get her. I don't care that she can feel the obvious proof of my arousal pressing against her.

"I should go." Even my voice sounds different—gruffer, thicker.

"Stay." She holds me tighter and looks up at me with her heart in her eyes. In that one instant, I get why Flynn married Natalie without a prenup. If he feels even a fraction of what I do gazing down at Aileen, I get it. I'd give her everything I have with no questions asked if it meant she would look at me, just like that, every day for the rest of my life.

Without breaking the intense eye contact, I lower my lips to hers, which are swollen from our earlier kisses.

Her hands slide up my chest to link around my neck, trapping me.

I've never let any woman trap me. I do the trapping, not the other way around, but in this case, I can't be bothered to care about details that would've mattered with anyone else. Here with her, the only thing that matters is *more*—of everything. All the reasons why I'd planned to stay away are long gone as I lift her into my arms, carry her to the sofa and come down on top of her, losing my fucking mind in a kiss.

A fucking *kiss*. When was the last time a kiss alone was enough to take me to the brink of release? A million years ago when I was new to such things. But this... *This* is new to me, the *feeling* that comes from kissing her, the desperation, the craving. I've never experienced anything remotely like it, and I can't get enough.

It's like the highest of highs with no drugs required. That thought is yet another reminder of the many reasons I should not be making out with Aileen on her sofa. But when I pull back from her, she whimpers, her fingers grasping my hair to keep me from getting away. I have zero ability to do what I know I should. Losing the power that saved my life ought to terrify me, but I can't spare the brain cells to think it through, to ponder the implications of what I'm giving up to her.

How can I think of anything but her when she's wrapped around me, the heat of her pussy pressed tight against my cock, which is so hard, it aches?

The one thing I know for certain is I can't let this continue toward its inevitable conclusion, not with her little girl injured and sleeping in the next room. If—or I probably should concede to *when*—this happens, I want to be completely alone with her so I don't have to hold anything back.

"Aileen," I whisper against her lips. "Sweetheart..."

She looks up at me, seeming as dazed as I feel. Her lips are puffy and swollen, her cheeks flushed, and her eyes are wide with wonder that makes me want to say fuck it to propriety and anything else that doesn't have me inside her right fucking now. I'm shaking from the effort it takes to hold back. I can't remember the last time I held back like this. It's far more common for me to take what I want than it is to show restraint.

"What's wrong?"

"Absolutely nothing." Other than the fact that I've lost my mind, my heart and everything else to her, I'm fine. Better than fine. Being with her like this is *amazing*.

"Why did you stop?"

"I didn't stop because I wanted to." I caress her face, my fingertips gliding over her soft skin. She's so incredibly responsive that even a light touch has her hips rising, seeking me out. I bite back a groan of frustration.

"Then why?"

A very good question. "Because when we do this, I want to be completely alone with you so we don't have to be quiet." I nuzzle her neck, and she arches into me. "And I want to take my time."

She trembles, and I feel it everywhere, especially in my cock.

"I should go."

"No." She tightens her hold on me, and I love that. I love that she wants me so much. No one has ever wanted me the way she does. Women want me for what I can do for their careers and the things I can buy for them. They don't want me for *me* the way Aileen seems to. "Don't go. Not yet."

I sag into her, my painfully aroused body molding to hers.

"It feels so good to be held by you. It's been such a long time since anyone held me, and it's never felt as good as it does with you."

And she's so refreshingly honest. If she thinks it, she says it. When she asked me earlier if she'd done something wrong, she nearly broke my heart. I'm not used to refreshing honesty from women. I'm far more accustomed to games, intrigue, cat-and-mouse and hidden agendas. With Aileen, what you see is what you get, and I have a feeling I ain't seen nothing yet.

Aileen

I'm so relieved he didn't leave. He's obviously conflicted about what's happening between us, but for the life of me, I can't figure out why. The attraction between us runs hotter than anything I've felt for any man, even the one who fathered my children. He's easy to talk to and so sexy, I can barely breathe from wanting him.

I snuggle into his warm embrace, breathing in the arousing scent of his cologne or shampoo or something that drives me crazy wanting to imprint it on my senses so I'll never forget it.

"What did you mean before when you said I can do better than you?"

His body goes tense, and I feel it because we're pressed together so tightly that I feel everything, especially the hard length of his arousal against my belly. I want to rub shamelessly against him, but he's right. We can't lose control with Maddie in the next room. I'm slightly appalled that he was the one who thought of her. Don't judge me. When you've gone as long as I have without sex, and you're underneath the hottest guy you've ever met, *stopping* isn't the first thing on your mind.

"I'm not the right guy for you—or your kids."

My hands are all over his muscular back, learning the feel of him.

He shivers under my touch, which fills me with a sense of my own power and a desire to figure out what's standing in our way. "I want to understand why you think that. You were so great with Maddie—and with me—tonight. You were everything we needed, and the way you reacted when you saw her trip..."

I fell even harder for him in that moment, not that I can tell him that. I'm afraid to scare him off by letting him know just how crazy I am about him. I already said too much, telling him I moved here in large part because he's here.

"I reacted the way anyone would."

"No, you reacted the way someone who *cares* about her would."

He releases a tortured-sounding sigh. "You don't know me, Aileen. Not really."

"I want to know you. Doesn't this feel good to you?"

"It feels too good."

"How is that possible? How can something feel too good?"

His fingers slide over my face. "You're so sweet and beautiful. Your kids are amazing. You've done such a great job with them."

"Thank you." Why do I feel a huge 'but' coming here?

"It's just that I'm not really... I'm not capable of..."

All at once, I figure it out. My body, which was on fire for him a few minutes ago, goes cold with realization. "It's because I had cancer, isn't it? Don't worry. If you get involved with me, I won't saddle you with my kids if I die."

He startles the same way he would if I'd hit him with a Taser. "*What?*"

"It's okay. I get it. You're a single guy with a big life and career. The last thing you need is two kids who aren't yours. I'd never do that to you. I plan to ask Flynn and Nat to be their guardians if anything should happen to me, but I haven't had a chance to talk to them—"

He kisses me. "Stop." He kisses me again, thrusting his tongue into my mouth, igniting the flame that's been on low burn since he slowed things down a few minutes ago. Leaning his forehead against mine, he says, "My reluctance has nothing at all to do with you, your kids, the cancer, or any of the things you just said. I swear to God, it's not that."

"Then *what* is it?"

"There're things... about me... If you knew me, really *knew* me, you wouldn't want me."

He sounds so sad and defeated, both of which are in stark contrast to the man I've come to know over the last few months, that I barely recognize this Kristian. He's usually so confident and almost cocky in his self-assurance, which I find wildly attractive in him when those qualities would be a turnoff in any other man. He and his Quantum partners have more than earned the right to a little swagger.

"You can't possibly know that for certain."

"I do. I know it for certain."

"I'm not going to beg for a chance to prove you wrong. I'm only going to say that I like you and I like this." I tighten my hold on him. "I like being with you and kissing you, and I liked leaning on you earlier when Maddie was hurt. I probably liked that a little too much."

"I liked it, too. I like it all."

"Then maybe..." I summon the courage to go for what I want. Having cancer has left me less afraid than I used to be. I'm painfully aware that life is short and we've got to seize the moment, especially when the moment is lying in my arms, hard and hot and sexy and so tormented. "Maybe we could spend some time together and see what happens. It doesn't have to be serious or committed or anything like that."

"So you'd be okay if I did this with someone else?" he asks, sliding his lips over mine.

"I'd rather you not do that with anyone else ever again, but I don't get to decide that for you."

His eyes flare with potent desire. "You're so brave and honest."

"I've learned the hard way that time wasted is time we never get back. I don't believe in playing games or mincing words." I guide his head to my chest and run my fingers through his thick, wavy hair. I've wanted to do that for so long that I take full advantage while I can. "I'm not asking for anything you don't have to give me, Kristian. I just want to spend time with you and have the chance to get to know you."

"I want that, too. I want it more than I should."

I don't understand. Maybe I never will. But what I already feel for him is more than I've felt for any man, and if this is all he's capable of, I'll take it. A little of him is better than nothing.

Kristian

It's well after three o'clock when I pull a blanket over Aileen and leave her sleeping on the sofa. I need to go before Maddie wakes up and catches me still here. I have no idea what she'd have to say about me sleeping over, and I don't want to make anything difficult for Aileen, even if she's made everything difficult for me.

This wasn't supposed to happen. I'd made my decision, and I'm not known for waffling. Usually, I decide, and I never look back. But with her... She has me questioning everything.

I'm too keyed up to go home, so I drive back to town and head for the office. It's not unusual for me to work all night while the place is quiet. When I pull into the Quantum parking lot, I see that Sebastian's truck is still parked outside. Instead of going upstairs to the office, I head down to the club, where I find Sebastian cleaning the bar area.

Hip-hop thumps through the speakers, loud enough to wake the dead. Drake, if I'm not mistaken. We saw him in concert with Future last summer. Flynn got us backstage, all-access passes. That was a great night, one of many I've had with my Quantum family. I wave a hand to get Seb's attention so I won't scare the shit out of him.

He sees me and turns the music down to a dull roar. "What's up?"

"Not much. Good night?"

"Busy as hell. Best thing you guys ever did was open this place up to new people. We're raking it in."

"Glad to hear it." He's Hayden's closest friend from childhood. The two of them grew up together, albeit on opposite sides of the Hollywood tracks. Seb's mom was Hayden's family housekeeper.

"Drink?"

"Please."

He pours me a Grey Goose and soda with a twist of lime. I've been a vodka fan for as long as I can remember—which is far longer than it should be. I had my first drink at twelve, when other kids my age were in sixth grade. I was never a kid. Childhood was a luxury I couldn't afford.

"How's Maddie?"

"Better now. Watching her get stitches was brutal."

"The poor baby. I've never seen so much blood. Scared the crap out of everyone."

"Yeah, poor Aileen. Hell of a thing to have happen on day two in a new city."

"I'm sure she appreciated having you with her at the hospital."

"Uh-huh." I take a sip of my drink, letting the vodka burn through me, offering the sweet relief I can only get from alcohol and kinky sex. The combination of the two is my favorite thing. Or it was until a certain woman came into my life, making me question everything—including my favorite things.

"You all right?"

"Yep."

"You sure?"

I look up at him. "I'm sure."

"Glad to hear it."

I'm about to ask for another drink when Melody Gorman, a woman we all know well, slides onto the barstool next to me. She's a teenage boy's wet dream with curves on top of curves, thick, shiny auburn hair that falls almost to her waist and the face of an angel. "Hi, Kris," she says, smiling at Sebastian, who puts a glass of white wine in front of her.

I glance at Sebastian, who raises a swarthy brow and grins. I should've known he wasn't here alone.

"Mel. Where'd you come from?"

"Long day on set today. Seb was good enough to loan me your sauna and shower. Hope you don't mind."

"My sauna and shower are yours. You know that." She's Aileen's polar opposite in every possible way. She's lush where Aileen is sparse. She's Hollywood glamour while Aileen's idea of style is "mom chic," if that's even a thing. Whatever it is, it works for me.

Staring down at pure, stunning beauty, I feel nothing for Melody. She's an old friend, someone I've played with many times in the club, but she may as well be a stranger rather than a woman I've been inside of too many times to count.

"You're looking a little tense, Kris," she says, resting her hand on my arm.

It takes everything I have not to recoil from her touch, to pull back my arm and tell her she has no right to touch me. Not anymore. But I don't do that, if for no other reason than I don't want to deal with the questions or the speculation it would generate. A tiger like me doesn't change his stripes practically overnight without people noticing, and I want to be left alone with my changes until I figure out how the hell I'm going to deal with them.

"You want to work it off?" she asks, glancing at Sebastian, who raises his brows.

"Nah, I'm good, but thanks for asking." The thought of touching another woman after being with Aileen generates the same sick feeling I had when I contemplated playing with Evie last night. That queasiness is another thing that's all new to me.

Other than my Quantum partners and our close friends, I've never felt *loyal* to a woman before. It's another emotion that I have no idea what to do with. My insides are churning, and the vodka doesn't have its usual calming effect. All the things I rely on to keep me sane are letting me down tonight, and I feel a spark of anger toward Aileen. How dare she do this to me? I was minding my own business at my friend's wedding when *she* showed up and ruined me.

She shouldn't be allowed to get away with that.

I no sooner have that thought than I'm flooded with guilt. It's not her fault that I've lost my fucking mind over her. It's *my* fault. I know better than to indulge myself with the kind of thoughts I've been having about her and her kids and white picket fences and puppies and happily ever after. Shit doesn't work that way in my world, and it would do me good to remember that.

"Ready for a refill?" Seb asks as he wipes down the bar until the mahogany shines, his pride in the club always apparent.

"I'm gonna head out." I don't want to be here, and I don't want to be home. The only place I want to be is on a sofa in Venice Beach.

Fucking *hell*.

"Have a good night, Mel."

"You do the same."

Seb walks me to the elevator and puts a hand on my shoulder. I hate that my first impulse is still to flinch and defend, even when there's no need for that with him. "I know you said you're fine, but you don't look fine, brother. If there's anything I can do…"

"Thanks, man." I give him a bro hug. He's one of the good guys, and I'm lucky to have him as a friend. I want to tell him there's nothing he or anyone can do about the dilemma that has me by the balls. I'm going to have to work it out for myself, and because my sanity is at stake, I'm going to do that by staying the fuck away from her.

CHAPTER 7

Kristian

Not even six hours later, I'm on her doorstep with a box of doughnuts, two coffees, a chocolate milkshake and the morning *LA Times* tucked under my arm. It occurred to me at about five o'clock that her car is still at Flynn's, so she's stuck at home. Around the same time, it occurred to me that we have at least a dozen people on our payroll who I could call and instruct to pick up the car and get it to her.

But I didn't do that.

No, I showered, shaved, got dressed for work and found myself at Kettle Glazed in Hollywood, getting breakfast and driving to Venice Beach to deliver it in person.

I'm nothing if not a glutton for punishment.

Aileen comes to the door, and the first thing I notice is that the dark circles that were under her eyes when we first met are back, indicating a restless night.

She lights up with delight at the sight of me. "Hi."

When was the last time someone was that happy to see me? Never that I can recall.

"Come in." When she steps aside to admit me, my gaze is drawn to the silky, formfitting robe she's wearing. Everything about her is petite and delicate and fragile, which is why I can never unleash my inner beast with her. I'd break her in half.

"How's Maddie?" I ask, sticking to safe terrain.

"Still sleeping. She was up a few times during the night."

I hand her a coffee. "I figured you might need this."

"God bless you."

Her pleasure in simple things is refreshing. "It's got cream but no sugar. Wasn't sure how you took it."

"Just like that. I gave up sugar in my coffee years ago." She takes a sip and makes a sound that reminds me all too much of last night and the interlude on her sofa.

I let my eyes shift to the "scene of the crime," and my cock twitches with appreciation of the memories.

Knock it off, I tell myself—and my cock. *That's not why you're here.*

Isn't it?

Shut the fuck up!

I'm not sure who my inner voice is talking to, but he's got my attention. I keep my eyes on her face and resist the urge to let them wander. "I was thinking that your car is at Flynn's, and you might need a ride to get it."

"That's so nice of you. I was just starting to think about how I was going to retrieve my car and my son."

"I'll take you."

"Don't you have to go to work?"

"I said I'll take you." That comes out sharper than intended, and I immediately regret that. "Sorry."

"Are you okay?"

I'm starting to get fed up with people asking me that, especially her, because it's completely her fault that I am anything but okay. "I'm fine. I own the company. I get there when I get there."

"All righty, then."

I'm fucking this all up. "And I sound like an arrogant douche, which wasn't my intention."

She smiles, and her amusement pisses me off. I'm off my game with her, and that too makes me crazy. I'm never off my game with

women. Unlike most men, I've never found them particularly complicated or hard to figure out. But she is different. She's unlike any
woman I've ever known, and that has me off-kilter and out of sorts. I
don't even know what I'm doing here when I vowed, *only a few hours
ago*, for fuck's sake, to stay away from her.

"I only meant that I have time to take you. If you want me to."

"I want you to." She reaches for my hand, and I meet her halfway,
giving her my hand, again before I consciously decide to. If she only
knew the power she has over me. It's frightening. "Let's go outside
and have our coffee."

Like the lap dog I am with her, I let her lead me to the deck,
where we sit next to each other on the same chairs we occupied last
night.

"I love having a deck and a yard and being able to have my coffee
out here in the morning."

"It's pretty. Ellie did a nice job with the yard and gardens."

"I can't believe she did everything herself. I'm so envious. I want
to know how to do all that. She said she'll teach me."

I hang on her every word, filing away each new piece of information she offers, adding them to the growing collection of things I
know about her.

"I'm used to having a super I could call to fix things. I don't want
to be that kind of tenant for Ellie."

"I'll help you if you need something."

"That's sweet of you to offer, but I want to be able to do it myself.
I'm used to being self-reliant."

My inner Dom wants to stand up and rage against that statement.
I want her to rely on *me* and only *me*. *I thought we weren't doing this*,
my annoying inner voice says. I want to tell him to shut the fuck up.
He's not in charge here. I am. Needing to move, I get up. "How about
a doughnut? You gotta try one of these. They're all the rage in
Hollywood."

"I won't say no to that."

I go inside to retrieve the box of doughnuts, forcing myself to
calm down while I'm in there. I hate being out of control and off my

game. Control has been the centerpiece of my life. Maintaining it has allowed me to go from a homeless street urchin to the top of my profession. Losing it is not an option, and I'd do well to remember that. After a few deep breaths, I return to the deck with the box of doughnuts.

She watches me with insight that rattles me. It's like she can see inside me, which puts me at a distinct disadvantage.

I open the box and present it to her, the sugary scent flooding my senses—and hers.

"Mmm," she says, licking her lips.

Naturally, my cock stands up with interest at the movement of her tongue over her lips.

"Is that chocolate frosted glaze?"

"I believe it is."

"Oh my God. Sign me up for that." She takes the doughnut, and I close the box, putting it on the table next to us. "You're not going to make me eat alone, are you?"

"I don't do sugar," I tell her as I return to my seat.

"*Ever?*"

"Ever."

"*Why?*"

"I eat clean—no sugar, nothing processed, very few carbs."

She cringes. "I don't think I could do that. I love carbs."

"I do, too, but after not eating them for years, whenever I do, I feel sick. So, I avoid them. But you go ahead and enjoy that doughnut. Don't mind me."

She takes a bite and then another, before putting it on a napkin and depositing it on the table.

"You don't like it?"

"I'm sure I'd love it if I could actually taste it. The chemo messed with my taste buds, making everything taste funny. They say it'll get better eventually. Any time now."

The word "chemo" fills me with anxiety. I want to know exactly what she had, how she was treated, what the long-term prognosis is, how she feels right now. I want to know everything. I want to know that she's getting the best possible care. But I can't ask. I don't have the right to.

"It's a lot," she says softly.

"What is?"

"Me and my kids and my illness. I'd understand if it's too much—"

"It's not." It's way too much. All of it, especially the way she makes me feel, but I'd never tell her that.

"Kristian—"

I reach for her hand and link our fingers. "It's not too much." *We're not getting involved here, remember?*

Shut up. Just shut the fuck up.

"Could I ask you something?"

Anything. "Sure."

"What exactly is it that you do at Quantum? I know you're a producer, but I'm not sure what that means."

Her question puts me on much safer ground, even if holding her hand is better than the kinkiest sex with other women. "Basically, it means that I pull together the pieces for every project. I find the material, bring it to my partners, decide with them what we're going to do—and what we're not going to do. The role is a little different at Quantum than some other production outfits, because we do most of our projects 'in house,' meaning the partners star, direct, film, etc. Right now, I'm preparing for the release of *Insidious* while guiding four other films through the various stages, from financing to discovery to casting to filming to postproduction to distribution to release to release on DVD. It never ends. At the top of our list right now is the project we're doing based on Natalie's story. It's Flynn's passion project, and we're excited about it. On top of *all* that, I'm also the managing partner, in charge of personnel and HR, among other things."

"Wow," she says. "You must have insane organizational skills."

"I guess I do, but I also have an amazing team that supports me. They don't let things fall through the cracks."

"It's impressive."

"What is?"

"All of it. Everything you do. And for what it's worth, I'm a huge fan of Quantum's films. I think I've seen *Camouflage* a dozen times."

"That was a very special film for us."

"It was incredible."

"I'm glad you thought so."

"*Everyone* thought so."

I smile at her, pleased by her approval of my life's work. "That's nice to hear. Sometimes I wonder if what we do matters—"

"It does matter. When I was so sick I couldn't do much of anything, I watched movies like a fiend. I don't know that I would've gotten through it without being able to lose myself in other people's stories. They kept me from spending too much time thinking about my own situation and freaking out about what was going to happen to me and my kids."

"I hate to think of you sick and afraid."

"It was a rough year, but I'm better now."

I'm tied up in knots. I want to ask if she's going to stay that way, if she needs more treatment, if I need to be terrified that I'm going to lose her after only just finding her. I can hardly breathe as these thoughts come over me, one after another.

The baby monitor on the table crackles to life when Maddie coughs.

Aileen releases my hand and gets up to go to her daughter. "I'll be right back."

"Take your time." I have no fewer than ten million things I need to get done today, but none of them matter when stacked up against what Aileen needs. So I wait, and I try not to think about what it means that I'm here, that I'm captivated, that I'm terrified.

Aileen

He came back. I'm so full of giddy joy this morning I don't know what to do with myself. When I woke alone, I feared that maybe he'd changed his mind. But I didn't have to wait long to find out he hadn't.

I step into Maddie's room and find her sitting up, her eyes bright and alert, which is a huge relief after the trauma of last night.

"Hi, baby." I sit on the bed and smooth the hair back from her face. Washing the blood out of her hair is my priority now that she's awake. "How're you feeling?"

"Okay."

"Does your head hurt?"

"A little." She yawns and then grimaces. "Ouch."

"You're going to need to take it nice and easy today."

"I don't want to take it easy. I want to go to the beach and go swimming."

"We'll be back to doing that in no time, but today is a rest day. We'll snuggle and read books and watch movies and relax."

What sounds like a perfect day to me doesn't appeal to my high-energy child, but she'll do what she's told because she always does.

"Mr. Kristian came to check on you, and he brought doughnuts."

Her eyes light up with delight. "He really came to check on me?"

I'm touched that she cares more about him than the treats he brought. "Of course he did. He was worried about you. Everyone is."

"That's nice of them. Is Logan here?"

"No, he slept over at Natalie's house, but Mr. Kristian is going to drive us over there to get him. Our car is still there. But first things first, we need to get you in the shower to get you cleaned up. Do you feel up to that?"

"Uh-huh."

Aware that Kristian has put his workday on hold for us, I hustle Maddie through a shower and get her dressed. She can eat her breakfast in the car on the way to Nat's house. When we're dressed and ready, I grab a small bottle of apple juice. "Good to go," I tell Kristian, who's still on the deck, typing on his phone.

He glances up at me, and before he can school his features, I see everything I've ever wanted looking at me with heat and desire and affection. Then he smiles, and it's all I can do not to turn into a puddle of need when the dimples make a rare appearance. "How's our patient feeling this morning?"

"Good," Maddie says. "My owie hurts."

He gets up, grabs the box of doughnuts and comes to us, sliding the screen door open and crouching to Maddie's level. "I'm sure it does, but you were so brave last night. Such a big girl."

My daughter leans into me, suddenly going shy in the face of such powerful male charm. Like her mother, she's only human, and he's quite something.

"Kristian brought us yummy doughnuts." I take the box from him and let her choose one.

"Thank you."

"You're welcome." He stands, takes the aviators from the top of his head and puts them over his eyes. "Shall we, ladies?"

We head out to the car, and what was perfectly fine last night in the middle of an emergency has me second-guessing today as I strap Maddie and me into the passenger seat. "Please don't crash. This is so against the law, it's not even funny."

His hand lands on my knee, sending a powerful surge of longing through my body. "You're totally safe with me. All of you. I'd never let anything happen to you."

I sigh, because how can I not? He's perfect, and if I could spend every day for the rest of my life just like this—my arms around my children and his arms around me—I'd never want for anything.

Whoa, Nelly. Back it up, sister. Talk about getting ahead of yourself. If he had any idea the thoughts I'm having about him, I'd probably never see him again. Even with my better judgment raining on my lovely parade, I can't help how I feel. It's been different with him since the first day I met him, and I've begun to accept that I'll always feel more for him than I probably should, especially since he's going to be one of my bosses.

PC—or pre-cancer—I might've talked myself out of feeling the way I do about him. It's not practical or advisable, but I don't care. AC—after cancer—I know life is short and feelings like the ones I have for him don't come around every day. I'll be damned if I'm going to run away and hide the way I would have before life gave me a mighty bitch slap and a potent reminder that time is finite, good health is a gift, and life is to be celebrated and lived to the fullest.

I want him. I want his hand on my knee in the car. I want his big, strong, sexy body wrapped around mine in bed at night. I want him to really know my kids. I want him in our lives—any way I can get him—and his actions last night only make the wanting more so in the bright light of this glorious Southern California day.

"Would you like to come for dinner later?" I ask him, trying to affect a casual tone. I think I pull it off quite convincingly. "I want to thank you for everything last night."

"You don't have to thank me. I was happy to be there with you both."

"Still, we need to eat. You need to eat. And I'm a very decent cook, if I do say so myself."

He keeps his gaze, covered by those maddening sunglasses that seal off his gorgeous eyes, on the road, so I can't tell what he's thinking. After a long silence, he says, "Sure, that sounds good. What time?"

"Around six thirty? Or is that too early for you? I could feed the kids and then—"

He squeezes my knee, which shuts me up. "Six thirty is fine. What can I bring?"

"Nothing. You've already done more than enough for me. Let me do something for you."

He glances at me quickly and then returns his attention to the road. "You don't have to do anything for me, Aileen."

"Why not? Is friendship a one-way street in your world?"

"No," he says, sounding uncomfortable with the direction of the conversation.

I should let it go, but I can't. "Let me tell you how friendship works in my world. You arrange for me to have a car and a job and a whole new life. You rush to the aid of my injured child, accompany us to the ER and stay with me until you're certain I'm not going to have a complete meltdown afterward. Then, you show up this morning when you certainly have better things to do, bearing doughnuts and the offer of a ride to pick up my car. After all that, I'll need to make you dinner every night for a year to properly thank you."

After another long silence, he says, "I didn't have better things to do this morning."

"Right," I say with a laugh. "If you say so."

"I say so." He squeezes my leg again, and I swear to God, if my child hadn't been injured and strapped to me, I might've been tempted to throw off my seat belt and make myself at home on his side of the car. One squeeze is all it takes to make me *crazy* for him.

"My mommy is a really good cook," Maddie says. "She makes yummy chicken and mac 'n cheese, too."

"I love chicken," he says, seeming more comfortable talking to her than he is talking to me.

They keep up the chatter about silly things all the way to Flynn and Nat's house. Kristian's hand remains on my leg except for when he needs to shift the car. Each time he shifts, he puts his hand right back on my leg, making me yearn to be alone with him. But that's not to be. Not now anyway.

Kristian has the code to the gate and punches it in. It swings open to admit us, and we pull up next to my car, which is right where I left it last night. So much has happened since then that my head spins as I try to process it all. He gets out of the car and comes around to help with Maddie, who's still a little wobbly on her feet. Seeing that, he scoops her up into his arms, and she goes to him like it's something she's always done.

My heart swells to an unhealthy size, watching him carry my little girl.

She winds her hands around his neck, and he tightens his hold on her.

It's too much for me, and not enough at the same time.

Kristian walks right into the house like he's done it a million times before, which he probably has. These people are family to each other, and they've made us feel so welcome among them.

We find Natalie and Logan at the pool, where he's splashing around while she keeps a close eye on him.

Logan jumps out of the pool and rushes over to us.

Kristian puts Maddie down, and Logan hugs her tightly.

Again with my heart. It can't take the overload of emotion today, and it's only ten o'clock!

"Are you okay, Maddie?" he asks, pulling back for a look at the bandage on his sister's forehead.

"Uh-huh, but I had to get *shots* in the head!"

"Holy crap. Did it hurt?"

"So bad."

He winces. "I'm glad you're okay. You wanna swim?"

"She shouldn't get the bandage wet," I tell him.

"She can put her feet in." He takes his sister by the hand and gently leads her to the steps, waiting for her to get settled before he lets go of her.

"He's incredibly sweet to her," Kristian says.

"He's almost always like that," I say, keeping my hand flat on my chest as if that alone will contain the emotion.

Natalie hugs me. "He's been so worried. How you holding up, Mama?"

"As long as she's fine, I'm fine."

"Did you get any sleep?"

I glance at Kristian, who's expressionless as he keeps an eye on the kids. "A little."

Natalie's eyebrows lift, but thankfully, she doesn't say anything.

"I should get to the office," Kristian says.

"Flynn's already there. I'll be glad when this premiere is behind us."

"There'll be another one before we know it," he says. "Keeps us in business."

"I guess so, but no one told me celebrities work so hard."

Kristian laughs. "They make it look so glamorous when it's a ton of work."

I want to hug him, but I manage to control myself. Barely. "Thank you so much for the ride and the doughnuts. And everything else."

"No problem. I'll see you later."

"Okay."

"Bye, guys," he calls to the kids.

"Bye, Mr. Kristian."

"Have a good day, ladies."

I watch him go, because the view is as good from the back as it is from the front, and after he goes inside and slides the screen door closed, I find Natalie watching me as closely as I was watching him.

CHAPTER 8

Aileen

The second he's out of earshot, Natalie pounces. "Do I see progress?"

"A little."

She takes me by the hand and half drags me to the chair next to where she was sitting. "Do tell. Leave nothing out."

Leaving out the more personal elements, I fill her in on what happened after we got home last night and how he surprised me by showing up this morning bearing breakfast and the offer of a ride to pick up my car.

"He's so into you, it's not even funny," Natalie says. "And the poor guy has no idea what to do about it."

"I like him so much."

Natalie bites her lip, making me wonder if there's something on her mind.

"What?"

"I just... I want you to be careful with him. He's very... complicated."

"What do you know that I don't?"

She shakes her head. "Nothing I can tell you. It has to come from him, if and when he chooses to tell you."

"Natalie! Come on! You can't drop something like that on me and then not tell me what you mean."

"I've already said more than I should."

"Can you give me a hint?"

"No."

"Are my children and I safe with him?"

Her eyes bug. "Yes! It's nothing like that. God, I'm making a mess of this. When I say complicated, I mean private and personal and... Shit. I suck at this."

"You have to tell me what the hell you're talking about, or I'm going to lose my mind wondering."

"It's not my place to tell you his personal business. That's up to him."

"How do you know about his personal business?"

Again, she bites her lip, her eyes darting around until they land on the kids. Logan is swimming in circles in front of Maddie, who's telling him what to do, as usual. They're thoroughly occupied and far enough away from us that I'm not worried about them overhearing our conversation.

"If I tell you this, you have to swear to God on a stack of Bibles you'll never tell anyone where you heard it or that you even know about it."

"I swear to God." I'm so desperate to know, that I'd swear on my own life at this point.

"Do you know what BDSM is?"

"Uhh, yeah. I saw the movies. What about it?"

"He's into it. They all are. *We* all are."

If she had told me that pigs were flying in hell, I wouldn't have been more stunned by this information. "You, Flynn..."

"He introduced me to it after we were together, and I've become a fan. To say the least."

Speaking of fans, I need one. And a cigarette. "You're serious."

"Dead serious. The only reason I'm telling you this is I watched what happened when Hayden kept his interests from Addie when they were first together. They nearly missed out on having something great because he wouldn't share it with her. I don't want to see you get any further down the road with Kristian if you don't think that's something you want. If I've learned anything from these guys, it's that being a part of the lifestyle isn't a choice. It's *who* they *are*."

I have no idea what to say.

"Flynn would kill me for telling you this, Aileen."

"Thank you for telling me. That actually explains a lot." I'm having visions of being bound and at his mercy. If the flash of heat that travels through my body is any indication, the idea intrigues me.

"Whoa," Natalie says. "Are you all right?"

"Of course. Why?"

"Your face is all red and flushed."

"It's the sun. I'm not used to it."

"Hmm, are you sure you're not imagining all sorts of scenarios that have you at Kristian's mercy?"

"Stop," I hiss at her and glance at my kids, who're thankfully still occupied by the pool.

She laughs. "Thought so."

And then another thought occurs to me. "It's not like that could ever happen with us."

"Umm, why's that, exactly?"

"I'm a single mom. It's not like I can run off and have any kind of sex, let alone kinky sex, whenever I want."

"You have friends who would happily take your kids any time you want to get your groove on."

"You have your own life to lead and your own kinky sex to have. You don't need my kids around your neck."

Natalie reaches out to squeeze my arm. "We love you. We love your kids. And we love Kristian. I'd like nothing more than to see you two together. I think you'd be good for him, and vice versa."

"Why do you think that?" I'm not even ashamed of the fact that I'm wearing my heart on my sleeve when it comes to him. I can't hide that I'm fiercely interested.

"There's something about him. I can't put my finger on it, but there're times when he reminds me of some of the kids I had in my class, the ones who came to school hungry and wearing dirty clothes. It's hard to explain what I mean, but there was something in their eyes that I've seen in him, too."

My heart aches at the thought of him being hurt or lost in any way. I want to swoop in and fix it so that nothing will ever hurt him again. "He's a rich, powerful, successful man."

"Now. But I honestly have no idea where he comes from. No one talks about his past, and I've never heard mention of a family."

"I want to know everything about him. I'm like a fourteen-year-old crushing on the football team captain. I feel so out of my league with him."

"Maybe he feels out of his league with you. Did you ever consider that?"

"Seriously? Look at me and then look at him. He's not the one out of his league."

"You, my dear friend, are gorgeous and sweet and joyful. You have nothing to worry about, and judging by the way he looks at you, he sees what I do."

"You're very sweet to say so, but it's been such a long time since I had any interest in a man. Hell, I haven't had sex since I was pregnant with Maddie."

"Whoa..."

"I know! There're probably cobwebs in there."

Natalie loses it laughing.

"What's so funny, Mommy?" Logan asks.

"Nothing," I reply. "Nothing at all." I give Natalie the stink eye as she continues to laugh.

"Sorry." She wipes tears from her eyes. "It was the cobwebs that did it."

"Not all of us can be lucky enough to have a hot, sexy, kinky movie star in our beds to keep the cobwebs away."

She snorts. "No cobwebs growing around here. That's for sure."

"I can only imagine."

She looks over at me. "Could I ask you something?"

"Of course."

"You never talk about the kids' father, and I haven't wanted to ask. But I'll admit I'm curious."

I fix my gaze on my babies, the only good things to come from a relationship that caused me more heartache than joy. "He left us right before Maddie was born." There's so much more to the story, but it's not something I talk about, even with my closest friends. Years after it happened, it's still so painful to think about.

"Oh God. I'm sorry, Aileen."

"He's never met his daughter."

"That must've been so awful for you."

"It wasn't the best time in my life. That's for sure. For a long time after he left, I was terrified about what would become of me and the kids. He never sent me a dime after he left. It was tough, especially living in the city, which is so expensive. But I found a decent job working as an admin for a financial services company, and I had a lovely older woman in my building who took the kids for me when I was working. She was a godsend. We were doing okay until I got sick." I look over at her. "You and Flynn can't possibly know what a difference you made for us after he made that huge donation to the fund the school set up."

"That was *all* him. I can't take any credit."

"You introduced him to us. None of it would've happened without you."

"We're both glad you got the help you needed."

"In some ways, he saved my life by introducing me to Doctor Birnbaum. Everything was better after that."

"Do you have someone out here that you'll see?"

"He referred me to a colleague at UCLA who's part of the same research study. I have an appointment for a check-up with him next week while the kids are at camp."

"I'm sure everything will be fine."

"I hope so, but it'll be a few years before I'm completely out of the woods, and even then, it can always come back."

"That's not going to happen," Natalie says emphatically.

"And you know this how, wise one?"

"Just a feeling I have. I predict you're going to fall madly in love with an intense, sexy man who'll fall in love with you and your kids, and you'll all live happily ever after."

"You may be reading too many romance novels."

"Ha-ha, but mark my words. You're going to end up with him."

"Could I ask you... In the event that my life doesn't work out like a romance novel..."

"What?"

"Would you take the kids? I know it's a huge thing to ask—"

She holds up a hand to stop me. "Of course we would. Don't spend one more second worrying about that. It's never going to happen."

"But if it does..."

"We'd take them, and we'd love them like our own. I promise."

My eyes fill with tears. "Thank you."

"But I don't want to talk about things that're never going to happen. I want to talk about you and that hot, sexy man who's gone over you and things that *are* going to happen."

My stomach knots with excitement and a twinge of anxiety. I'll never deny that I want him fiercely. But can I be what *he* wants? That I don't know, and I haven't the first clue what to do with this new information Natalie has given me.

Kristian

I have meetings on top of meetings, people needing answers to a litany of questions only I can answer. We have the premiere of Quantum's new film *Insidious* Saturday night, and there're a million details to be seen to, media requests pouring in, and all I can think about is Aileen and how amazing it was to hold and kiss her last night.

Recalling how responsive she was makes me rock hard in the middle of my workday, which is just what I need with people in and out of my office, the phone ringing off the hook and my assistant, Lori, waiting for me to sign a stack of checks.

"What's up with you today, Bossman?" she asks, hand on her hip, annoyance radiating from her. With chin-length dark hair and big green eyes, she's a gorgeous, energetic twentysomething I hired right out of USC a couple of years ago. She's since become essential to me, which is why I put up with her impertinence.

"Nothing."

"Your head isn't in the game. Something's up."

"Did I miss the part on your résumé that said you went to shrink school?"

"Ha-ha, very funny. I know you, and I know when you're not paying attention, and you're definitely *not* paying attention today. Case in point, you just signed your lunch order." She cracks up laughing as she holds up the deli menu. "Apparently, you want the Kristian Bowen for lunch, not to be confused with the always popular Clark Gable." She has a good laugh at my expense that makes me smile even though I hate to encourage her.

"I'll have the Paul Reuben with an extra pickle, no pun intended."

She raises a brow in question because I rarely eat sandwiches.

"I'm having a craving for pastrami," I tell her.

"You got it." She heads for the door but turns back. "I heard you say everything is fine, but I know you. Something's up. If you need anything, I hope you'll ask."

"There is one thing..."

"What's that?"

"I want to invite someone to the premiere on Saturday, but she has kids. Everyone else we know will be there, too, so I need a babysitter. Do you know anyone who might be willing to stay with two very good kids who are five and nine? I'll pay a thousand dollars."

"My roommate, Cecelia, will do it."

"She will? Really?" I've met her a few times, and she seems nice.

"Yep. She's going through a bad breakup, so she's sitting around at home at night. It'll be good for her to have something to do."

"Shouldn't you check with her first?"

"I'll text her and let you know for sure, but I'm almost positive it'll be fine."

"Do you think she might be willing to spend the night?" I'm getting way ahead of myself, and I know it, but I can't seem to stop the train from leaving the station and hurtling down the tracks.

"I'm sure she'd be fine with it. I'll ask her and let you know."

"Tell her fifteen hundred to spend the night."

"Wow. You must really like this woman."

Recognizing a trap when I see one, I go back to my email, avoiding the question. She gets the hint and leaves me to work in peace, but now I'm on edge waiting to hear if Cecelia, who's a nurse in her mid-twenties, will babysit for Aileen on Saturday so I can take her to the premiere. Then another thought occurs to me, and I buzz Addie, asking her to stop by to see me when she gets a chance.

She pops her head in fifteen minutes later. "You rang?"

"Come in. Shut the door."

"What's up?"

"Your friend Tenley, the stylist..."

"What about her?"

"Would she be able to help me out with something for Saturday night?"

"Kinda short notice."

"I know, but I'm willing to pay whatever she wants."

"Let me ask her." Standing before me, she fires off a text.

Part of me can't believe I'm doing all this before I've even asked Aileen to come with me, further proof I've gone around the bend over her. However, I want my ducks in a row in case she agrees to be my date.

My date. When was the last time I had anything as pedestrian as an ordinary date? Except, if she says yes, nothing about this date will be ordinary *or* pedestrian, because I'll be with her.

"She says for you, she'll make it happen. She wants to know who, what, when and where?"

"Could I let her know all that tomorrow?"

Addie sends the text and nods. "She says she'll hook you up."

"Thanks, Addie."

"No problem. Do I get to ask who, or do I already know?"

"You already know." I release a button on my shirt, because it's suddenly warm in here. It's not like me to share my personal business with others. The first lesson to surviving on the streets was keep your mouth shut. It's a lesson that's stayed with me.

Addie claps her hands and lets out a squeal. "Oh, I *knew* it! I told Hayden you two are going to end up together."

"Don't get ahead of yourself—and don't jinx me. It's very new."

She eyes me curiously, making me squirm ever so slightly. "Why don't you seem happier to have found someone special?"

"What? I'm happy."

"No, you're not."

"And you know better than I do how I feel?"

"I've known you a long time, Kris. You've been 'off' all week. I thought you were excited for her and the kids to get here, and then you didn't show up to welcome them. Jasper said you were sick, but were you really, or was it something else?"

For someone who never had a family of my own, it's still unsettling to me that there are people in this world who know me as well —or better—than I know myself. I fix my gaze on a pen I balance between two fingers, which is better than looking at her.

"Kris... Talk to me. Tell me what's wrong."

"Nothing is wrong."

"Don't lie to me—and don't lie to yourself. You're better than that."

"No, I'm not." The words come out harsher than I intend, and she's taken aback by what I said and how I said it.

Hands on hips, she glares at me. "What the hell is that supposed to mean?"

Sighing, I sit back in my chair, resigned to having this conversation whether I want to or not—and I definitely do *not* want to talk about it with everyone I know. However, my friends aren't going to let me get away with my usual avoidance tactics in this case. "She deserves better than me. I... I don't know how to be soft or gentle or sweet, and someone like her, that's what she needs. She's been through so much..."

Addison comes around my desk and leans back against it. She's so close now, there's no avoiding her. "You were all those things when Maddie got hurt. You reacted instinctively and gave them everything they needed—and then some, if I know you, which I do. Maybe you've never had to give those things to a woman before, but don't tell me they aren't in you, because I know better."

Her faith in me is overwhelming. "I'm afraid..."

"Of *what*?"

"I'm afraid to touch her. What if I scare her or hurt her? She's already had too much pain in her life. It would kill me to cause her more."

"*Talk* to her. Tell her what you want. She may surprise you. Just ask Hayden what happens when a man isn't honest with the woman he loves." She winks. "He'll tell you how much easier it is to *communicate* than it is to hide from it."

"You're tougher than she is."

"I wouldn't say that at all. She's raised two great kids and battled cancer—on her own. She might be the toughest woman I've ever known."

I hadn't thought of it that way until she put it so bluntly.

"One thing I can tell you from personal experience is that there's nothing a strong woman hates more than to be underestimated."

That's another good point. "What if..." It takes all the courage I can muster to express my deepest fear. "What if she says she's into it and it turns out to be more than she can handle?"

"I assume you'd work out things like limits and safe words in advance?"

"Of course, but that's not what I'm afraid of."

"Then what is it?"

"What if I scare her?"

"If you tell her everything ahead of time, including how you are in a scene, she'll know what to expect and it won't scare her."

"And what if it's too much for her, and she doesn't want me like that?"

"Then at least you'll know how she feels and can go from there. You can't operate in the dark on this. That nearly ruined me and Hayden before we ever had a chance to be together, and that would've been tragic."

There can be no denying how happy Hayden has been since he allowed himself to fall in love with Addie. He's gone from being a cranky pain in my ass to a smiling, dopey fool—and it's all because of the wise woman who's gotten me to say more about what goes on inside me than I've said to anyone. Ever.

And she's right. I should be talking to Aileen about this, and I will. Tonight. As soon as her kids go to bed, I'll lay it on the line and let the chips fall where they may.

Suddenly, I feel like I'm going to be sick.

CHAPTER 9

Aileen

The kids and I have a long, tedious day as I try to keep Maddie quiet and comfortable. I feel sorry for Logan, who wants to go to the beach or the park or something, but he's stuck at home with us. Only the anticipation of Kristian's arrival keeps me sane as I deal with unusually whiny kids.

Maddie's wound hurts, so I give her some Tylenol and put her down for a nap, hoping the medicine will kick in while she rests.

Then I give Logan some badly needed attention, which involves watching *Minions* with him for the nine hundredth time, or at least that's how it seems to me. He loves those movies and is sucked in as always as he reclines against me on the sofa, allowing me to run my fingers through his hair while he watches.

Maddie's accident rattled him as much as it did me, which is why he's a little clingier than usual today. I don't mind it, though. As he gets older, he's less snuggly with me, and I miss my little boy who always wanted me to hold him, even when he was almost too heavy for me to lift.

They're growing up too quickly for my liking, so I take full advantage of the chance to hold him close without him squiggling out of my embrace the way he normally does these days when I try to hold him.

The movie doesn't grab my attention, so my mind wanders to the information Natalie gave me earlier. I'm still trying to wrap my head around what it means, and I'm dying to get online so I can do some research. But I can't do that with my kids underfoot. I know almost nothing about the lifestyle or how it works, but I'm incredibly curious. More than anything, I want to know about how it pertains to him. What does *he* like? And how will I find the courage to broach this topic with him? The thought of saying something like, *hey, I hear you like it kinky* makes me feel like I've plugged myself into an electrical outlet. Every cell in my body has been tingling for hours now.

I feel guilty for allowing my thoughts to go in this direction when I'm snuggled up to my son, but ever since Natalie filled in some major blanks for me earlier, it's almost all I can think about.

I swear the clock is moving in reverse.

I must doze off, because I come to when Logan stretches as the movie ends at five thirty. One hour to go.

"What's for dinner?" he asks.

"Chicken and mac 'n cheese."

"I'm starving."

That's my cue to get up and start dinner. As I bread the chicken the way the kids like it, I recall Kristian telling me he eats "clean," so I keep one piece free of breading for him and make a big salad to go with the mac 'n cheese I make from scratch for the kids. Natalie thought of everything when she supplied us with groceries, and I'm again thankful for her generosity.

With the chicken and mac 'n cheese in the oven and the salad in the fridge, I check on Maddie and tell Logan I'm going to take a shower. I want to look as nice as I can for Kristian, so I take my time getting ready. I find a cute dress from my single days in one of the boxes I shipped from New York. It didn't fit me after I had kids, but now I've lost so much weight, I can wear it again. It's black with cherries on it. The neckline does good things for my breasts, the one place I still have a little extra flesh after my illness.

My cancer was caught early by my gynecologist, during a routine visit. I had a lumpectomy and then a second surgery to remove the one lymph node that came back questionable. Technically, I was diagnosed at stage three because of the lymph node involvement, but my doctors told me it hadn't spread any farther, and they felt confident going with the lumpectomy over the more radical mastectomy. The chemo they'd recommended as a "precaution" had nearly killed me, but that's over now. At least I hope so. That was the worst part, by far. It made me so sick I couldn't eat for weeks. I honestly believe that Flynn getting me in to see Doctor Birnbaum saved my life. He believed I'd been given a nearly lethal dose of chemo that might've killed me if I'd continued that course.

I can't bear to think about all that when I have so many better things to focus on with a sexy man coming for dinner. I do what I can with my short curly hair, put on mascara, a hint of blush, some concealer to hide the signs of the nearly sleepless night, and top it off with lip gloss I bought before I got sick and have never worn.

I leave my bedroom, look in on Maddie again and go to the living room where Logan is playing with his superhero action figures. Iron Man is his favorite, and that's the one he's holding when he looks up at me and does a double take.

"What?" I ask him.

"Nothing. You look... nice. Really nice."

I realize it's been a long time since he saw me make an effort with my appearance and vow to make it a more regular thing so he won't worry about me as much. "Thank you."

"Why did you get dressed up?"

"Because Mr. Kristian is coming over for dinner." I take a seat on the footstool to bring me closer to him.

"Is he your boyfriend?"

"I don't know if I'd call him that, but if he was, how would you feel about it?"

He shrugs. "It's okay." Despite what he says, I see something uncertain in his expression.

I nudge him with my knee. "Tell me the truth."

"He looks at you funny."

My stomach drops to my toes. "He does?"

"Uh-huh." Iron Man takes flight over Logan's head. "That means he likes you."

I want to ask how he knows these things. "You think so?"

"Duh," he says with the grin I love so much. "Even I know that."

"What do you think of him?"

"He's cool. He was really nice to Maddie last night when she got hurt."

"Yes, he was."

"It's okay if you like him, Mom. I don't mind."

"That's good to know. Thank you."

A knock on the door has my heart doing backflips. He's here. I jump up to open the screen door for him, and I'm struck once again by how beautiful he is. Dark wavy hair, incredible blue eyes, made more so by the light blue shirt he's wearing, and a body to die for. He's carrying a huge armload of flowers and a bag.

I hold the screen door for him. "Come in."

"For you," he says, handing me the gorgeous and fragrant arrangement. I recognize lilies and snapdragons and my favorite, white hydrangeas. I love that he included them, which means Natalie must've told him they're my favorite.

"They're beautiful. Thank you."

He offers a small smile as his gaze lands on my lips, letting me know he wants to kiss me but won't with Logan looking on.

I burn for that kiss.

"Hey, Logan."

"Hi."

"How's Maddie?"

"She's napping. The cut was hurting earlier." I nod toward the kitchen. "Want to help me put these in a vase?"

"Um, sure."

In the kitchen, I put the flowers on the counter and turn to him, resting my hands on his hips. "Hi," I whisper.

"Hi, yourself." His voice is gruff and sexy, and I wish I could be alone with him. That thought is unprecedented for me. I'm not the kind of mom who yearns to be free of her kids. I love being with them, and they're never too much for me. The three of us have been a unit for so long. But now...

His lips brush against mine, clearing my brain of every thought as I process his nearness, his scent, the tingle of his late-day scruff against my face.

I take a deep breath.

He shifts his attention to my neck. "Long fucking day," he whispers.

"Were you busy?"

"Yeah, but that's not what made it long."

"No?"

He shakes his head. "Waiting for this made it long." His arms slide around me, bringing me in close to his fully aroused body.

My reaction is instantaneous, my legs are like rubber bands wobbling under me. The last thing I want is to put a stop to something that feels this good, but we can't do this now. "Kristian..."

"Hmm?" He seems to be breathing me in, which I find wildly erotic.

"The kids."

He freezes, raises his head and takes a step back, but his eyes... His eyes are on fire for me. "I'm sorry."

"Don't be. I wanted that as much as you did."

"I'm not sure that's possible."

Realizing he wants me so fiercely makes it that much harder to turn away from him, to put the flowers in a vase, to try to focus on finishing dinner and getting Maddie up so she won't be awake all night.

I'm distracted by his presence and the way he continues to glance at me as I make small talk with him and the kids during dinner on the deck. I pick at my food because it tastes funny, and I'm too wound up to eat.

Kristian watches me while talking to Logan about the game room at his house that my son loved so much when we were there. "You'll have to come over and play again soon."

"Can I, Mom?"

"Sure, we can do that."

"Tomorrow," Kristian says. "We'll order pizza and play games."

"That'd be *awesome*," Logan says, smiling widely.

"What do you say?" I ask him.

"Thank you, Mr. Kristian."

"You can call me Kris if you want. All my friends call me that."

I can see that Logan is thrilled to be elevated to friend status, and I send Kristian a warm smile. He can't possibly know what his kindness and attention toward my kids means to me—and them.

"Can I play, too?" Maddie asks.

"Of course you can. I have the original Frogger game that you'll love. You have to jump the frog across the water from one log to another. I bet you'll be good at that."

"I *love* frogs," Maddie says, her eyes dancing with animation that's a welcome relief after a rough day.

"I know. I saw your frog blanket last night."

And he pays attention. *Swoon.* You can stick a fork in me. I'm all done. This man...

"Frogs and horses," Logan says disdainfully. "That's all she cares about."

"Like you care about video games and gadgets," I reply.

He sticks his tongue out at me.

Laughing, I mess up his hair. "Truth hurts, kiddo."

I make the kids help clean up after dinner, and they work together to put away the food and load the dishwasher while Kristian and I remain outside to give them room to work. Other than mediating a couple of disagreements, I don't get involved.

"They're great kids," he says softly, so only I will hear him. "Polite, funny, cute, sweet, helpful, well-behaved. They must have a fantastic mother." Under the table, his hand finds mine, and he links our fingers.

His touch makes me warm all over. "Thank you. I got lucky with them."

"It takes more than luck to end up with kids who load the dishwasher and clean the kitchen without protest."

"I've always made them help. It's second nature to them by now."

"What time do they go to bed?" he asks, waggling his brows at me.

That's all it takes to set me on fire for him. "Eight. Maddie might be tough tonight because she had a big nap."

He sits back and puts his feet up on the chair that Logan occupied. "That's okay. I don't have anywhere to be."

And I'm supposed to function after hearing that?

I supervise the kids through showers and pajamas. I read them two stories and allow Maddie to listen to some music with her headphones for a while to help her fall asleep after the long nap. I pray that she isn't up all night, because it seems I have plans.

I shiver thinking about kissing him last night and then in the kitchen earlier, not to mention the information Natalie gave me and how I might broach that topic with him.

"Are you cold, Mom?" Logan asks me, misinterpreting my shiver.

"Maybe a little."

"Put a sweater on. I don't want you to get sick again."

He touches my heart when he worries about me. "I'm totally fine," I tell him as I lean over to kiss him good night. "I promise."

"Can we go to the beach tomorrow?"

"We'll see how Maddie feels in the morning."

"I'll feel fine in the morning, so we can go to the beach."

"We can't do anything until everyone goes to sleep." I turn off the lights and leave the door propped so I can hear them if they need me. "Sleep tight, guys. I love you."

"Love you, too," Logan says, his voice heavy with impending sleep.

"Mama," Maddie says. "Can I have a drink of water?"

"Yep. Be right back." I go into the kitchen and fill a plastic tumbler with ice and water, putting a cover on it so I won't be changing sheets in ten minutes, and take it back to her, kissing her one more time. "Close your eyes and go to sleep."

"Okay."

I tiptoe from the room because Logan is already out cold and return to the deck.

Kristian holds out a hand to me. "Everyone settled?"

I take his hand and let him guide me onto his lap. "For now." I'm so caught up in the thrill of being back in his arms I can barely breathe. I feel so safe and comfortable with him, but in the back of my mind, lurking like a dark shadow, are the things Natalie told me about him. Am I crazy to get more involved with someone whose lifestyle is so totally different from mine? Probably, but I can't seem to dial back the out-of-control feelings I have for him.

"I want to ask you something," he says.

I'm immediately on guard. "Okay..."

"The premiere for our new film *Insidious* is Saturday night. I was wondering if you might like to go with me."

"To a *film premiere in Hollywood*?"

He laughs softly. "Yes, that's the plan."

"I... I have the kids, and what would I *wear*?"

"I've already arranged for a sitter for the kids and a stylist for you —that's if you want to go."

My heart beats so hard and so fast, I fear I might hyperventilate. He wants to take me to a *premiere*—as his *date*.

"Aileen? Are you breathing?"

I laugh. "Barely. Who did you find to watch my kids?"

"My assistant Lori's roommate, Cecelia. She's twenty-five and a nurse at the UCLA Medical Center."

"And she wants to *babysit* my kids?"

"Apparently, she's going through a bad breakup and could use the diversion."

"What does she charge per hour?"

"Don't worry about it. I'm paying her."

"I don't feel right about that. They're *my* kids."

"Please let me take care of it. I asked you to come with me. I don't want it to cost you anything."

As I think it over, I roll my bottom lip between my teeth. I'm not used to relying on anyone else when it comes to my kids, but it seems to mean a lot to him that I let him do this for me. "I'd want the kids to meet her before I leave them with her."

"That can be arranged." After a pause, he says, "She agreed to spend the night."

He says that so casually, as if he hasn't dropped a bomb into the middle of our conversation. After another long pause, he gives me a gentle shake. "Hello? Earth to Aileen. Come in, please."

"I, um..."

"No pressure, sweetheart. If you'd rather come home, that's totally fine. I just wanted to give you the option of a night away."

I want everything he's offering with a fiery yearning I haven't felt in... well... *ever*.

"If you want to think about it, that's totally fine."

"No."

His brow lifts even as his face falls with obvious disappointment. "No?"

"I don't want to think about it. I want to go with you and be... with you." I feel overheated and overwhelmed as I take the biggest leap I've ever taken. Whatever this is that's happening with him, I want it. I want *him*.

His low groan, the tight squeeze of his arms around me and the hard press of his erection against my bottom let me know he's every bit as affected by what's happening between us as I am, and there's comfort in that. "How will I live until Saturday?" He raises a hand to my face and turns me toward him for a deep, sensual kiss that makes my head spin.

How will *I* live until Saturday?

His other hand lands on my leg and slides upward as he kisses me with deep strokes of his tongue.

"Mommy." Maddie is at the door to the deck.

I turn away from the kiss and get up, thankful for the darkness that makes it so she can't see that I'm on his lap kissing his face off. Kristian releases me, and I get up on wobbly legs to go to my daughter. "What's wrong, sweetie?"

"Logan is snoring."

Every cell in my body hums with unfulfilled desire as I usher her back toward the bedroom. "I thought you were listening to your music?"

"I was, but then I wasn't, and Logan is snoring so I can't sleep."

"Get back in bed."

She does what I tell her while I gently turn Logan so he's not on his back. It's a delicate operation, but thankfully, he doesn't wake up. "There," I whisper to Maddie. "He'll be quiet now. No more getting up unless you feel sick." I kiss her and tuck her in. "Okay?"

"Okay, Mommy." Her thumb finds its way into her mouth, and her eyes close.

I stroke her hair and rub her back, hoping to help her relax.

I'm reeling from Kristian's invitation, the knowledge that we'll have a full night together in a few days and the desire that beats through me like a separate heartbeat. When I'm confident that Maddie is settled for the night, I get up to leave her and return to Kristian on the deck.

"All set?" he asks, extending his hand to bring me back to his lap.

"I hope so."

"Should I go?"

"Do you want to?"

"Not even kinda."

I laugh at the blunt statement. "Then don't."

His arms encircle me as he nuzzles my neck. "I keep telling myself I shouldn't be here. I shouldn't allow this to happen, but I can't stay away. I can't help myself."

"I wish you didn't feel so conflicted."

"There're things... about me... Things you don't know, and if you did, you might not want this."

"Do you mean the BDSM?"

He goes rigid with shock. "How in the hell do you know about that?"

"I hear things."

"Jesus," he mutters.

"Does it make you angry that I know about that?"

"Angry? No. I'm surprised more than anything."

"Because I know?"

"Not that so much as the fact that you're still here."

"Did you think it would frighten me?"

"It should."

"Why?"

He huffs out a breath and shakes his head. "If you knew me, *really* knew me, you wouldn't want me."

I hear despair in his words, and that touches me deeply. "Remember when you said you can't stay away, you can't help yourself?"

He nods.

"I feel the same way." I smooth the hair back from his forehead. "I can't help wanting to be with you. I want to know and understand you, including the things you think will frighten me."

"I'm not used to your kind of honesty."

"Let me tell you what having cancer does to a person. It makes you realize life is short and precious and every minute matters. It makes you intolerant of bullshit."

He cups my face and runs his thumb over my lips. "It makes you a refreshing change of pace."

"Will you talk to me about the reasons you feel so unworthy of me?"

He shakes his head. "I don't talk about that stuff with anyone."

"That's not going to fly with me."

He looks at me with surprise.

"Can I tell you a story?"

"Sure."

"I want to tell you about the man who fathered my children."

CHAPTER 10

Kristian

I'm still reeling from the fact that she knows about the BDSM. She also knows I'm hiding things from her, and yet she's still here, snuggled into my arms, about to share part of herself with me. It's all I can do to keep breathing while I wait to hear what she'll say.

"I met Rex the summer after I graduated from college. I was at the Jersey Shore with my college friends for a week, and he came to a party we had at the house we rented. We hit it off immediately. He was charming and sweet and sincere. I was used to guys who talked a big game but didn't deliver. That wasn't him. He called when he said he would, showed up when he said he would, he had a good job in the finance sector, came from a nice family. He checked all my boxes, and I fell deeply in love with him over the next few months."

I hold her hand as she speaks, needing the connection, even as the thought of her in love with another man makes me seethe. What can I say? I'm hardly rational where she's concerned.

"We got pregnant with Logan by accident. I wasn't ready to be a mom. I'd only just graduated from college and was focused on trying to start my career in marketing. I cried for days, but Rex... He was rock solid and so excited to be a father. Eventually, his excitement led to mine, and I began to accept that my plans had changed.

"Looking back now, I can't believe I was ever anything less than thrilled to be a mom, because my kids are the best thing to ever happen to me. We talked about getting married, but we never got around to it between work and taking care of Logan. Rex was a good father to Logan, but during that first year, he began to go missing for hours at a time, and when I'd ask where he'd been, he never had a good explanation. I was afraid he was cheating on me. We weren't married. We had a new baby. I was tired all the time. Our sex life had become almost nonexistent by that point. It was frightening to me because he made most of the money we lived on, and I couldn't conceive of how we'd get by if he left us."

It kills me to hear her talk about being afraid or lonely. I gather her in closer to me. "Hold on to me."

She puts her arms around my neck, and I stand to carry her inside, sliding the screen door closed behind me. I debate between the sofa and her room and choose her room, putting her down on the bed and crawling in next to her.

She snuggles into my arms. "Much better."

Stroking a hand over her short hair, I say, "Tell me the rest."

"I finally confronted him about his absences, and he assured me there was no one else, that he loved me and Logan and wanted our life together. For a few years, things were good, and then, when I was pregnant with Maddie, he began to disappear again, once for two days. I heard from the wife of one of his colleagues that he'd lost his job, and I panicked. I had no idea what to do or who to call. When he finally turned up, he'd been badly beaten. His face was so swollen, I barely recognized him. I wanted to take him to the hospital, but he refused. I tended to him until he recovered, and then I demanded he tell me where he'd been. He broke down. I'd never seen him cry before. He told me he'd been hooked on cocaine since before he met me, and he couldn't lead the double life anymore."

I gasp because I didn't see that coming. I'm not sure where I thought this was leading, but it wasn't there. "God, Aileen."

"There I was with a four-year-old, a baby due in two months, a part-time job, a three-thousand-dollar-a-month apartment and a drug addict boyfriend. And how, I asked myself, had I not known? With hindsight, though, I could see the signs were all there. I just didn't put them together. I asked him to go to rehab, and he refused. I told him he had to leave, even though I was terrified of being alone with two kids. I helped him pack his bags. He kissed Logan good night, hugged me, said he was sorry he couldn't be what we needed, and he left. I've never seen him again."

"Jesus. I don't even know what to say."

"I had Maddie by myself while a lady in our building watched Logan for me. The next day, I brought her home from the hospital, and the three of us have been a family ever since."

I hold her tight against me, my heart beating hard and fast. I've never wanted to protect anyone from further hurt more than I do her and her kids.

"What about your family?" I ask.

"My mom died from ALS when I was fifteen."

"That's awful. I'm so sorry."

"It was awful. I wouldn't wish that disease on my worst enemy. My dad remarried a couple of years after she died and had a second family with his new wife. They live in Louisiana, and my three half-siblings are in high school now. We don't see much of them."

"No other siblings?"

"Just me."

"We have that in common. I always wanted brothers. Flynn, Jasper and the others at Quantum are the siblings I never had."

"Do you understand why I told you about Rex?"

"I think so."

"I don't do secrets, Kristian. That's my line in the sand."

I have so many secrets, things I've never told anyone, that it would take a lifetime to share them all with her. This would be a really good time to tell her I can't do this. I can't be what she wants or needs, because my secrets would horrify her. I should get up and leave. I should walk out her door and never look back. But I can't bring myself to move, to do what I know I should. I don't know *how* to share that part of myself with her, because I've never shared it with anyone.

We all have our secrets, as we found out recently when we learned that Henry Kingsley is Jasper's father, and Jasper is a British marquess in line to inherit a dukedom. I come from the opposite end of the social spectrum, the side that people tend to overlook and forget about.

"Kristian?"

When she says my name, I realize I've zoned out and left her hanging. I take her hand, linking our fingers, unable to be this close to her without wanting to touch her. "I don't know how to do this."

"To do what?"

"This. A real relationship. I've never done it before."

"*Ever?*"

I shake my head, feeling the old bite of shame at having to admit such a thing. How does a man get to almost thirty-seven years old without ever having a girlfriend? I'll tell you how, and it'll give you nightmares. "I keep telling myself that I should go, that I should walk away while I still can, but it's already too late for that. I can't make myself go when I know it would be the best thing for you and your kids."

"*Why* do you say that, Kristian? I want to understand what you think is so wrong with you."

"Everything is wrong with me."

She sighs with exasperation as I tell her nothing and everything at the same time. "I don't know what that means."

I keep my gaze fixed on our joined hands, needing that connection in more ways than one. "You and your kids, you're a family. Until I became part of Quantum, I'd never been part of a family before."

Her eyes fill with sympathy that makes me mad. I don't want her to feel sorry for me. But I don't let her see the anger. As always, I bury it deep inside with a lifetime's worth of rage. "What about your parents?"

"I never knew my father, and my mother was murdered when I was three."

She gasps. "Oh my God, Kristian..."

"I've never told anyone that. Even my closest friends don't know."

I expect her to ask me why I haven't told them, but she doesn't. Rather, she releases my hand, moves closer and puts her arms around me, her fingers sliding into my hair. "I'm so sorry that happened to you."

She doesn't know the half of what happened to me.

"Do you... Do you remember her?"

"Vividly. I also remember hiding in the closet when she was killed. He never knew I was there."

She tightens her hold on me, and in her arms, I'm the little boy who watched the life leave his mother, who was left alone with her body for four endless days until someone heard me crying and called the cops. Every minute of those four days is seared into my memory, never to be forgotten no matter how much I wish it could be.

"What happened to you? Afterward?"

"I survived."

Aileen

My heart breaks for the three-year-old who lost his mother to murder.

He raises his head, his gaze fierce. "I don't want you to feel sorry for me. That's not why I told you."

"I can still be sorry that such a thing happened to you, can't I?"

"I've worked long and hard not to be defined by the things that happened to me before I had control of my life. I don't tell people about it because I don't want to be pitied."

That word... Control... It stands out to me after what Natalie told me about his sexual preferences. I'm filled with desire and curiosity. I want to know everything there is to know about him.

"I understand," I tell him, even if the lump in my throat makes a liar out of me.

"I heard you when you said you don't do secrets, and I respect that, but there are things I just don't talk about because it's shit I'd rather forget than resurrect."

I have so many questions, but I can't ask. Not now anyway.

"You should tell me to go."

"Why?"

"Because you deserve someone who can be tender and sweet with you and your kids. That's not me."

"How can you say that after the way you took care of Maddie and me last night? Or how you made sure we had everything we needed when we moved? How can you say that when you kiss me the way you do and touch me with such reverence?"

He stares at me, seeming stunned by the revelations.

"I want you to do something for me," I say, summoning the courage I'll need to take the next step with this complicated, sexy man.

"I'd do anything for you."

Does he hear himself? He's saying everything I've ever wanted to hear from a man—and he means every word he says to me. That alone is such a priceless gift after what I went through with Rex. "I want you to stop warning me off you. I'm a big girl, and I can make my own decisions for myself and my children. I want you in our lives, or you wouldn't be here."

"You don't know everything you should to make that decision."

"I should be warning you off me."

"What? Why?"

"In case you haven't heard, I've been diagnosed with a sometimes-fatal illness that is currently under control but leaves a huge question mark hanging over the rest of my life. You'd be crazy to get involved with me. Not to mention I have two little kids who'll always be in the way of whatever is happening between us."

For the first time in a while, a smile tugs at his lips. "You think you're so clever, don't you?"

"I'm not being clever. I'm simply stating that I'm not the best risk either."

His big hand cups my face as he stares down at me. "Please don't talk about you dying. That's not going to happen."

"It will someday."

"But not any time soon."

"You can't possibly know that."

"I know it," he says as he brings his lips down on mine, kissing me with a fierceness he hasn't shown me before now.

I slide my arms around his neck and fall into the kiss that sets my body on fire for more of him.

Apparently, it does the same to him, because he ends up on top of me, the hard ridge of his erection pressed against my core. I raise my hips, needing more, and he groans into my mouth.

"You make me so crazy, Aileen. I've never wanted anyone the way I want you."

His confession makes me feel light-headed and empowered—a heady combination.

I lay my hand on his chest and begin to unbutton his shirt, wanting to feel his skin next to mine. I'm immediately hit with fears that he'll find my body unattractive. I have scars and stretch marks and sharp hip bones. The thought has me stopping halfway through the job of unbuttoning his shirt.

"What's wrong?"

"I'm not really back to where I was before I got sick. You might think—"

"I think you're beautiful, sexy and desirable." His lips skim over the sensitive skin on my neck. "If you knew how much time I spend thinking about you, you'd have another reason to run away from me."

My fingers dig into his muscular bicep. I don't remember desire feeling like this, or maybe it's just that nothing has ever felt quite like this. I'm on the verge of forgetting my kids are asleep right across the hall. "I think about you just as much."

His hand is on my leg, sliding up under my skirt. "We need to talk about some things before this goes any further."

"What things?" I ask, barely able to string together two words while I wait to see what he'll do.

"Things like limits and safe words and what it really means to submit."

I swallow hard and realize I'm trembling.

"Does that frighten you?"

I shake my head. "It excites me."

Exhaling, he drops his head to my chest. "Aileen..."

I run my fingers through his hair because I've wanted to for so long, and now I can any time I want. "What's wrong?"

He raises his head to meet my gaze. "I'm trying to figure out how I'll survive until I can have you to myself on Saturday."

I finish unbuttoning his shirt and push it open as I raise my hips, hoping he'll take the hint to keep going.

"The kids..."

"Are asleep. Nothing wakes them after they're asleep. It's okay."

Groaning, he cups my pussy over my underwear. "So hot and wet."

"That's all for you."

He withdraws his hand and lies back on the bed, arm over his face, leaving me to wonder what's wrong. "Sorry," he says after a long silence. "I... If I touch you the way I want to, I won't be able to stop, and we can't do what I want to do with your kids across the hall."

My heart—and the rest of me—goes haywire as I imagine the things he wants to do. I have a feeling my imagination is no match for the reality of him. I let my gaze travel down his chest to the huge bulge in his pants that has me reaching out, before I even consciously decide to, and placing my hand on that rigid flesh.

His groan is quickly becoming one of my favorite sounds. "Aileen..."

"Let me."

When his hands fall to his sides, I recognize his surrender and get up on wobbly legs to shut and lock my bedroom door. Returning to the bed, I unbuckle his belt and free him from his pants, gasping at the size of him. *Dear God.* For the longest time, all I can do is stare.

"Sweetheart, you're killing me here."

"I haven't done... anything... in a long time. That's not going to fit."

He cracks up laughing. "Wait till you see all the places it'll fit."

My face is on fire with desire as an array of salacious images flashes through my mind like a raunchy movie starring the sexiest man I've ever met. "I'm going to pretend you didn't say that."

Smiling, he covers my hand with his and shows me how he likes to be touched. "Yes," he says, "just like that." He closes his eyes and sinks back into a pillow.

Leaning over him, I draw the broad head into my mouth and apply gentle suction.

"Oh fuck... Aileen... Oh my God. Don't stop, baby. *Please don't stop.*" The words are like a chant. He guides me with a hand on the back of my head as I take as much of him as I can—which isn't much, but that doesn't seem to matter to him. "Aileen, honey..." He gives my hair a gentle tug to dislodge me. Grasping his cock, he directs it away from my face and comes all over his chest.

Watching him lose control is the sexiest freaking thing I've ever seen. I get up to grab a towel out of the bathroom and use it to clean him up. He watches me intently, and when I'm done, he takes my hand and gives a gentle tug to bring me down on top of him.

Wrapping his arms around me, he says, "Tell me to go."

I shake my head. "I don't want you to go." I drop my gaze to his lips, and the next thing I know, he's turned us so I'm under him and he's kissing me again like his life depends on it. My dress is raised up and over my head, leaving me in a skimpy pair of panties and a bra that fortunately match. He releases the front clasp of my bra and pushes the cups aside, bringing my chest into contact with his.

At that moment, I can't be bothered worrying about scars or bones or stretch marks, not when his heat is all around me and his big body is anchoring me to the bed.

"Wait," he says when I begin to squirm, looking for more. "I want to remember what this feels like." He drops his head to my shoulder.

I wrap my arms around him, and we stay like that for a long while.

"I think this might be the single most perfect moment of my entire life," he says after a long silence.

The emotion I hear in his voice makes my heart flutter in response to him. "The first of many."

CHAPTER 11

Aileen

He kisses me again, so hard that my lips will be bruised tomorrow, but I can't be worried about the future when the present requires my full attention. Then he's kissing his way down the front of me, and I freeze, worried about the scars from my surgery and how he might react to them.

"Kristian, wait..." I try to cover my left breast, the site of the lumpectomy.

He nudges my hand out of his way. "I have scars, too. Just because you can't see them doesn't mean they aren't there. Everything about you is beautiful to me, especially the part about you being alive and here with me."

It's the perfect thing for him to say, and I don't resist when he moves my hands to my sides. I let him take a good long look at the part of me that I'd never let anyone see if it were up to me. He kisses a line from the bottom of the scar to the top, which is right below my nipple. I have another scar in my armpit where the node was removed.

"You said it's been a long time for you. How long are we talking?"

"Since Rex."

He draws in a deep breath, holds it, releases it. "We need a safe word, something that stops everything if you aren't digging what's going on."

"Am I going to be unsafe with you?"

"Never," he says fiercely. "You've never been safer than you are with me."

I've seen him eight times in my life, and I already know that's true. "Then why do I need a safe word?"

"Because that's how this works. You have a way to stop it at any time. That's the *only* way this works."

"What will we do that I might want to stop?"

"We'll do everything."

"That's too vague." I drag my finger down his chest to his abdomen, outlining each muscle and loving the way they quiver under my touch. "Tell me what you like."

He captures my hand and stretches it up and over my head. "I want to bind you to the bed so you can't move and blindfold you so you can't see. I want you totally defenseless against what I might do to you. I want you to wonder what's coming next. I want you on the razor's edge of desire so sharp, it hurts."

Holy shit. I'm already there, from his words alone. But it's more than the words. It's the heat in his eyes and the gruff tone of his voice that put me there.

"Does any of that frighten you?"

"No," I say, but the quiver in my voice gives me away. "Is there more?"

"So much more." He cups my breast and pinches my nipple, lightly at first, but then with increasingly more pressure. "How would you feel about clamps?" His expression changes. "Ah, fuck. Forget that. I never should've asked you that."

I'm having trouble keeping up. "Why?"

"You had breast cancer. Of course you don't want nipple clamps. I was out of line asking you that."

I cover his hand, which is now flat on my belly. "I like that you forgot, even for a moment, that I had cancer and treated me like any other woman."

"You're not like any other woman."

His sweet words go straight to my heart. "I want to be normal again, Kristian. If you treat me like I'm still sick, that'll hurt me."

"So that's a yes to nipple clamps?" he asks with a teasing smile.

"That's a yes to everything."

"You have no idea what *everything* entails."

"I want to know, and I want you to teach me."

Groaning, he drops his head to my chest. "I can't talk about this anymore tonight, or I won't be responsible for what happens with your kids across the hall."

Knowing he wants me so badly is such a huge turn-on. In fact, I don't think I've ever been more aroused in my life than I am right now. I shift my legs, seeking relief from the relentless ache.

"Is someone feeling needy?" he asks.

"Mmm." I stroke his hair and back, wanting to touch him everywhere now that I'm allowed to indulge the many fantasies I've had about him since we first met.

"We can't have that." He kisses a path straight down the front of me, using his lips and tongue to set me on fire for him while he cups my breasts and gently runs his thumbs over my tight nipples.

I feel his teeth against my hip bone and nearly levitate off the bed.

"Easy, baby. I'll take care of you."

I'm a quivering, trembling mess of tingling nerve endings by the time he eases my panties down my legs, tossing them aside as he kneels on the bed between my legs, his hands flat against my thighs as he gazes down at what he's uncovered. I wonder if he can see how wet I am and begin to feel embarrassed.

"Stop thinking I don't like what I see. Look at me."

I force my eyes to open and meet that intense gaze that's becoming so familiar to me.

"Can you see how hard I am for you?"

I drop my eyes to his groin, where his huge, hard cock indicates that he likes what he sees. He likes it very much.

"Any questions?"

"No," I say with a nervous laugh.

"I never again want you to think you're anything other than perfect to me. Do you hear me?"

I nod.

"The proper response would be 'Yes, Sir.'"

I hold his gaze, realizing the importance of this moment. If I give him that, I'll be crossing a line that can't be uncrossed.

"The choice is always yours, honey," he says softly. "You have all the power here. Do you understand?"

I swallow hard and lick my lips, drawing his fierce gaze to my mouth. "Yes, Sir. I understand."

"Good." He bends over me. His lips skimming against my inner thigh make me want to beg for more, but I sense that begging will only prolong the agony.

His broad shoulders force my legs apart, until I'm spread before him like a sacrifice.

My pussy is still bare from the chemo. The hair never grew back, not that I'm complaining, and judging from the way Kristian stares at me, he has no complaints either.

"Tell me this pussy belongs to me—and only me."

"It's yours," I say breathlessly. "It's all yours."

A low growl rumbles through him, and my hips jerk, wanting him closer. If he doesn't do something—*anything*—soon, I'm going to lose it. "Is my baby feeling needy?"

"God, *yes*," I say in a voice that doesn't even sound like me. "Please, Kristian..."

"What's my name here?"

"Sir. Please, Sir."

"Tell me what you want."

I want to cry from frustration and need and the clawing, craving desire that's all new to me. I'm so wet and hot and achy. "I want your tongue. And your fingers."

"Where?"

Realizing he's going to make me say it is like dumping gas on the already out-of-control flame burning inside me. "My pussy. I want your tongue and fingers on my pussy. In me..."

"I always want you to tell me what you need. Will you do that?"

Though it doesn't come naturally to say such things out loud, I bite my lip and nod. With each minute, I begin to get a better idea of what it'll be like to be intimate with him, to be dominated by him. And though I'm uncomfortable and slightly embarrassed by the things he makes me say and do, I want more.

He strokes me first with his fingers, sliding them through the flood between my legs and then driving them into me, curling them to reach the spot deep inside that makes me cry out from the overload of sensation that hits me all at once.

"Shhhh," he says. "Don't wake the kids before I make you come at least twice."

The noise that comes out of me is barely human. Then he adds his tongue, and I'm completely lost to him, ruined for any man who isn't him. His tongue is everywhere, licking in long strokes that make me crazy. Then he sucks my clit into his mouth and runs his tongue back and forth, taking me right to the brink of release before backing off, leaving me panting and sweaty.

"So hot and sweet and tight," he whispers, fucking me with his fingers while ruining me with his tongue.

"*Please...*" His arm across my hips ramps up the desperation because I can't do anything to ease the ache.

"Is this what you want?" he asks, sucking on my clit as he drives his fingers into me again.

I detonate. That's the only word I can think of to describe the explosion that rocks me, taking me right out of myself and into a realm I never knew existed. I come down slowly, and the first thing I'm aware of is Kristian kissing away my tears while his fingers continue to move in me, milking the last waves of the epic orgasm.

I'm blinded by the tears that keep coming.

"Talk to me, baby. Tell me you're okay."

My lips are dry, so I lick them and look up to find him watching me now with concern rather than desire. "I'm okay."

"Are you sure?"

Nodding, I reach for him and bring him down on top of me, even as his fingers are still lodged deep inside me.

"Did it feel good?"

I laugh, because how can he ask me that? "If it felt any better, I might not have survived it."

"That's just the beginning," he says, nuzzling my neck and ear, which starts the slow burn all over again, as if my body didn't just do something I would've thought impossible an hour ago.

"I've never felt anything like that. Ever."

"I want to fuck you so bad. I've never wanted anyone like this."

"Do it. Right now." I've clearly lost my mind, but I can't be bothered to think about any of the many reasons why we shouldn't. Not when he's big and strong and hard in my arms, his erection throbbing against my belly.

"Not here. When I fuck you for the first time, I want to be completely alone with you."

I sob at the thought of having to wait days to feel him inside me, stretching me.

"We need to talk birth control. Are you on it?"

"I have an IUD to deal with my erratic periods." I don't mention the nonhormonal IUD also reduces my risk of cervical and endometrial cancer. Nothing kills a mood faster than the C word, and I've had enough of that word to last me a lifetime.

"Thank Christ, because I don't want to have to use condoms. Not with you. I've never had sex with anyone without a condom. Ever. Tomorrow, I'll get you proof that I'm clean."

That he wants me to be the first woman he has sex with without a condom fills me with elation, especially knowing what I do about his sexual proclivities.

He curls his fingers inside me, reminding me he's not finished with me yet. Just that quickly, I'm right back to the edge of release. "I want another one."

"I'm not sure I can."

His low rumble of laughter does wondrous things for his handsome face and lights up his eyes. I like that happy, joyful look on him and want to see it more often. He's so serious and intense most of the time. "Is that a challenge?"

"I already know better than to challenge you."

"Oh, but I so love a challenge. You wouldn't want to deny me, would you?"

I would deny him nothing, but it's probably too soon to say so. I just shake my head and let my legs fall open, inviting him to do whatever he wants to me. If the first time was about ravenous hunger, this time is all slow seduction. His fingers and tongue work in concert to keep me climbing, the orgasm growing and multiplying with every stroke. He keeps it up until I'm about to explode, and then, very subtly, he removes a finger from my pussy and presses it against my ass, demanding entry.

I explode. The second time is somehow greater than the first, if that's even possible. Every muscle in my body—hell, every *cell* in my body—is fully engaged, and when I begin to recover my senses, I discover his finger is firmly planted in my ass. The discovery triggers a second wave that he fully exploits, leaving me a quivering mess in the aftermath.

"So fucking hot," he whispers as he uses his free hand to stroke his cock until he comes all over my belly. "I can't wait to be inside you when that happens."

I can only whimper in response. He's demolished me, and we haven't even had sex yet.

He withdraws from me slowly, making me cry out again from the overwhelming sensations that rocket through me. He gets up and goes into the bathroom. I hear water running before he returns with a warm washcloth that he uses to clean me up. When he's finished, he puts a hand on either side of my hips and stares down at me, as if trying to drink me in.

"I've had every kind of sex a person can have," he says bluntly. "And this, with you, was the hottest sex I've had with anyone."

His raw confession makes my heart ache with something that feels an awful lot like love. "And we haven't even actually had sex yet." I go for levity in a desperate effort to recover my equilibrium.

A pulse of tension in his cheek has me running my finger over it, wanting to ease him.

"Saturday night... Yes?"

"I'll want to meet the sitter ahead of time."

"I'll have Lori set that up."

"And I want to pay her."

"You're not paying her. I invited you. I'm paying her."

"They're my kids!"

"I'm paying."

"Are you going to try to dominate me outside the bedroom, too?"

"Not at all, but some things are nonnegotiable. This is one of them."

When I begin to protest, he lays a finger over my lips. "Let me do this. I need to be able to do things for you and the kids. It makes me happy to do things for you—and them."

I sense that not a lot has made him truly happy in his life, so I'm loath to argue the point. "Within reason."

He flashes a victorious smile that has me wondering if I just made a huge mistake.

CHAPTER 12

Kristian

I carry the time I spent in Aileen's bed with me through the insanely busy day that follows those blissful hours. She's all I can think about. I relive every minute a thousand times and have the erection to prove it. I spend most of the day sitting behind my desk or at a conference room table, hoping no one notices my agitated state.

At noon, I text her because I can't wait another minute. *Pizza and games at my place tonight?*

We'd love that. What time and what can I bring?

Six thirty and only you and the kids.

Send me the address again.

I text the address and instructions for accessing the garage, giving her the code that will admit her to my building. Only Jasper, Hayden, Flynn and Marlowe have that code. And now Aileen has it, too.

Through an endless afternoon of meetings and phone calls and details, I count the hours until I can get the hell out of here and be with her again.

Flynn knocks on my door shortly after five. "You got a minute?"

"Yep."

We spent a big chunk of today talking logistics for the film we are making about Natalie's story.

Flynn closes the door.

"Everything okay?"

"I owe you an apology."

"What for?"

"Nat told me that she gave Aileen the 411 on you and the BDSM. She shouldn't have done that, and I told her so."

"It's fine," I say, waving away his apology. "She saved us a lot of time and angst by filling in the blanks for Aileen."

"Still, it wasn't her story to tell."

"Aileen said Natalie didn't want us to go through what Hayden and Addie did when he refused to let her into that part of his life. She does make a good point. We're all about the communication in our lifestyle, and yet we have the hardest time telling new people."

"You're taking this better than I thought you would. We all know how fiercely private you are."

"Aren't we all?"

"You take it to a whole other level. After fifteen years, sometimes I feel like I don't know you any better than I did the day I met you."

"You know the things that matter."

"Do I?"

"What's this about, Flynn?" I feel cornered, and I don't care for that feeling. It brings back too many memories I'd sooner forget.

"Nothing. I just wanted to apologize."

"No need. It's all good."

"So you and Aileen..."

"Night, Flynn," I say, forcing a smile.

"Just tell me one thing..."

I raise a brow in inquiry.

"You're being careful with her, right?"

The implication that I wouldn't be infuriates me. "Good night, Flynn." This time I say it without the smile.

Thankfully, he lets it go and leaves with a wave.

Why am I so damned mad that he felt the need to ask me that? I know he's only looking out for his and Natalie's friend, but still... It's offensive that he felt he needed to ask. But when I think about all the things he's seen me do with other women, the fury dissipates as quickly as it formed. He has every good reason to be concerned for his friend, and I can't blame him for putting me on notice that I'll answer to him if any harm comes to her at my hand.

That won't happen. I'd rather die than cause her harm.

I text him. *Sorry for being a dick. She's safe with me. I promise.*

All good, he replies.

My concentration is totally blown, and I can't wait another hour and a half to see her. I text her. *Cutting out of work early if you want to come sooner.*

We'll leave in ten.

I grab my keys and phone, leaving the piles of work I'd normally bring home with me. Fuck work. I have far better things to do tonight than work.

Lori looks up with surprise when I emerge from my office about two hours earlier than usual.

"Will you call this in for me?" I hand her a piece of paper where I've written the number of the pizza place and the order for a large cheese, a large veggie and a house salad.

"That's a lot for one person," she says, giving me a curious look that I ignore.

"Did you ask Cecilia to call my friend?"

"It's all set. She's going over there tomorrow to meet her and her kids. And she's thrilled to have the chance to make some extra money."

"Tell her it can be a regular thing if she wants it to be."

"I'm sure she will. She has hideous student loans." Lori props her chin on her upturned fist, settling in for a good gossip session that I have every intention of avoiding. "Does someone have a *girlfriend*?"

"Oh damn." I check my watch. "Look at the time. Gotta run. Call in that order."

"Yes, sir, Bossman."

When she calls me sir, it does nothing for me. But when Aileen did it last night... *Stop or you'll be hard before you get on the elevator.*

It seems every Quantum employee has a question for me that has to be answered before I reach the elevator and press the Down button, determined to make my escape without further delay.

The doors open, and Addie walks out, looking flushed. Her lips are swollen, and there's a bite mark on her neck.

"Oh, hey, Kris."

"Addison. Are you coming from the directors' suite by any chance?"

"How'd you know?" she asks, having the good sense to look a little guilty.

Laughing, I shake my head. She's made Hayden so damned happy that what do I care if they're taking a little "break" at the end of the workday? Addie keeps Flynn ruthlessly organized and has done wonders for Hayden's surly disposition. That makes her one of our VIP employees. "It's written all over your face—and your neck." I kiss her forehead and get on the elevator. "Have a good night."

She sticks her hand between the doors to keep them from closing. "Tenley has an appointment with Aileen tomorrow. I told her to give Aileen the full treatment, including hair, nails and makeup. Hope that's okay."

"That's what I wanted. Thank you."

"Not a problem. Flynn tells me I'm excellent at spending other people's money."

"You have to do what you're good at."

"Exactly! Can you tell him that?"

"I'll make a point of it."

"I know we're not talking about this, but I'm really happy for you and Aileen."

"Don't jinx us."

"Wouldn't dream of it." She removes her hand, and the doors close.

On the ride to the ground floor, I realize I'm smiling like a crazy loon as an unfamiliar feeling bubbles up inside me. What the hell is that? Whatever it is, I've never experienced it before, but it sure does feel good.

$\mathcal{A}ileen$

The kids are almost as excited as I am to go to Kristian's for pizza and to play in the game room that Logan tells me is "sick." I didn't see it the last time we were there. Flynn took the kids upstairs while I stayed with Natalie, Addie, Ellie and Marlowe downstairs. Of course, Kristian was there, too, which is the primary reason I never made it upstairs.

Traffic is a beast, and the slow crawl into town gives me far too much time to relive last night for the three thousandth time. I've been distracted and off my game with the kids today, which of course they noticed.

Logan keeps eyeing me, even now that we are in the car.

At a stop light, I glance over at him. "What's up?"

"Nothing."

"Are you lying?"

"No."

"Logan..."

"Are you sick again?"

"What? No! I feel great."

"Oh." He deflates before my eyes, as if he's releasing a breath he's been holding all day. "That's good."

I glance in the rearview mirror to make sure Maddie still has her headphones on as she watches *Frozen* for the millionth time on the iPad. "Can I tell you a secret?"

"Uh-huh."

"You can't tell anyone."

"Duh, Mom. I know what a secret is." The words drip with disdain that makes me wonder what the teenage years will be like.

"What would you say if I told you Mr. Kristian might actually be my boyfriend now?"

"That's cool. I told you before that I like him."

I glance over at him, noting the wistfulness in his expression.

"What're you thinking?"

"That it might be nice to have a dad. Someday."

Oh God. He breaks my heart. "It's still very new. But today, when I was kind of zoning out—"

"Kind of?" he asks with a goofy grin.

"Okay, totally zoning out... I was thinking about him."

"That's a lot better than you being sick again and not wanting to tell us."

"Yes, it certainly is." I reach for his hand and curl my fingers around his. "Don't worry about me getting sick again, okay? Everything is fine, and I'd tell you if it wasn't." Telling them the first time around was one of the hardest things I've ever had to do.

"Okay."

"So you don't care if I have a boyfriend?"

"I don't care. I want you to be happy."

"I'm happy with you and Maddie."

"That's different."

"Yes, it is," and I'm stunned that my nine-year-old already knows that there're different kinds of happy.

We arrive at Kristian's building a short time later, and it takes me a minute to find the entrance to the parking garage. I lean out the window to punch in the code he gave me, and the door opens to admit us. I park in an empty space.

"*Whoa*," Logan says, taking in the fancy sports cars that line the opposite wall.

Do they all belong to Kristian? Holy crap. Of course, I know he's loaded, but to see proof of his staggering wealth is somewhat overwhelming.

"Do you think he'll let me check them out?" Logan asks.

"I'm sure he would."

"That'd be so cool."

I love to see him so excited and animated. During the bleak months of my illness, I had reason to wonder if any of us would ever be excited or animated about anything again. But those days are far behind us now, even if the residual trauma lingers in all of us.

Maddie fell asleep during the drive, so I unbuckle her from her booster seat and lift her into my arms. She's gotten so big recently. I won't be able to carry her for much longer. I no sooner have that thought than the elevator dings, and Kristian is there to greet us.

My heart kicks into overdrive, and my mouth goes dry at the sight of him and the way he looks at me... No one has ever looked at me like that, and I feel dizzy until I realize I'm holding my breath.

"Let me take her," he says, reaching for Maddie.

He lifts her effortlessly into his arms, curling one arm protectively around her while using his free hand to ruffle Logan's hair. "What's up, my man?"

"Are those cars all yours?"

"They are."

"Holy cow. What kind are they?"

Pointing to each one, Kristian says, "McLaren MP4, Rolls-Royce Phantom, Audi R8, Tesla, BMW M6 and Mercedes G-Wagon. I keep a bright red Lamborghini in New York."

"Whoa. Can I sit in them?"

"Sure. Why don't we do that after dinner?"

Logan smiles up at him. "Okay."

"Will you push the Up arrow on the elevator?" Kristian asks him.

"Yep." Logan runs ahead of us to summon the elevator.

Kristian curls his free hand around my neck, bringing me in for a quick kiss. "Longest day *ever*," he says gruffly.

That's all it takes to put my girl parts on full alert. "For me, too."

He gives me a small smile before releasing me to give Logan his full attention, encouraging him to push the button for the penthouse and showing him how to work the key card that gives us access to his home—all this while continuing to hold my sleeping daughter.

Then he hands me the key card, and the meaningful look we

exchange is full of so many things, I can't process them all. "Keep that so you can come over any time you want."

We've been here five minutes, and I'm already dying to be alone with him. But that's not going to happen tonight. We arrive in Kristian's spacious contemporary home with the windows that look out over the Hollywood Hills. He gently puts Maddie on the sofa and pulls a light blanket over her.

"Is it normal for her to be so tired?" he asks.

"Not usually, but after her night in the ER and the time-zone change, she's still catching up."

"Can we go play games now?" Logan asks.

Kristian glances at me. "You want to stay down here with her while I take him up?"

"Sure. I'll wake her in a little bit so she's not up all night."

He turns on the TV and hands me the remote. "Pizza should be here soon. You can buzz them up from the intercom next to the elevator."

"Okay."

He places his hands on my son's shoulders. "Come on, Logan. Let's go shoot some stuff."

"Awesome!" Logan bounds up the stairs to the second floor, where I assume Kristian's bedroom is also located.

I take a seat on the sofa, curling my legs under me and hugging a throw pillow. I'm torn between wanting to be upstairs with them and here with Maddie. I decide to let her sleep for another half hour and entertain myself by watching the news. I'm interrupted when the buzz of the intercom startles me, even though Kristian told me to expect it. I fumble with the intercom, pressing the wrong button before I find the correct one.

The elevator opens, and the young delivery guy greets me with a smile as he hands over two large pizzas and something in a brown bag. "Thanks so much."

"Any time. Tell Mr. Bowen that Mitch said hi."

"I will." He's gone before I can ask if Mr. Bowen tipped him.

Kristian and Logan come down the stairs, apparently racing to see who can reach the bottom first.

Logan is laughing as he jumps from the third step to land a second before Kristian.

"Nice move," Kristian says, smiling at my son. "Have you considered a career as a stunt man?"

"You think I could do that?" Logan looks up at him with a wistful expression that tugs on my heart and makes me realize I'm not the only one becoming invested in this relationship.

"You can do anything you set your mind to," Kristian tells him as he gets out plates and cutlery, moving around the kitchen with easy familiarity that has me wondering if he cooks.

There's so much I still don't know about him, and I want to know everything. I kiss Maddie awake.

Her eyes open, and she smiles at me.

"You want some pizza?"

Nodding, she sits up and looks around at where we are. Kristian's apartment is an upscale bachelor pad, complete with comfortable leather furniture, glass tables and vintage Hollywood artwork.

I help Maddie up and usher her toward the counter, where Kristian has set up dinner around the bar.

As he lifts Maddie onto a barstool and offers her lemonade, I wonder if he has any idea how good he is with kids. Some people are awkward and clumsy around them. He's a natural.

"I'm surprised you'll eat pizza," I say to Kristian.

He winks at me. "It's gluten free."

"Of course it is."

"That room is *awesome*," Logan says around a mouthful of cheese pizza.

"I want to play, too," Maddie says.

"As soon as you finish eating," Kristian tells her. "I'll teach you how to play Frogger. It's my favorite."

"I remember that game," I say, sharing a smile with him. "I loved it when I was a kid. I didn't think it existed anymore."

"I had a heck of a time tracking down a machine that still works, but I found one in San Pedro a couple of years ago and fixed it up."

"You did that yourself?"

"Uh-huh. I like to tinker."

"Do you cook, too?"

"How'd you know?"

"The way you move around the kitchen was a dead giveaway."

Since we're on one side of the counter and the kids on the other, they can't see when he lays his hand on my leg, making me forget where we are and who is watching. I go completely stupid in the head, until his thumb moves ever so slightly, jarring me out of the stupor to remind me I can't let this happen. Not here or now anyway.

I try to push his hand away, but he won't be pushed.

Without missing a beat in the conversation he's having with the kids about the amusement park at the Santa Monica Pier, he continues to stroke my inner thigh with his thumb while chowing down on pizza and salad. I add "master multitasker" to the list of things I've learned about him.

Thanks to Kristian scrambling my brain cells, I'm still working on my first piece of pizza when the rest of them finish.

He finally removes his hand from my leg and leans in to kiss my forehead. "Take your time, hon. I'll entertain the troops. Come on up when you're done. Third door on the right."

They take off, leaving me with a rare moment of total peace and quiet. Except for when they're in school and I'm at work, the kids and I are usually together. Money has always been tight, and I hardly ever leave them with sitters, other than the lovely woman in our former building who watched them for free whenever I needed her. So it's truly unusual for me to have someone else to entertain them. I ought to curl up on the sofa with the Kindle app on my phone, but I want to be where they are—and where *he* is—so I put the leftover pizza away, clean up the kitchen and head upstairs to find them.

Third door on the right, he said... I glance into the other rooms, one of which might be a guest room. Another is a gym. At the far end of the hallway, past the third door on the right, are open double doors that I decide to investigate. I duck my head into the room and see a king-size bed that's been hastily made. It's covered by a navy blue duvet and has gray accent pillows. The furniture is cherry, maybe, pretty but not fussy.

I can hear the kids in the game room, so I resist the urge to further explore and go to see what they're up to. I step into a full-on arcade that has every conceivable game—pinball, pool, air hockey, driving games and others I can't easily identify. But what I see before me truly stops my heart—Maddie standing on Kristian's feet, his arms around her as he teaches her how to play Frogger.

I can't even...

He glances over his shoulder, sees me there, and the look that passes between us is so full of emotion that my heart contracts almost painfully. Then Maddie needs him, and he returns his attention to her, but I'm left reeling from the knowledge that I'm falling in love with him—fast and hard.

CHAPTER 13

Flynn

I can't let it go even though I know I should. Natalie was trying to help her friend, but it wasn't her place to tell Aileen about Kristian's sexual preferences. Trust is a critical element of our lifestyle, especially in light of who we are to the rest of the world. Natalie knew she could trust Aileen, and Kristian doesn't mind that she told her. But that might not always be the case, and I have to make sure she understands the critical need for discretion.

I find her in our home office on the computer, probably tending to foundation business. She's been an absolute godsend as the director of the foundation I started to aid the cause of childhood hunger. The carnival fundraiser we're holding at a private estate is coming up in a few short weeks, and she's been frantically busy seeing to the details.

"Hey," she says, smiling up at me. "I didn't hear you come in."

That's because I didn't want her to hear me come in. She expects me to go around the desk to kiss her the way I normally would, but that's not going to happen.

"I want you in the bedroom prepared to serve your master in five minutes." After delivering my order, I turn and leave the room, but not before I catch the stunned expression on her face. Nope, she didn't see that coming. Excellent.

In the nearly six months we've been married, she hasn't given me reason to discipline her, so I'm giddy with excitement over my plans for the evening. Any time I get to spend with her is the best time I've ever spent with anyone, no matter what we're doing. But knowing she gets me, that she understands my needs and isn't hesitant about tending to them, makes me love her that much more fiercely.

I go into the living room and fix myself a drink, my favorite Bowmore whisky burning a path through me, heating me up from the inside and killing the last of the fury I felt after Natalie told me what she did. At breakfast, she admitted to feeling guilty about spilling the beans to Aileen about Kristian's sexual preferences.

I'd never touch her in anger. Ever. She's everything to me. If you'd told me a year ago that I'd be so slavishly devoted to any woman, I would've scoffed. Not me. No way. I was determined to preserve and protect my freedom, until that fateful frozen day in Greenwich Village when her demon dog, Fluff, "attacked" me during a shoot, changing both our lives forever. Since then, I've experienced the kind of happiness I thought only existed in the romantic movies we churn out in Hollywood.

It pains me to wait fifteen minutes, but I want her wondering what's up. Not that it's unusual for me to order her into position. We have some sort of sex, often kinky, every day. But it is unusual for me to come home from work and order her into the bedroom without any preliminaries. By now, she's on edge, trying to figure out what's going on. That's right where I want her.

I'm euphoric with anticipation as I secure Fluff—I've learned the hard way, with teeth in my ass, not to allow her anywhere near us when we're having sex—and head for the master bedroom.

Natalie is right where she's supposed to be, beautifully nude and on her knees at the foot of the bed, her head bent in supplication that makes me immediately hard. She's so fucking beautiful and all mine for the rest of our lives. How did I ever get so lucky? I ask myself that every day.

"You need to be punished, my love. Do you know why?"

"N-no. Sir." She quickly adds that second word.

The slight stammer makes me even harder, as does the sight of her tight nipples. She might be unnerved, but she's also excited.

"Look at me."

She lifts her head and shows me the gorgeous green eyes she used to hide behind brown contacts. That was before the whole world knew her story. Now she has no need to hide from anyone, least of all me. "Did you talk to Aileen about something that's none of your business?"

Her lips part on a gasp, and her big eyes get even bigger. She's so damned cute that I want to say to hell with the punishment. But I can't do that. It's my job as her husband and her Dom to teach her about our lifestyle and correct her when she makes mistakes. So far she's taken to it like the proverbial duck to water. This is the first time she's stepped outside the lines, and even though it was for a good cause, I can't let it go. "Answer me, Natalie. Did you tell Aileen something that's none of your business?"

"Y-yes... But—"

I hold up my hand to stop her from continuing. "Please stand and bend over with your elbows on the bed."

"Flynn—"

"Is that my name here?"

"Sir, please... Let me explain."

"You already explained why you did it. Now you have to take your punishment."

"Wh-what is my punishment?"

"A sound spanking. I think twenty is a good number, don't you?"

"N-no, Sir. It's not a good number."

"Thirty?"

"No!"

"Twenty it is, then. Hurry up. I'd hate to have to add more because you're not moving fast enough."

She scurries from her knees into position over the bed, casting a nervous glance at me over her shoulder.

"What's your safe word?"

"Fluff."

"And when should you use it?"

"Any time it gets to be too much."

"What happens if you use it?"

"Everything stops."

"That's right." I caress her soft, supple backside, loving the tremble that rocks her body. Her responsiveness to my touch is such a huge turn-on. "Tell me why you're being punished."

"B-because I told Aileen about Kristian's kink."

"And why shouldn't you have done that?"

"It's n-not my business."

"Exactly." I deliver the first of twenty spanks to the lower part of her right cheek.

She cries out in surprise and then moans when I rub the spot, turning pain into desire.

"Count for me."

"One," she says through gritted teeth.

The second one lands on the exact same spot, which will hurt, but this is about punishment after all. "Two."

"Tell me you understand why we expect you to keep our secrets."

"I do," she says, sniffing. "I'm sorry. I shouldn't have—"

The third spank comes down on the lower part of her left cheek. "Th-three."

"No, you really shouldn't have, sweetheart." I rub the spot and watch closely as she squirms, trying to find some relief from the ache between her legs. "Do you need your safe word?"

"No."

I deliver ten more in rapid succession, not giving her time to react before the next one lands. "Are you losing count, sweetheart? Do we need to start over?"

"No! That's thirteen."

"More than halfway there."

A sob erupts from her, and I'm tempted to stop.

"Do you need your safe word?"

She shakes her head.

"Words, sweetheart. Give me words."

"No, Sir."

I'm so damned proud of her. She's strong and determined and all mine. I give her five more spanks. Her bottom is now a fiery pink, and the scent of her desire makes me crazy, especially when I notice that her inner thighs are wet. "Two more and then we're done."

She grasps the quilt and drops her head. Moving her hair out of the way, I stroke her neck and down her back, drawing out the suspense that much longer. She's quivering madly when I deliver number nineteen, rubbing the spot until I hear her moan.

"I think my baby might be enjoying her punishment a little too much." To make my point, I slide my fingers through the flood of moisture between her legs. "Ah-*ha*! I thought so."

She makes a noise that can't be called a groan or a grunt. It's somewhere in between. I love her like this, submissive to me, allowing me to control her pleasure and her pain. It's the greatest feeling, the highest of highs, to know she trusts me so implicitly.

I grasp my cock and push into her. "Don't come. Not yet."

Despite the flood of moisture, we're always a tight fit, and I'm careful not to hurt her. It takes a good ten minutes before I'm fully inside her—my favorite place to be. Reaching under her, I cup her gorgeous breasts and toy with her nipples. Her inner muscles clamp down on me and I count backward from a hundred to hold off the orgasm that wants out—right now. But I'm not finished with her. Not yet.

I slow the pace, knowing it will make her crazy, and I'm not disappointed.

She raises her hips, looking for more, but I don't give it to her.

"Flynn!"

"Is that my name in here?" I deliver the twentieth and final spank, and she ignites, coming so hard, she takes me with her, even though I'm nowhere near ready. "Did I tell you to come?" I ask her when I catch my breath and my head stops spinning.

"It's not my fault." Under me, her body is soft and relaxed even as her pussy twitches with strong contractions that make me hard all over again.

"Whose fault is it?"

"Yours."

I take a gentle bite out of the back of her shoulder, making her startle and then laugh. I want to see her gorgeous face, so I withdraw from her and stretch out next to her on the bed, running my fingers through her long silky dark hair. Her lips are curved into a small, satisfied smile that pleases me.

Resting my hand on her pink ass, I gently caress her. "Do you understand why I had to punish you?"

She opens her eyes, meets my gaze, and a punch of emotion hits me, as if it's the first time all over again. "I'm sorry I told Aileen about Kristian. I was only trying to help them along. Is he really mad?"

"Not at all. He said you did him a favor."

"Then why..."

"Why did I punish you?"

She nods and rolls her bottom lip between her teeth. She's so adorable, I almost forget what I was going to say.

"You can't tell people about us. Even people you know well and trust. I need to know it won't happen again, Nat. That's really important to me."

"It won't happen again. I'm sorry I stepped out of line. I just want them to be as happy as we are."

"I know, honey, and I get why you did it. Your intentions were good. But—"

She lays a finger over my lips. "It's okay. You don't have to say it. I know why I can't tell anyone, and I hope you know I'd never tell anyone who could hurt you or the others. Aileen loves us all. The information is safe with her. But I won't do it again. I promise."

"Thank you." I kiss her softly, wanting to give her sweetness after her punishment. I twirl a length of her hair around my finger. "How was your day?"

"Now you ask," she says with a teasing grin. "It was busy. Things are coming together for the fundraiser. I also had an appointment with Dr. Breslow."

I freeze with shock. She hates doctors, especially gynecologists, after the trauma of her rape exam years ago. "Why did you go there without me?"

"I have to go alone at some point. Why not now?"

"You don't ever have to go alone, Nat. Is something wrong?" The thought of something being wrong with her terrifies me.

"Nope." She flashes a mysterious smile. "In fact, in about eight months, our duo is going to become a trio."

I'm stunned speechless. Nothing in my life could've prepared me for this moment. My brain goes completely blank, and my heart... My heart feels like it's going to explode from the blast of joy that overtakes me. And then I remember the punishment, the rough sex, and I'm appalled and terrified. "Did I... I didn't... Are you hurt? What we did..."

Still smiling, she places her hand on my chest, on top of my wildly beating heart. "I'm completely fine, Flynn. If anything hurt, I would've stopped it."

"I can't... We can't... You..."

Laughing now, she wraps her arms around me and brings my head to rest on her shoulder. "It's a baby, not a bomb, and I swear I'm completely fine. Nothing has to change between us."

"This changes *everything*. No more rough stuff."

"I love your rough stuff. You wouldn't deny me, would you?"

"Don't do that."

"What am I doing?"

"You're trying to manipulate me. As long as you're pregnant, the most you're getting from me is good old-fashioned gentle missionary."

"Then I'll have to hit the club to find someone who can take care of my needs."

My hand comes down on her ass before I remember I just put a stop to such things for the foreseeable future.

Natalie laughs right in my face. "Please tell me you're not going to turn into a crazy lunatic while your wife is pregnant."

"Define 'crazy lunatic.'"

"Withholding sex and treating me like I'm fragile or breakable. If you do that, our baby will be an only child."

"Our baby," I whisper. My eyes flood with tears. I'm going to be a *dad*. Natalie and I are going to be *parents*. I never thought I'd get married again, let alone fall madly in love with the perfect woman for me. And now, a baby, too…

She brushes away my tears with her fingertips. "Are you happy?"

"You have to ask?"

"I just want to be sure."

"I had no idea this kind of happy was possible until I found you."

"Until Fluff found *you*."

"Thank God for her." I kiss my wife, the mother of my child, my one true love.

CHAPTER 14

Kristian

I have the best time with Aileen's kids. They're fun and funny and polite. They scream when a game goes their way and laugh it off when it doesn't. They ask the best questions and never stop talking the whole time we're playing. We take a short break to go down to the garage so they can sit in each of the cars. We stop in the kitchen for some ice cream before returning to the game room. They try every game at least once, and I enjoy teaching them the finer nuances of each one.

Aileen lets out a squeak that gets my attention. "Oh my God! It's almost ten! We have to go."

"Not yet, Mom," Logan says without taking his eyes off the screen. He's on a roll with a driving game and is racking up an impressive score.

"You guys finish up the games you're playing," I tell them. "You can come back any time you want." With them happily occupied, I take their mother by the hand and lead her out of the room.

"You're incredibly good with them," she says.

"Am I? Really?"

"Really."

"They're great kids. I've had the best time with them."

"Thank you."

"You don't need to thank me for having fun with your kids. I love being with them, almost as much as I love being with their mom." I prop an arm over her head and pin her to the wall with my body. "I've thought about last night all day today. It's *all* I've thought about."

Her gaze drops to my mouth. "Me, too."

Because I can't wait another second to kiss her, I bring my lips down on hers.

Her hands slide up from my chest to meet behind my neck, her fingers combing through my hair in a soothing caress that makes me crazy for more of her. "Stay here tonight. I have plenty of room for you guys. We'll put the kids to bed and have some time for us."

"We can't do that."

"Why not?" I cradle her sweet face in my hands, compelling her to look at me. "The kids would love it. I even have extra toothbrushes and T-shirts they can sleep in." I bend my head to nuzzle her neck. "I'm dying to hold you and kiss you and touch you, and I don't want you driving home at this hour." I feel her capitulation in the way she draws me closer.

"I can't sleep with you."

"I know." I kiss a path from her collarbone to her ear and then roll her earlobe between my teeth. "Stay."

"If you're sure it's no problem—"

Elated to know we'll have more time together, I kiss the words right off her lips. "It's no problem." I release her and will my raging erection into submission so I can face the kids without embarrassing myself. "Hey, guys," I call into the game room. "Your mom says you can stay over tonight."

"Yes!" Logan fist-pumps the air above his head.

"But you have to go to bed as soon as those games are done."

He gives that news a thumbs-down but doesn't protest any further.

To Aileen, I say, "See, that was easy."

"They like you."

"I like them. And I really, *really* like their mom." I kiss her again. "Let's get them settled."

It takes half an hour to tear the kids away from the games, get them changed, their teeth brushed and tucked into bed in one of my four extra bedrooms.

"Your mom will be right next door if you need her. And if you go right to sleep, I'll get some more of those doughnuts Maddie liked for breakfast."

"Mr. Kristian is spoiling you guys with pizza and games and doughnuts."

"It's okay, Mom," Maddie says. "As long as we don't overdo it."

I muffle my laughter behind my hand.

"That's right, sweetheart," Aileen says when she kisses her daughter good night.

What must it be like, I wonder, to have your mom tuck you in and kiss you good night every night, without fail? These kids have no idea how lucky they are to have her.

"I want a story," Maddie says, sounding whiny.

"You got to stay up *two hours* past your bedtime. No stories." Aileen is firm but loving with her daughter, who apparently knows when to quit. "Sleep tight. Love you guys."

"Love you, too," Logan says as he turns to face the wall.

"Love you, Mommy," Maddie says.

Their sweetness has my emotions all out of whack. I've never had such a close-up view of a mother loving her children the way they should be loved. In my world, it didn't work like this. Mothers neglected their children. Forgot to feed them. Forgot to buy them new clothes when theirs stopped fitting. Forgot their birthdays and didn't get them anything for Christmas.

Kids in my world never felt safe or loved or coddled or any of the things Logan and Maddie will take for granted because they won't know it any other way. And for that, I'm thankful. I never want them to know how it could've been if they hadn't had the amazing good fortune to be born to their wonderful mother.

The thoughts resurrect painful memories that I'd much sooner forget than relive, especially when I have so many good things to focus on, such as the sexy, adorable mom who's turned my life upside down. My trip down horrible memory lane leaves me feeling unsettled—and unworthy. How can I hope to be any sort of positive influence in the lives of Logan and Maddie when I have no idea how it's supposed to be done? No one ever taught me how to be part of a family.

Queasy and sick with fear that I'll somehow screw up the sweetest thing that's ever happened to me, I go downstairs. While I wait for Aileen to join me, I pour a shot of Grey Goose and down it, chasing it with another one. When she appears in the kitchen, eyeing the bottle and the shot glass, I wonder if this is what it's like to get caught drinking by your mom. I wouldn't know.

"Drink?"

"Um, sure."

I fix her a glass of the chilled chardonnay that she likes and hand it to her. She takes a tentative sip, eyeing me over the edge of her glass. "Is everything okay?"

"Uh-huh."

She puts down her glass. "What happened between the game room and the kitchen?"

Jesus. The woman sees right through me. It's like she can lift my hood and peer inside where all my secrets are hidden from everyone but her. I consider denying that anything happened, but I already know that's not going to fly with her. "I was watching you with your kids and thinking about how lucky they are to have you."

"I'm lucky to have them."

"They'll never know how lucky they are."

She comes around the counter to stand in front of me, looking up at me with those big, expressive eyes. It's the weirdest thing, but her eyes remind me of a pencil box I was given one year in school when I showed up without any school supplies. It had a picture of a cat on it that had big, kind eyes that made me wish for a pet or someone real who'd look at me the way that cat did. I can't tell her that her eyes remind me of a paper cat on an old pencil box, but for the longest time, that paper cat brought me comfort when nothing else did. Now I have her and those amazing eyes that look at me and make me feel things I've never felt before. Things that scare me.

"Tell me what you were really thinking."

Stunned, my first impulse is to take a step back, to retreat, to run for the closet. But I have a sinking feeling she'd follow and force me out of hiding. "I don't know how to do this." Part of me is angry that she's forcing me to say things I'd rather not share with anyone —even her.

"Do what?" she asks, the picture of patience and calm.

"Be part of what you have with the kids. I'm afraid I'll make a goddamned mess of it."

She places a hand on my chest and takes another step to close the distance between us. "When I came into the game room earlier, you know what I saw?"

I shake my head. I'm so riddled with insecurities that I'm unable to breathe or even blink out of fear that she'll see me for the fraud I am.

"I saw my daughter, surrounded by a man for the first time in her life. She's never had anyone who'd allow her to stand on his feet so she could get a better view. She's never had anyone to teach her how to play Frogger. These might seem like small things to you, but they're huge to me—and to her."

The words and the feelings they conjure make me feel raw and unprotected from the barrage of emotion. "This is all new to me. I don't know what I'm doing."

"You're doing *great*. Do you see the way Logan looks at you? Like you're a superhero."

I shake my head. "He shouldn't think of me that way." For the first time in my life, I'm ashamed of the things I did to stay alive, things that make me so much less than I want to be for Aileen and her beautiful kids.

"Why not?"

"Because! He doesn't even know me. None of you do. If you did..." I shake my head, filled with anguish.

"Are my children and I at any risk of harm by spending time with you?"

"No." I'm almost offended she would ask me that. "Of course not."

"If we were in danger, would you try to keep us safe?"

"I'd do anything it took to keep you and your children safe." I'm overwhelmed to realize I speak the truth. I'd literally take a bullet for any of them, and when, exactly, did I start to feel that way about them? I suppose from the beginning, if I'm being honest.

"Then what else do we need to know?"

"So many things."

"Did those things make you the man you are today? The same man who ran to my daughter's aid when she was injured and allowed her to stand on his feet while he taught her something new? The same man whose every word my son hangs on, waiting for more? Or the man who makes me want things I thought I'd never have? Did those things make you that man? Because I like that guy so much. *So, so much.*"

"Aileen." I drop my forehead to hers. I'm overwhelmed and humbled by her, and falling for her so fast and so hard, I don't know which end is up anymore. My arms slide around her, bringing her in as close to me as I can get her. She makes me feel like I'm ten feet tall and can conquer the world, as long as I have her by my side.

"Everyone has a past, Kristian. Everyone has done things they aren't proud of. No one is perfect, least of all me."

"You're as close to perfect as anyone can be."

She laughs. "If you say so."

"I say so, and I don't want to hear you say otherwise."

She curls her hands around my neck and looks up at me. "I know this is all new for you, but you're doing great so far."

"Would you tell me if I wasn't?"

Nodding, she says, "If you want me to."

"I do. I need you to tell me if I screw up."

"Can I tell you when you do great, too?"

"I guess."

"Why is it so hard for you to hear that you're a good man, Kristian?"

"I don't know. I guess maybe because no one has ever thought so before."

"That can't be true. Your friends think the world of you. I see that every time I'm around you all."

"It's different with you and the kids. You guys make me want to be more. Better."

"You don't need to be anything other than exactly who you are. That's enough for us."

My heart is so full, it feels like it might explode. And then she goes up on tiptoes to kiss me so softly and so sweetly that I nearly break down. I don't deserve her. I don't deserve her children. But goddamned if I know how to resist her—or her kids. I fall into the kiss, losing my mind along with my heart. I can't seem to stop it no matter how much I know I should. I'm completely lost to her.

I wrap my arms around her and lift her.

She gasps in surprise, breaking the kiss. "Where're you taking me?"

"To my room so we can spend some time alone. If that's okay."

"It's okay."

"Hold on to me."

"I love when you say that." She drops her head to my shoulder and tightens her arms around my neck.

Here, in my arms, is everything I never dared to dream possible until she walked into my friend's wedding and changed my life forever. It took me a while to realize that's what she did, but I can no longer deny it, nor do I want to. I carry her upstairs, stopping outside the kids' room to peek in.

"Are they asleep?" I whisper.

"Out cold."

That's what I want to hear as I continue to my room at the end of the hallway, leaving the door open so she can hear her kids if they need her. We can't do what we did last night, but I'll take whatever I can get.

Her lips brush against my neck, and I feel as if I've been electrocuted. Then she does it again.

"Are you enjoying yourself?" I ask her.

"Mmm-hmm. Very much so."

I'm never going to survive her if she can make me hard as a rock simply by kissing my neck. It usually takes a hell of a lot more than that to get me fired up.

We stretch out on my bed, and she curls up to me, her body aligned with mine. "Can we talk about something else?"

"Anything you want." As I rub circles on her back, I remind myself that I'm not allowed to let desire get the best of me tonight. Not with her babies sleeping right down the hall.

"I want to talk about the BDSM and how it works. I want to understand it."

All the air leaves my body in one long, tortured exhale.

"I did some research today, and I have so many questions."

"Like what?" I ask, my voice gruff with desire.

"There're so many different aspects to it, so I guess I'm wondering what you like."

What do I like? What *don't* I like? How can I explain it in a way that won't terrify her? "I like to control my partner's pleasure."

"How?"

I scrub my hand over my face. In all the months since I first met her, I've been unable to picture her in the context of my kink, which is another first. Usually, that's the first place my mind goes when I meet someone who interests me sexually. But that hasn't happened with her.

She tugs at the hand that's covering my face. "Do you not want to talk about this?"

"What if we weren't about that?"

"What do you mean?"

"I mean when I'm with you, I might not need it to be more than it already is."

She ponders that, rolling her lip between her teeth. "From what I read, most people who are heavily into the lifestyle can't turn it on and off like that."

"That's true, but that doesn't mean it *can't* be turned off under certain circumstances."

"So, what you're saying is that you want that with other women, but not with me?"

Fuck. I'm bungling this. "No, that's not it. I'm saying I might not *need* it because it's already so much *more* with you. Does that make sense?"

"Is it because you think I'm fragile? Because I was sick?"

Yes, in part. "No."

"I'm not fragile. I *was* sick. I'm not anymore."

"I know that, sweetheart."

"I don't want to be treated differently because I used to be sick."

"I understand that."

"So you'll teach me about what you like?"

Releasing a deep breath, I realize she's got me cornered. If I decline to teach her, she'll think it's because I think she's fragile. "Here's the thing... I *feel* things for you, things I've never felt for anyone, and the thought of touching you with anything other than reverence makes me a little sick. It doesn't make me hot to think about restraining you and denying you orgasms or fucking your ass or clamping your nipples or anything I'd normally do with women who mean nothing to me."

I glance down to find her face flushed and her lips parted. Fuck, did hearing that turn her on? It seems like it did. I have to know. I dip my hand under the skirt of her dress and cup her mound. Heat radiates from between her legs, providing confirmation that my words aroused her.

"What if I want those things? Would you do them if I asked you to?"

I'm trapped between a rock and a very hard cock.

"Do you want them?"

"I want everything with you, Kristian."

CHAPTER 15

Aileen

I can't believe I just blurted that out. Way to scare him off. But he doesn't look scared. No, he suddenly seems almost dangerously aroused.

"Do you understand what it means to be sexually dominated?"

"I think I do, but why don't you tell me so I can be sure."

"It means that I control every aspect of your pleasure. I say what, I say when, I say how many times. And you," he says, tipping my chin up to force me to meet his intense gaze, "you can stop it all with one word that's agreed to in advance, which means at the end of the day, you're the one with all the power."

"Is it okay to tell you that it excites me to think about doing those things with you?"

"Ah, yeah," he says, his voice rough, "it's okay."

"So, you'll do them with me?"

"Not until you have a chance to see what you'd be getting into. Up close and personal."

"Where?"

"At our club."

"You'll take me there?"

"If you're sure it's what you want."

"I want you, and this is part of you, so I'm sure it's what I want."

"I'll take you to the club. Eventually."

"Soon. You'll take me soon."

"Who's the Dominant in this relationship?" he asks, a teasing smile curving his lips.

I gaze up at him. "You are. Sir."

"Jesus, Aileen. You're playing with fire, and you don't even realize it."

I cup his erection and drag my fingernail down the length of it. "Yes, I do."

He trembles and then he pounces, rolling on top of me and devouring my mouth in a kiss that's pure sex.

I curl my arms around his neck and my legs around his hips. "Is it Saturday yet?" I whisper against his lips.

His low growl makes me crazy with wanting him. Even at the beginning of my relationship with Rex, before it went so wrong, I never wanted him the way I want Kristian—as if my life depends on having him. I should be protecting myself—and my kids—from the way he makes me feel. I've been down this road before and found it pitted with potholes. And with how many times Kristian has warned me off, I ought to be terrified and running away.

But that's not what I'm doing. No, I'm kissing him and pressing my core against the rigid length of his erection and thinking about the things he said he wanted to do with me and wondering how long I'll have to wait to be dominated by him.

DESPITE MY GOOD INTENTIONS, I FALL ASLEEP IN KRISTIAN'S BED AND spend the entire night with his arms wrapped tight around me. It's the best sleep I've had since I was diagnosed, and for the first time in ages, I wake ahead of the kids. Thank goodness for that, because I'm not sure they're ready to see me sleeping in his bed—or in his arms.

I move carefully, hoping I won't wake him as I make my escape.

His arms tighten around me. "Don't go," he says in a voice rough with sleep.

I love knowing what his voice sounds like first thing in the morning. "I have to or we're going to get caught."

"Five more minutes." He presses his erection against my bottom, and I dissolve into a puddle of want.

That's all it takes.

Then he cups my breast and catches my nipple between his fingers.

"Kristian... Don't. We can't do this now, and I'll be a mess all day if we start something we can't finish—again."

His low chuckle makes me smile. "Glad I'm not the only one walking around in a state of agony."

"Is it agony?"

"To want you more than I've ever wanted anyone and not be able to have you? I can't think of a better word to describe it."

"Neither can I."

"Soon, sweetheart. We'll have an entire night together, and we'll make it count."

"I can't wait."

His hand is on my leg, moving up and under the hem of the dress I never removed last night. We both slept in our clothes, which is just as well since I never made it out of his bed.

I stop his hand from its intended destination between my legs. If he so much as touches me, I'll forget that my kids are sleeping right down the hall and will be up any minute.

Kristian groans as his fingers twist around mine. "I really hope you guys like Cecelia."

"I'm sure we will."

"Don't forget that Tenley is coming today, too. She talked to you, right?"

"She's coming at two."

"I told her you're to have anything and everything you want. I want you completely pampered."

"I don't need all that."

"I want you to have it. Let me do this for you. I want our first offi-cial date to be special."

"It'll already be special because I'll be with you."

"Do you have any idea what you're doing to me?"

I'm not sure what he means. "What am I doing?"

"You're making me fall so hard for you that my head is spinning. The more time I spend with you, the more I want. The more I touch you, the more I crave you. I can't concentrate at work or sleep or do anything but think about you. You're making a hot mess of my life."

Smiling and filled with the giddy joy I feel whenever he's nearby, I try to get free of his tight embrace. "I'll just go so you can get back to normal."

"You're not going anywhere," he says in a low growl that sets me on fire with longing.

"But you just said I'm making a mess of your life."

"It's the best feeling I've ever experienced. Please don't ever take it away from me. I'm not sure I'd survive it."

"Kristian... Let me go. I want to turn over so I can see you."

He loosens his hold on me, just enough that I can turn to face him.

I rest my hand on his face, his morning beard prickling my palm. "In case it matters, you're doing the same thing to me."

"It matters." He kisses me, and I forget all about how I'm supposed to get up before the kids catch us together. I forget every-thing that doesn't include him and how it feels to be surrounded by him, consumed by him.

"Mom!" Logan's voice brings me crashing back to earth.

Kristian releases me, and I get up so quickly, I stumble in my haste to get out of Kristian's room before my son catches me there.

"Easy, sweetheart," he says.

I glance over my shoulder, and the sight of him propped up on one elbow, sexy and disheveled as he watches me with hungry eyes, will stay with me until I can be alone with him again. It's going to be another long-ass day.

~

TENLEY ARRIVES RIGHT ON TIME, ROLLING A RACK OF GOWNS INTO MY home like it's no big deal. To her, it probably isn't. To me—and to Maddie, who vibrates with excitement at the thought of a fashion show—it's the biggest of big deals. I can't believe that one of Hollywood's top stylists has come to my house to dress me for a premiere that I'm attending with Kristian. I feel like a princess.

Tall and thin with long dark hair, Tenley is as put together as you'd expect a Hollywood stylist to be, with the skinniest jeans I've ever seen, a top that clings to her full breasts, sky-high heels that she runs around on the way I do tennis shoes and a gigantic purse filled with the tools of her trade. *Sleek* is the word that comes to mind.

She hugs me like we're old friends, even though we've only met a couple of times, once at Flynn and Nat's wedding and the last time I visited before the move. She came to Kristian's with her sexy boyfriend, Devon Black. "I'm so happy to have the chance to dress you." With her hands on my shoulders, she leans back for a closer look. "When Addie told me you're Natalie's friend who had cancer, I couldn't wait to find the *perfect* dress for you. And let me say, you look *marvelous.* Your hair is so cute, and you've gotten some sun."

"Thank you." I'm overwhelmed and delighted by her enthusiasm, and I try not to flinch at being described as the friend who had cancer. I know she means well—and so did Addie.

"I gotta say, you landed yourself one hell of a catch, too." As she talks, she removes dresses in zipped bags from her rack. "That Kristian Bowen is some kind of sexy and *ultra* mysterious. Everyone is curious about him."

I'm unprepared for how it feels to hear a gorgeous, sexy woman talk about Kristian that way. A knot of dread forms in my belly. How in the world will I ever keep him interested in me when women like her find him sexy and mysterious? Before I can let the jealousy sink its nasty claws into me, Maddie comes bounding into the room, stopping short at the sight of Tenley and her rack of dresses.

I hold out my arms to my daughter, who steps into my embrace.

"Maddie, say hi to Miss Tenley. She's going to help Mommy find a dress for the movie premiere."

"Hi," Maddie says shyly.

"Hi, Maddie. Are you going to help me find the perfect dress for Mommy to wear?"

Maddie nods.

"Excellent! Let's get started."

I try on ten gowns, each of them more spectacular than the one before. How I'll ever decide on one of them is beyond me.

"I want you to try one more," Tenley says, a calculating look in her eye. "I saved this one for last for a reason." She holds up a champagne-colored gown that's the simplest of the lot, and I love it immediately.

"Won't I look washed out in that color?" I ask, aware of how pallid my skin still is after my illness.

Tenley waves a hand. "Don't worry about that. We'll make sure you're glowing."

"I like that one, Mommy," Maddie says.

"I do, too. Let's see how it looks on." Maddie comes with me into my bedroom when I change into the gown. She carefully zips me in like she's been doing it all her life. I turn to face her, and her mouth drops open.

"You look so pretty!"

"Really?"

She nods. "So, so pretty."

I face the full-length mirror behind the door. The gown hugs me through the breasts and ribs and then flares at the waist, making me look slightly less waifish than I did in many of the others. My shoulders and collarbones are too prominent for my liking, but there's nothing I can do about that between now and Saturday night, so I try not to dwell on the things I can't change. "Let's see what Tenley thinks."

Maddie goes ahead of me to the living room. "Mommy looks so pretty!"

"Does she?" Tenley asks.

"Uh-huh. Show her, Mom."

I feel oddly shy emerging from my bedroom in this dress. Everything about it is different. Judging by her expression, Tenley agrees. "Holy smokes. That's the one! I had a feeling it might be. I wanted you to try on the others so you'd know perfection when you saw it."

"Do you think he'll like it?" I ask Tenley, feeling madly vulnerable. I barely know her, but she knows Kristian, and I want him to be proud to have me with him Saturday night.

"Um, yes, Aileen," she says with a grin. "I think he'll like it. Let's talk about shoes!"

She leaves an hour later, promising to get the gown back to me by Saturday morning after a few alterations to make it a perfect fit. I've chosen an incredible pair of Jimmy Choo heels, and I almost faint when Tenley tells me that Flynn's brother-in-law Hugh, a Beverly Hills jeweler, will provide a loaned diamond necklace, bracelet and earrings for the occasion.

Cinderella has nothing on me.

"That was so much fun!" Maddie says after Tenley leaves. Logan hid out in his and Maddie's bedroom the entire time she was there, and I let him know it's safe to come back out.

"Did you find something you like?" he asks.

"Wait till you see," Maddie says. "Mommy looks like a princess."

"That's cool."

The doorbell rings, and I go to answer it.

"Hi there. I'm Cecelia. You must be Aileen?" With blonde hair, blue eyes and a gorgeous smile, she's the epitome of a Southern California girl.

"Yes, please come in." I introduce her to Logan and Maddie. "Miss Cecelia is a friend of Mr. Kristian's, and she's going to stay with you guys when we go to the movie premiere."

"You can call me Cece," she tells the kids. "That's what my friends call me."

We chat for a few minutes, and then she asks if the kids like the beach.

"We love it," Maddie replies.

"Why don't we take a walk over and check out the playground?" Cece suggests.

"Can we, Mom?" Logan asks.

"Sure, let's do it."

As the four of us make the short walk to the playground, Cece asks the kids a bunch of questions that get them talking about their favorite classes at school, the friends they left behind in New York, the summer camp they're going to and what they like best about their new home—the beach.

"We have some cool new friends, too," Logan says. "Mr. Kristian has the best game room ever and so many sick cars. He let me sit in them last night and pretend to drive."

They like her, and she's great with them, which is a huge relief. I want this time alone with Kristian so badly, but more than that, I want to be sure my kids are safe and happy with their new sitter.

"It's so good of you to do this," I say to her when the kids are occupied on the swings.

"I'm happy to. I just went through a bad breakup, so it helps to keep busy. Plus, I have crazy student loans from nursing school, and Kristian is making it well worth my while."

I begin to wonder just how much he's paying her to watch my kids. Before I can ask her, my phone chimes with a text from him.

Where are you guys? I'm at your house.

My heart immediately skips a beat and does a somersault in my chest—all that from knowing he's nearby. *At the playground across the street.*

Be right over.

I run my fingers through my hair and wish I'd worn something more exciting than a tank top and an old pair of cutoff denim shorts. "Kristian is coming over."

"If you guys want to go grab some dinner or something, I'm not doing anything tonight. I'm off duty at work for a couple of days."

I'm so tempted. Would it be wrong of me to leave my kids for a few hours with someone they just met?

"Cece," Maddie calls, "come push me."

"I'm coming." She jogs over to the swings and has Maddie giggling within minutes.

"Push me, too," Logan says.

She alternates like an old pro, pushing one and then the other while keeping up a steady stream of chatter about their favorite movies, their favorite food and what kind of ice cream they like best.

They like her. She likes them. She's a nurse, for crying out loud. She's more qualified to be with them than I am. Would it be wrong to take some time to myself? I've done it so rarely that the thought of leaving them makes me sick with guilt.

Then his arm slides around me from behind as he kisses the back of my neck, and the guilt is trumped by pure lust when the scent of his cologne fills my senses. I'm a bad, bad mother.

"How's it going?" he asks, keeping his arm around me as he waves to the kids.

"Good. They like Cecelia."

"Thank God."

I pause, but only for a second before I look up at him. "She said she's not doing anything tonight if we want to go grab a bite to eat. Or something."

His fingers dig into my shoulder, and his jaw tightens with tension. "What did you say?"

"I told her I'd see if you wanted to."

"You had to ask?" His eyes are covered by his sunglasses, but I don't need to be able to see his eyes to know what they look like. "Are you comfortable leaving the kids with her?"

"I think so. I feel a little guilty, though."

"Why?"

"I've hardly ever left them with anyone other than the woman in our building who watched them for me."

"We don't have to, Aileen. Not until you're comfortable with her. For what it's worth, I've known her for a couple of years through my assistant, Lori, who's her roommate."

"It's worth a lot. In fact, I was just thinking that as a nurse, she's more qualified to be with them than I am."

"That's not true. No one is more qualified to be with them than you are."

I lean my head against him, and it feels so natural to stand there watching my kids with his arm around me and my head resting against his chest. I could get used to this. "You're out of work early."

"I couldn't get shit done from wanting to be with you."

That decides it for me. I need to spend some time alone with him. I call the kids over, and Cece follows, keeping a close eye on them, which I appreciate.

"How would you guys like to hang with Cece for a little while?"

"Can we?" Maddie asks while Logan looks on, his expression giving nothing away.

"If you want to. Cece said she's free tonight and can spend some time with you guys while I go to dinner with Mr. Kristian."

"What'll we do for dinner?" Logan asks.

Kristian pulls out his wallet and hands him three twenties. "How about you take these lovely ladies out for pizza?"

Logan takes the money, brightening considerably at being given such responsibility by Kristian.

"I know a great place that we can walk to," Cece says.

Kristian hands Logan another twenty. "Get ice cream after, too."

"Awesome," Logan says. "Let's go, you guys."

"Wait a minute." I point to my cheek, and my son rolls his eyes as he comes over to kiss me.

Maddie does the same.

"Love you guys."

Cecelia and I exchange phone numbers, and I give her the key to the house.

"Are they allergic to anything?" she asks.

"Not that I know of."

"Bedtime?"

"By nine at the latest, if you can get them there. They can take their own showers, but Maddie might need a little supervision."

"No problem. We've got this, right, guys?"

"Yep," Maddie says.

"Can we go now?" Logan asks.

"Sure, I'll see you in the morning. Love you."

They take off with Cece, shouting, "I love you, too," over their shoulders.

The second they're out of earshot, Kristian says, "Come home with me."

CHAPTER 16

Aileen

I look up at him, and he kisses me, right there on the playground with the sun setting behind us. The beach is crowded, but everything and everyone fades away until there's only him, holding me and kissing me with the kind of passion I never knew was possible until he showed me how it could be.

"Come home with me, Aileen," he says again, much more urgently this time.

With our bodies tightly aligned, I can feel how badly he wants me. "Let's go."

He keeps his arm around me as we walk—so quickly I have trouble keeping up with him—back to my house, where his car is parked in front.

"I should change." I'm beginning to feel panicky about whether my legs need to be shaved or if I'm sweaty from the walk to the beach.

"You don't need clothes for this date." He holds the car door open, imploring me to get in.

I get in the car. Who cares if my legs are shaved when a hot, sexy man who makes me crazy with desire wants to take me home and have his wicked way with me?

The minute the car is moving forward, his hand is on my leg, his heat branding my skin.

Now that the moment is upon me, I'm riddled with worries and insecurities and…

"Stop it," he says, his voice a low, gruff growl. "Whatever you're thinking that's making you tighter than a drum, knock it off."

I remind myself to breathe, to try to relax, to remember this is Kristian, who has been so good to me and my kids. I have nothing to fear from him, but even knowing that, I worry about whether he'll want to dominate me, if I'll be enough for him, if he'll—

"Aileen."

The single word is like a command. "Yes?"

"Stop." After a long pause, he says, "Nothing will happen unless you want it to, and everything about you is perfection to me. Whatever you're thinking, however you're blowing this up in your mind, don't. If you had any idea how much I want you, you'd get out at the next light and run away."

"I'm not going anywhere."

"Neither am I, so stop worrying."

"It's been a really long time for me."

"I know that, sweetheart. I'll take good care of you. I promise."

His sweet words go a long way toward calming my nerves, but they don't do anything to stop the tingling on the surface of my skin or the ache between my legs that intensifies the closer we get to his place. Traffic is heavy this time of day, and it takes longer than it should.

"Fucking hell," he mutters when we have to sit through one light a second time.

His impatience is endearing.

"You were good with Logan back there, giving him the money and asking him to take the girls out to dinner."

"I could tell he wasn't completely sold on staying with Cece."

"You don't believe me when I tell you you're great with them, but there's another example. I would like to know how much you're paying her to stay with them for the premiere."

"That's between me and her."

"I want to know."

"I'm not telling you."

"I'll get it out of you."

His huff of laughter makes me smile. I love him. I no sooner have that thought than I'm sucking in a deep breath and my heart all but stops at the realization.

"What?" He looks over at me, concerned.

"N-nothing." *I love him.* Oh my God, I really do. I have, probably, from that first day at Natalie's wedding when I was introduced to him and felt the earth shift under my feet. Before that, before him, I wouldn't have believed it possible to take one look at someone and feel everything there is to feel. But that's exactly what happened at the wedding, and every time I've been with him since then, the feeling has grown and multiplied.

Ten minutes later, we pull up to his building, where he punches in the code. In the garage, he tells me to wait for him and comes around to help me out of the car, taking my hand to lead me to the elevator. Once inside, he wraps both arms around me and kisses my neck. His erection is hard and hot against my belly, and I rub against him, making him groan.

"Are you hungry?" he asks.

"Not for dinner."

"Jesus, Aileen. Throw gas on a wildfire, why don't you?"

Laughing, I kiss his neck and under his chin. "Sorry."

"No, you're not. Do you want to check on the kids?"

"You wouldn't mind?"

"Of course not. I don't want you to be distracted by anything but me for the next few hours."

I shiver in anticipation of *hours* alone with him. As I withdraw my phone from the back pocket of my shorts, I realize my hands are shaking. I put through a call to Cece, who answers on the first ring.

"Hi there."

I smile when I hear Logan say in the background, "I told you she would call."

"Tell him he's always right."

"I will," Cece says, laughing. "We're having a great time. Don't worry about a thing."

"Do they want to talk to me?"

"Sure, here they are."

I talk to both of them, reminding them to be good for Cece and do what she tells them to. They're excited about going for ice cream, and I'm getting in the way of their good time. "Have fun," I tell Maddie the second before the line goes dead. "I'm already yesterday's news."

"They're in good hands and having fun. The same could be said for you." He drops his hands to my ass and pulls me in tight against him. "The first time," he says against my ear, "will be fast. The second time, I'm going to linger, make it last."

"I think I'm drooling. Am I drooling?"

Smiling, he shakes his head. At some point, he removed his sunglasses, and those dazzling blue eyes are watching me intently. The elevator dings, and I startle. I immediately feel foolish for being so jumpy.

"You're getting wound up again," he says, his hand on my lower back as he directs me into the apartment.

We go straight to the stairs, and he steers me to his room with his hands on my hips.

"I want you to wear these shorts every day."

"Really? Why?"

"Your ass is so hot in them. When I got to the park earlier, the first thing I saw was you in these shorts. I wanted to do this, right there in front of everyone." He drops to his knees behind me and kisses the lower curves of my ass cheeks, taking a bite out of the right one.

I cry out from the surprise and the desire that shoots through me like a rocket, landing in a ball of heat between my legs.

"Mmm, yes, let me hear you. No holding back." He slides his hands up the backs of my legs and squeezes my cheeks.

He's hardly done anything, and I'm already about to come. Rising to his feet, he hands me a piece of paper he pulls from his pocket.

"What's this?"

"Recent test results that prove I'm clean."

I take a quick look, see what I need to know and hand it back to him. "Thank you."

"We need a word. One word that stops everything if it ever gets to be too much for you."

"Destiny." I've given this some thought since we first talked about safe words, and I keep coming back to that one.

"I like it."

I wrap my arms around his neck and gaze into the cool blue eyes that look at me with such desire. "It's a reminder that even if I can't handle what's currently happening, I'm not going anywhere, so you don't need to worry about that."

He kisses me and makes quick work of getting rid of our clothes. Then we're falling onto the bed, a tangle of arms, legs and lips that never stop moving as we sort ourselves. Knowing we're completely alone and have hours to indulge in each other goes a long way toward easing some of the tension I felt earlier.

I've read enough about sex and love and lovemaking after breast cancer to expect my body might not fully cooperate. I hope that doesn't happen now.

"What?" he asks, his lips busy on my neck.

I close my eyes against an emotional reaction to his concern. I've never been with a man who was so tuned in to me, and in light of what I know about Kristian's past, it's remarkable that he's so sensitive when no one taught him how to be.

"I'm... I'm not the same person I was before I got sick. I'm not as confident that everything will work the way it's supposed to."

"That's not for you to worry about. It's my job to make sure you feel good. Let me take care of you."

All righty, then.

"No thinking or worrying allowed." His lips skim over my collarbones and down to the tops of my breasts. "Just breathe and feel."

Breathe and feel. I can do that.

"I want you to know that since I met you, I've been unable to bring myself to touch another woman."

His confession shocks me. "You met me *five months* ago."

"Believe me. I know."

I'm reeling until he draws my nipple into his mouth and sucks gently, forcing me to give my full attention to what's happening right now. It's not quite the same sensation as it was before my surgery, but it feels amazing nonetheless. I try to take his advice to breathe and feel what *is*, rather than what used to be. And it feels pretty damned good to have his lips and hands setting my body on fire for him.

"I want to kiss you and touch you everywhere, but more than that, I want to be inside you," he says in that gruff voice that's such a turn-on. He takes himself in hand, his cock so hard, it's purple and leaking.

"Yes... I want that, too."

With his free hand, he tests my readiness.

I'm relieved to have dodged one of the more prevalent side effects of treatment—vaginal dryness. In fact, I seem to have the opposite issue, which apparently pleases him if his deep groan is any indication.

He aligns his cock with my pussy and gives a gentle thrust. "Nice and slow."

Oh. My. *God*. He's so big, it hurts, and not in a good way.

"Easy, sweetheart." Retreating, he gives me a second to breathe before he's back again, deeper this time.

My fingers dig into his back, seeking something to hold on to. At least I'm not thinking about my post-cancer body or vaginal dryness anymore. I can't think about anything but the insistent invasion that's starting to feel good.

"That's it," he says, beginning to move a little faster. "Yes, God, Aileen... Even better than I thought it would be. You're so hot and tight."

I can't think or breathe or do anything other than feel, which is just what he wanted. I'm consumed by him, surrounded by his appealing scent, the rub of his chest and leg hair against my sensitive skin, the movement of his lips on my face and the deep, tight strokes of his cock.

"Hands over your head." He reaches for them to pin me to the bed. "Is this okay?"

I look up at him and nod, loving the way it feels to be even lightly dominated by him. I wonder what else might be possible when he really lets go.

"Talk to me. Tell me how it feels."

"Incredible."

"That's a good word."

"It's a good feeling."

"Mmm, it certainly is. The best feeling ever."

After that, there're no more words, only deep sighs and gasps and a sharp cry when I come harder than I ever have before.

"Ah, *fuck*," he mutters as he drives into me, throwing his head back as he comes, his fingers digging into my shoulders.

Every part of me tingles and throbs in the aftermath of the most spectacular sex of my life. I had no idea it could be like that until he showed me what was possible. I can only imagine what he's capable of when he takes it to the next level. Actually, I probably lack the imagination to know what he's capable of, but I can't wait to find out.

Jesus. That was... I have no words to describe it. My brain is blank, but my body hums with energy and bone-deep satisfaction. What the hell is she *doing* to me? Before this, before her, the word *bewitched* was the name of an old TV show. Now it has taken on all-new meaning. I'm under her spell, captivated and bewitched by a woman for the first time in my life.

And God, it feels so *good*. I could get lost forever in the sense of contentment and well-being I experience every time I'm with her. It's like coming home and finding paradise at the same time. I've never been truly at home anywhere, except with my Quantum family. But this is different. She's all mine, and no one has ever been all mine.

I hold her closer, desperately afraid of losing her now that I've found her.

"Are you okay?" she asks.

"Yeah. You?"

"Oh yeah," she says with a dirty laugh that makes me smile. "Glad I didn't forget how to do that."

"You definitely didn't forget."

"What're you thinking about?"

I withdraw from her and move to my side, keeping her tucked up against me. "How good it feels to be with you, no matter what we're doing. But this..."

"*This* is the best." She slides her leg between mine, and that's all it takes to make me hard again. Laughing, she says, "That was quick."

"It's you." I cup her ass and squeeze, making her gasp. I'm already addicted to how responsive and eager she is.

"No, it's *you*." Her voice is husky and sexy. I could listen to her recite a grocery list, and her voice would turn me on.

"It's *us*. We're good together."

"So good."

I'm suddenly paralyzed with fear. Nothing this good can possibly last. It never has before. The last time I allowed myself to get comfortable somewhere, I received a hard lesson on why it's not prudent to trust other people with my emotions. I'd been in that foster home a year and had started to let down my guard around the family when they told me their son was graduating from college, and they needed the space I was taking up for him. I've never let that happen again, until now. My guard is so far down, it may as well not exist at all.

I should stop this while I still can, but damn if I can find the wherewithal to get out of bed while she is warm and soft and naked in my arms. I've learned not to risk more than I can afford to lose, and with her, I'm risking everything—my heart, my soul, my *sanity*—and I'm doing it with my eyes wide open.

Arranging her facedown on the bed, I leave a trail of kisses from her shoulders to her waist, noting the bones that protrude a little too prominently for my liking. I want to take care of her and make sure she's eating and healing and thriving, but still I worry I'll end up hurting her and her kids or being hurt by them when she moves on to someone who can give her softness and sweetness.

That's not me. That's never been me. No one ever showed me how to be those things. I'm all about harsh and aggressive and pleasing myself first and foremost. I haven't been that guy with her, but maybe it's time to give her a little taste of what she'd be getting if she hitches her wagon to me. Raising her to her knees, I roughly push her legs apart with my knees and take a bite out of her ass that will leave a bruise.

She lets out a mewling sound and arches her back, as if asking for more. I do the same to the other side and then hold her cheeks apart and give her my tongue—everywhere. Her sharp cries of pleasure feed the fire burning in me. I slide two fingers into her, curling them for maximum effect as I suck on her clit, and she explodes, screaming as she comes hard. I don't let up, continuing to give her my tongue and my fingers, sliding one of them into her ass and making her come again, even harder this time. I keep my finger in her ass when I press my cock into her pussy, which is still twitching with aftershocks.

I focus on the pleasure, and only the pleasure. I can't think about the white-picket-fence fantasy I've allowed to take me over since she arrived. That shit happens to other people. Not me. This is what I'm all about—raw, hard, dirty fucking. This I understand. This is what makes sense to me.

As I go at her hard and deep, I experience a twinge of guilt at knowing she'll be sore tomorrow, but that doesn't stop me. I wrap an arm around her midsection and hold her still for my fierce possession.

Fisting the quilt on my bed, she gives as good as she gets, her ass pressing back against me, taking everything I give her and crying out as she comes, squeezing my dick and my finger so hard that I lose the control I've been clinging to like a life raft in a storm.

I come down from the most incredible high to realize she's crying.

Her tears shatter me. Withdrawing, I turn her so I can see her face, which is wet with tears. "I'm sorry, Aileen. I'm so sorry. I didn't mean to hurt you."

She places her finger over my lips, quieting me. "You didn't hurt me. Well, you did, but it was the best kind of hurt."

I can't bear the tears that continue to leak from the corners of her eyes. Everything hard in me goes soft again at the sight of those fucking tears. I love her desperately, endlessly. I kiss away her tears. "Why're you crying?" The words come out harsher than intended, but her expression never changes as she gazes at me the way Natalie looks at Flynn and Addie looks at Hayden. Is it possible...

No. *Just no.* Don't go there. I don't dare to hope. Fucking hope has bitch-slapped me too many times to be tempted by it again.

"I can't believe I've lived this long without knowing *that* was possible. What if I'd died when I was sick without knowing—"

I kiss her again because I can't bear to hear her talk about how she could've died—or that she still could. I ache at the thought of this world without her in it, and I realize in one crystal-clear moment that I'll never be able to stay away from her, even if that might be what's best for both of us. I'm not strong enough to resist her.

I'm utterly terrified by the things she makes me feel, but I'm not going anywhere.

CHAPTER 17

Aileen

Kristian is quiet as he drives me home at eleven. He's been quiet since the second time we made love. He hardly said a word as he led me to the shower and washed every inch of me, sliding his hands over my body with the reverence of a man in love. He was quiet as he made us delicious veggie omelets that we ate at the bar in his kitchen.

He's told me he finds my honesty refreshing, but maybe I went too far before with the tears and what I said to him after the most intense sex I've ever had. I hadn't realized I was crying until he asked why. I'd been almost outside myself, if that makes sense, and when I came out of it, there were tears.

We're driving along the boardwalk in Venice Beach when I give voice to my fears. "Did I do something wrong?" I immediately hate myself for assuming I'm the problem. But what else can I do when I have no idea what he's thinking?

"Of course not." He reaches across the gearshift to put his hand on my thigh, the heat of his palm branding me the way it always does when he touches me this way.

"You've gone quiet on me."

"I'm sorry."

"If you don't tell me what you're thinking, I'll assume I did some-thing wrong or that you're disappointed after having sex with me."

"You did nothing wrong, and I am *not* disappointed after having sex with you. I'm the opposite of disappointed."

"What's the opposite of disappointed?"

"Euphoric? Stupidly hopeful? Enchanted? Bewitched? In so far over my head, I don't know which way is up? To start with."

"You feel all that?" I ask in a squeaky voice. "*For me?*"

"God, yes, Aileen. You've made a fucking mess of me."

"You're not... You're not happy about it?"

"I'm... confused."

My stomach starts to hurt. Confused is a long way from happy.

He brings the car to a stop outside my house, where only the living room is lit up, kills the engine and turns to face me. "I'm sorry if I made you feel uncertain." Running a finger over my cheek, he says, "That wasn't my intention. Tonight was incredible."

The light touch of his finger on my skin makes me shiver. "For me, too."

"I'm flying without a net here. I've never done anything like this before."

"Had sex?" I ask with a coy grin, hoping to cajole him out of the serious mood he's in.

"Had sex that *matters.*"

"Are you freaking out?"

"Little bit."

"We don't have to... If you don't want to... I mean, nothing says..."

Smiling, he wraps his hand around my neck and draws me into a soft, devastatingly sweet kiss. "We *do* have to, and I *do* want to, but you've got to be patient with me as I figure out how to do this. I'm the ultimate fixer-upper."

"Why're you so hard on yourself? If only you could see the Kris-tian that I see."

"Tell me about him."

"He's kind and generous and smart and sexy and so amazing with my kids, who're falling for him as fast and as hard as I am. He's successful and sweet and has incredible friends who'd do anything for him, which tells me he's the kind of man I want in my life, even if he doesn't think he's good enough for me and my kids. In his professional life, he's confident and self-assured, but in his personal life, he's filled with self-doubt. I'm trying to reconcile those two guys."

He stares at me for a second, his mouth opening and then closing. "How'd I do?"

"You summed me up rather well," he says gruffly.

"What're we going to do about this self-doubt in your personal life, which, from my vantage point, seems to be going rather well at the moment. Unless I'm mistaken..."

"You're not mistaken."

"Come in for a while." I need to sleep, and so does he, but I need more time with him more than I need sleep or anything else.

He releases his seat belt, and we walk in together.

Cece is on the sofa, curled up with a book. She smiles when we come in.

"Hi there. How were they?"

"They were great. We had a nice time. Logan is so smart, and Maddie is just the sweetest little girl." She puts the book into her bag and slides her feet into flip-flops. "Did you guys have a good dinner?"

I wonder if she knows exactly where we've been and what we've been doing. "We did," I say, trying to keep my expression neutral. I've never had anything to hide from a sitter before, and I feel the need to giggle all of a sudden.

"What time do you need me on Saturday?"

"Can you do five?" Kristian asks.

"Sure, no problem. What time do you expect to be back on Sunday?"

"By noon?" he says.

"That works for me."

I withdraw my wallet from my purse to pay her.

"All set," Kristian says, handing her some rolled-up cash.

I want to protest, but I won't argue with him in front of her. I show her out and thank her again.

"It was a pleasure. Your kids are adorable."

"That's so nice of you to say."

"I wouldn't say it if it wasn't true. See you on Saturday."

I watch her get into her car and wave as she drives off. "How much did you pay her?" I ask him.

"I don't recall."

"Kristian! Come on. You can't pay for my babysitters!"

He puts his arms around me. "Why not?"

I flatten my hands on his chest to keep him from distracting me. "Because they're *my* kids, and *I* pay for them."

"It makes me happy to do things for you—and for them. You want me to be happy, don't you?"

"Don't be manipulative."

His face lights up with a sexy grin and those dimples... Dear God, the dimples... It's not fair. How am I supposed to fight with those damned dimples?

"I know you've raised your kids all by yourself, and I so admire what a great job you've done with them, but you're not alone anymore." As he says those words, something that resembles fear skirts across his expression before he schools his features. He swallows hard. "You have to let me help out once in a while, because I want to, not because I feel I have to."

"Does saying that to me scare you?"

He nods.

"Why?" I ask, genuinely curious.

"Because as much as I want you, I'm still terrified I'll disappoint you. And the kids."

"Of course you will. No one's perfect, and I don't expect you to be. I'll probably disappoint you, too."

He leads me to the sofa and sits next to me, putting his arm around my shoulders to draw me in close to him. "Not possible."

"Yes, it is," I say, laughing. "You haven't seen me when I have PMS or when chemo brain kicks in."

His brows knit adorably. "What the heck is chemo brain?"

"Confusion, forgetfulness, memory failure, tripping over my own feet, to name a few things, and irritability when any of the above occurs. It can be as short-lived as a year after chemo, or it can last forever. I haven't had it too bad, but I'm definitely more forgetful and clumsier than I was before I had chemo. I'm also tired a lot."

"I hate to think about you going through such an ordeal by yourself with two kids."

"I had a lot of great support from Logan's school community and friends like Nat and Flynn, who stepped up for us."

"I wish I'd known you then."

"I'm glad you didn't. Anyway, you haven't seen me at my worst, by any means."

"I want to see you at your best, your worst and everything in between."

"Can't you understand that I want that with you, too?"

"I bet my worst is a whole lot *worse* than yours."

"I want you to do something for me."

"Anything."

"I want you to give yourself permission to enjoy this as much as I am."

"Are you? Enjoying it?"

"So much." I turn his face toward me so I can kiss him. "You can't tell?"

"Maybe you'd better show me again."

"Hold that thought for one second while I go check on my kids." I get up to go peek in on the kids, who are both sleeping soundly. Returning to the living room, I crook my finger at Kristian and then head for my bedroom. When he joins me, I close the door and lock it.

"What's going on?" he asks, raising a brow.

Sliding my arms around his neck, I go up on tiptoes to kiss him. "More of this maybe?"

"Mmm," he says against my lips. "I could be down with that."

"And I want to talk about the things you want." I swallow hard. "In bed."

"What we did tonight is more than enough for me."

"But that's not how you like it."

"Was there anything about what happened earlier that I didn't seem to like?"

"You know what I mean. You want more than that."

"Not with you." He kisses my forehead, the end of my nose and my lips. "With you, what we did was more than enough."

I pull free of his tight hold.

"Where're you going?"

"Over here." I sit on the edge of the bed and wrap my arms around my legs.

"What's wrong?"

"Why won't you be truthful with me?"

He slides his hands into his pockets. "I've been more truthful with you than I've ever been with anyone."

"Then tell me why you want those things with other women but not with me."

"I don't *need* it with you. It's already so much more just because it's you."

I want to believe him, but recalling what Natalie said about how Flynn and the others *need* kinky sex has me wondering if he's telling me everything.

"What if *I* want it?"

He sits next to me on the bed. "What if you want what?"

I lick lips that have gone dry. "The things you talked about before."

"You're going to have to be more specific."

"I want to submit to you."

He sucks in a sharp deep breath. "You have no idea what you're saying."

I'm not sure what compels me to move, but I find myself dropping to my knees in front of him. "Teach me."

"Aileen..."

Looking up at him, I go for my best innocent expression, hoping to tempt him. "Yes, Sir?"

Gritting his teeth, he says, "You're playing with fire."

"Will I get burned, Sir?" My heart beats wildly as I watch him try to decide how to proceed—and yes, I can *see* the dilemma he's grappling with.

Then he unbuckles his belt and opens his pants, freeing his cock. "Is this what you want?" he asks in a sexy growl as he strokes himself.

"Tell me what *you* want."

"Suck my cock."

Yes, please... "How do you like it?"

"Wrap your hand around the base."

I follow his direction, and he gasps when my hand brushes against his sensitive skin.

"Tighter."

I tighten my grip.

"Stroke it. Hard and fast."

My heart beats erratically, and I remind myself to breathe as I give him what he wants. With his hands propped behind him on the bed, his head falls back and his hips move in time with my hand. His eyes are closed, so he has no warning when I lean over him and draw the wide head into my mouth.

He gasps sharply, which fills me with satisfaction and a sense of my own power.

Pleasuring a partner has never turned me on the way it does now. I want him to love this. I want it to be the best he's ever had, so I devote myself to him, taking his cock into my mouth and retreating, lashing him with my tongue and sucking as hard as I can. He's so big that my lips are stretched to their limit.

He gasps and moans and thrusts his hips but doesn't try to take over the way I expect him to.

When I sense he's getting close, I cup his balls and roll them gently between my fingers.

"*Fuck,*" he mutters in that gruff, sexy tone I've come to love so much. "Aileen... Stop. *Babe...*"

I don't stop. Instead, I stroke him faster and suck him harder.

He explodes in my mouth, something I used to hate with Rex, but with Kristian, it seems perfectly natural to swallow every drop and lick him clean while he trembles in the aftermath. Falling back on the bed, he releases a deep breath and reaches for me.

I crawl on top of him.

His arms come around me, his lips skimming my forehead.

"How'd I do?"

He grunts out a laugh. "You ruined me."

"I want to be the best you've ever had, so tell me if there was something you want that I didn't do."

"Aileen..." He sighs. "Everything about you is the best I've ever had."

Well... As far as compliments go, they don't get much better than that. "Could I ask you something else?"

"Sure," he says, but I hear hesitance.

"This, between us... You aren't going to suddenly decide you can't do it and run away from me, are you?"

"No," he says, sounding resigned. "I'm not going to run away."

I raise myself up on one arm so I can see his face. "Is this what you want, Kristian? Am I what you want?"

He cups my face in his big hand, his thumb dragging over my lips. "I tell myself I should stay away so you can find a nice, normal guy who can be what you need. But the thought of any other guy touching you makes me insane with jealousy. I tell myself that you could do better, that you deserve better, but I can't stay away. I'm on my way back to you before I consciously decide to come here. From the second I first saw you, I've been a disaster, and that's all your fault."

I laugh through the tears that slide down my cheeks. Maybe you could hear those words from the guy you're crazy about and not cry, but I'm not that strong.

He kisses away my tears. "So yeah, you're what I want, what I need, what I *crave*, but you have to show me how to do this. I've never tried to have a normal relationship with a woman, let alone a mom of two precious kids. I'm scared to death that I'm going to fuck it up and hurt you guys somehow. That's my biggest fear."

His raw honesty touches me deeply, because I know it doesn't come naturally to him. "You will fuck up and you will hurt us, and we'll hurt you, and it'll be messy and difficult and awful at times. That's life and love and relationships. It's what happens when you *care*."

"I have this darkness inside of me, and you're all light and laughter and joy. It would kill me if my darkness dimmed your joy."

"Then let's not allow that to happen. Maybe my joy will defeat your darkness."

His lips curve into a small smile. "Wouldn't that be something?"

"Anything is possible if you have faith in me and us and what we're building together."

"I feel like a greedy little boy being offered ice cream for the first time in my life."

Does he have any idea how sweet he is? "You'd better lick it fast before it melts."

His eyes widen with surprise at my blatant invitation, but then he pounces, turning us over so quickly, my head spins. "Don't mind if I do."

CHAPTER 18

Kristian

I float through the next couple of days on a cloud of contentment unlike anything I've ever experienced. Work is insane as we prepare for the premiere, so time with Aileen is limited to stolen hours late at night. I go to her the second I break free of work, and she's always happy to see me.

Last night, I didn't get there until midnight. She met me at the door, took me by the hand, led me into her bedroom and undressed me without saying a word. I lost myself in her sweetness for hours. Today, I'm sleep-deprived and running on adrenaline and a kind of bone-deep happiness I've never known before. Apparently, I'm doing a piss-poor job of hiding my euphoria, because it's the number one topic of conversation at our partner meeting on the morning before the premiere.

They talk about me like I'm not in the room hearing every word they're saying.

"I've never seen him smile like that," Jasper says.

"I know!" Mo replies. "I didn't know he *could* smile like that. The dimples are on permanent display."

"You think he's in love?" Hayden asks.

"Could be," Mo says. "He's got the same dopey, gobsmacked look about him you had when Addie finally brought you up to scratch."

Flynn cracks up laughing at the dopey face Hayden makes at Marlowe.

"What're you laughing at?" she asks Flynn. "No one was dopier or more gobsmacked than you were when you first met Natalie."

Flynn holds up his hands in defense. "You won't hear me arguing."

All eyes turn to me, and I fight the urge to squirm.

"So," Hayden says. "What gives?"

"Are you talking *to* me now and not just *about* me?" I ask him, smiling so he'll know I'm joking.

"Don't be a smart-ass. Tell us what we want to know."

"Umm, I think I'll pass on that." I refer to the agenda Lori printed out for the meeting. "We've got a lot to cover this morning and interviews starting in an hour." We're back-to-back today with all the major entertainment shows coming in to interview Hayden, Flynn and Marlowe about *Insidious*.

Flynn plays a drug addict struggling to break free of a vicious opioid addiction, Marlowe is his therapist, and Hayden directed them both to Oscar-worthy performances. We're already hearing buzz about a repeat sweep for Quantum in next year's awards season.

"Come *on*, Kris," Marlowe says. "You gotta tell us something!"

I want to snap at her to mind her own business, but I'd never do that. These four people are the closest thing to "family" I've ever had, and they mean the world to me.

"Things are good." That's the understatement of the century. Things are *magnificent*.

"So you're over that 'flu' you had?" Jasper asks, using his fingers to make air quotes around the word *flu*.

"For the most part."

"What's this about the flu?" Flynn asks, looking to Jasper and then to me.

"Nothing," I say, giving Jasper a pointed look.

He smiles as he shrugs, the bastard. He likes knowing he's made me squirm. I suppose that's the least of what he owes me after I rode him about Ellie when they first got together. Payback is truly a bitch in this crowd.

Thankfully, we get back to business after that, but I'm painfully aware that I've dodged a bullet for now. I'm on borrowed time when it comes to my partners and their need to know everything that goes on in our group.

I'm usually right there with them, poking at whomever is going off the rails with a member of the opposite sex, but being on the receiving end of the pokes is another thing that's new to me. Until now, I've never given them reason to be curious about my love life. They've often witnessed it, such as it was, firsthand at our clubs here in LA and in New York, but now I can't imagine making love to Aileen with an audience, which is another massive change on top of the many others.

The day passes in a blur of frenetic activity, the kind I usually relish because it keeps me at the top of my game—where I do my best work. Today, I'm at the bottom of my game with my brain muzzy from lack of sleep, my attention split between work and wondering what Aileen and the kids are up to today and figuring out how many hours I have to put in at the office before I can see her.

Once again, it's after midnight when I arrive at her place, using the key she gave me. I've even got a bag with me tonight so I can shower in the morning and go straight to the office for a couple of hours to deal with last-minute issues before the premiere. We've given up pretending that we aren't spending every night together. So far, I've been lucky to avoid detection by the kids, but I'm sure it's only a matter of time before we get caught.

She says it's okay if they catch me there, but I'm anxious about whether that'll cause problems. She's told me they both like me and that I make her happy. And isn't that something? Her kids like me, and I make her happy. Hearing that is frosting on an already delicious cake.

Aileen is asleep, so I undress quietly, use the bathroom and then slide into bed, snuggling up to her warmth and finally relaxing after an endless, stressful day.

She turns over to face me. "So late tonight." Her voice is husky and sexy and sleepy. I marvel at how quickly I've become addicted to the sound of her voice and how easily I've fallen into the habit of sleeping with her, when I've always preferred to sleep alone. Not anymore. Now I don't want to sleep without her wrapped around me.

"I think we're finally ready." I tip her chin up to receive my kiss, and when her mouth opens to my tongue, I lose myself in her sweet sexiness. If there's anything better than this, I've yet to find it. I make slow, sultry love to her, our bodies moving together in perfect harmony, as if we've been doing this for years rather than days. I can't get enough of her. I'm drunk on her taste and her scent and the heat of her pussy around my cock as she comes with soft gasps that make me wild for her.

I lose my mind as I pound into her, captivated by a feeling I can only get from being with her this way. It's the highest of highs, and I'm truly addicted.

Her hands grasp my ass cheeks, pulling me deeper into her, and that finishes me off.

I collapse on top of her, my head spinning and my lungs burning from holding my breath. "I didn't mean to be so rough."

"I loved it." She has this blissed-out look on her face that I can see in the glow of the nightlight in the bathroom.

"You're not sore anymore?" I probably should've asked her that beforehand. She'd been too sore after the first night to have sex for a couple of days. I thought I'd die waiting for her to feel better.

"I'm fine. Don't worry."

I do worry. I worry about everything where she's concerned—her health, her happiness, her safety, her well-being, her kids... I'm happier than I've ever been, and all I can think about is how long will it last before the rug gets pulled out from under me the way it always does.

For now, right in this minute, I have everything I've ever wanted right here in my arms, and I tell myself that's enough.

But still... I worry.

Aileen

The pampering begins just after noon. I'm happy and tired and sore and elated and completely in love with the most extraordinary man. He's complicated and broody and sexy and loving and sweet and sometimes rough around the edges. And he's seen to every detail to make sure today is another in a string of magical days for me.

Not only has he made this amazing for me, but he asked Tenley to include my daughter, who is getting her nails done right alongside me. Her hair is in rollers, and her grin stretches from ear to ear. The cut on her forehead is healing nicely, and she doesn't complain about it hurting anymore.

Flynn came to pick up Logan to do "guy things," as he put it, while I get ready for my big night out.

I can't believe this is my life. A year ago today, I had just been diagnosed, and my future seemed anything but rosy. Now my illness feels like a distant nightmare that happened to someone else. I'm going to a Hollywood premiere with the man of my dreams, and we have the entire night to spend together. The last time I was this excited, the kids and I were on our way to Flynn and Nat's wedding, not knowing I would meet someone who would change our lives so profoundly.

The screen door opens, and Natalie pokes her head in. "Knock, knock."

"Hey, come in!" I'm thrilled to see her, as always.

"I was out doing errands and wanted to pop over to see if you need anything."

"Since Venice Beach is nowhere near your house, you need a better story."

"Fine," she says, laughing as she flops down on the sofa, "I wanted to see how you're holding up before your first big night in Hollywood."

"I'm freaking out. I can't believe I'm going to a premiere with Kristian and the rest of you."

"Try to think of it as just another date."

"Is that what you did when you went to the Golden Globes with Flynn?"

"Touché. I was a disaster."

"Then you know exactly how I feel."

"It's okay, Mommy. Mr. Kristian will make sure you don't get scared or anything."

"That's true, honey." She's right—he'll take care of me and make sure I have a wonderful time. I love that she knows that about him and has such faith in him. I'll have to tell him that later. It'll mean a lot to him.

"I can't wait to see the movie," Natalie says. "I haven't seen it yet. I wanted to wait to see it in the theater on the big screen."

"It's so cool that we get to see it before everyone else."

"That's what we get for s-l-e-e-p-i-n-g with the producers."

My face heats with embarrassment at realizing everyone has figured out we're sleeping together.

"What does that spell?" Maddie asks.

"Friends," Natalie says smoothly.

I take a closer look at my friend and notice she's unusually pale. "Are you okay?"

"I'm fine. Better than fine, actually."

The odd statement has me looking at her again. She makes a gesture of a hand over a pregnant belly that makes me gasp and then startle, earning a scowl from my nail technician.

Natalie laughs at my reaction.

I can't say a *word* about the scoop of the year with the nail ladies in the room, which of course Natalie knows.

She covers her mouth with her hand to muffle her laughter. I can't believe she dropped a bomb like that on me when I can't do or say a thing! And then I'm blinking back tears because my sweet friend is having a baby, and after everything she's been through, I couldn't be happier for her and Flynn. They've got to be over the moon with excitement.

Makeup people are next, and Natalie leaves to get ready herself before we have a minute alone to celebrate her big news. We'll have to do that later.

Tenley shows up around four, helps me get dressed and opens a velvet box from Flynn's brother-in-law Hugh, the jeweler. She drapes me in diamonds—necklace, chandelier earrings, bracelet and ring that she advises me to wear on my right hand unless I want the entire town buzzing about being engaged to Kristian. I never would've thought about such a thing, although the thought of being engaged to him does crazy things to my insides.

"How much is all this worth?" I ask, breathless from excitement—and the fear that I might lose one of the priceless pieces.

"About one-point-five."

"*Million?*"

"Uh-huh."

She's so matter-of-fact about it, but I suppose it's an everyday thing to her, when to me it's another first in a once-in-a-lifetime day.

I reach up to touch the necklace, to make sure it hasn't moved, while Tenley buzzes around me, making last-minute adjustments.

Maddie knocks on the bedroom door. "Can I see, Mommy?"

"Come in."

She steps into the room as I turn toward the door. Her eyes shine with delight. "You look like a *princess!*"

"I feel like one, too."

"You're *so* pretty."

"Thank you, baby. Come here and give Mommy a hug."

"No sticky fingers," Tenley says.

"My fingers aren't sticky," Maddie replies indignantly. "Don't worry." She comes over to carefully hug me.

I wrap my arms around her and kiss the top of her head. "You'll be a good girl for Cece tonight, right?"

"Uh-huh."

"She said you can make popcorn and watch movies. Doesn't that sound like fun?"

"I don't want Cece to sleep over. I want you."

Uh-oh. "I'll be back before you even know I'm gone."

"What if I need you?"

"You can call me. I'll have my phone with me the whole time, and I'll call you before bed to tuck you in. Okay?"

She thinks about that for a minute.

I hold my breath the entire time.

"Okay." She spins around and leaves the room.

I let out the breath I was holding.

"Whoa, you dodged a bullet," Tenley says.

"No kidding." I'm rattled by the near miss with Maddie. I've left them so infrequently with others that I worried about how they'd react to the plan for tonight. They've seemed fine about it, but with rubber now meeting road, Maddie is having second thoughts. Thankfully, second thoughts didn't turn into a full-blown meltdown.

Cece is due any minute, and Kristian will be here soon, too. Hopefully, my luck will hold with the kids.

Logan comes bounding into the house, back from his outing with Flynn, and runs straight for my room, stopping short when he sees me decked out.

His mouth falls open as his eyes widen. "*Wow.* You look so good. Really, really good!"

"Thanks, buddy." I'm delighted by his reaction and thrilled that they're seeing me looking healthy and vibrant after my illness. "Did you have fun with Flynn?"

"Uh-huh. We went to a skateboard park, but he had to go home and change into a monkey suit. What is that, anyway?"

"That's what guys call tuxedos," I say, smiling.

"They should call them penguin suits rather than monkey suits."

"You're absolutely right. They should." I hear Maddie talking to Cece in the living room. "Sounds like Cece is here."

Logan spins around to go see her.

"Your kids are so sweet, and you're stunning," Tenley declares, taking a last critical survey of my appearance.

"All thanks to you."

"It was my pleasure. I hope you have a wonderful time."

"I'm sure I will. By the way, I meant to ask earlier... If you're here with me, who's tending to Addie and Natalie and the others?"

"Some of my people. They wanted you to have me."

"Probably because I needed the most work."

She shakes her head. "Addie said it was because you most deserve to be treated like a princess, and I couldn't agree more." Squeezing my hand, she says, "Have the best time ever."

"I will," I say softly, moved nearly to tears by the kindness of my sweet friends. "Thank you again."

"Any time."

Tenley leaves the room, and I have two minutes to myself before Maddie comes to tell me that Kristian has arrived. I take a couple of deep breaths to calm my nerves and the butterflies in my belly. I'm nervous and excited and filled with anticipation about the night I get to spend with him. "Here goes," I whisper to the reflection in the mirror. The woman looking back at me is healthy, strong and confident. She fills me with confidence as I turn to leave the room and see him coming toward me, too sexy for words in a black tuxedo.

He stops short in the hallway, his eyes flaring with heat and desire.

I've never felt more in my life than I do in the ten seconds it takes for him to recover and come the rest of the way to me.

He slides an arm around my waist, bringing me in close to him. "You are *beyond* beautiful."

"In this old thing?" I joke so I won't cry and ruin my makeup.

"Exquisite," he whispers in my ear, sending a shock wave of need rippling through me.

"You're rather exquisite yourself." I never want to forget this perfect moment with him.

"I've got nothing on you. Every guy there will be wishing he could be as lucky as I am."

"*Right.*"

"It's true."

It's not true, but for one night, I'm going to allow myself to believe it is.

CHAPTER 19

Kristian

I'm blown away. I had no idea what to expect when I arrived, but knowing Tenley, I assumed Aileen would look amazing. But she's *magnificent*. The dress, the shoes, the makeup, the diamonds... She takes my breath away, and I wish we didn't have somewhere to be so I could skip straight to the plan for later. I've thought a lot about what she said the other night, how she wants to understand my lifestyle and give me what I need. I promised to take her to the club, and tonight, after the premiere, I'm going to keep that promise.

Once she's had a chance to see the action up close and personal, if she still wants me to teach her, I will. But if she decides it's not for her, that's fine, too. I'm finding I don't need the kink the way I have in the past, which is another change I'm trying to process on top of many others.

In a way, I feel like I'm being reborn and remade with her, and this new version of me is far better than the old one. I like the way I look to her and how she makes me want to be the best version of myself. No one has ever made me feel the way she does.

I carry her overnight bag as we say good night to Cece and the kids, and I escort her to the chauffeured Bentley that's waiting for us at the curb. I wave off the driver and hold the door for her myself, waiting until she's settled to close the door and go around to get in on the other side. The second I'm seated, I reach for her, and she slides across the seat to snuggle up to me. I press a button to close the window between us and the driver.

"Is this one of your cars?"

"Nope. This one is rented because I wanted the privacy screen."

"Why? What's going to happen back here?"

"You'll have to wait and see." I nuzzle her neck. "But anything is possible."

"Mmm." She tips her head to give me better access. "I have to tell you something Maddie said earlier when I was nervous."

"What did she say?"

"That I didn't need to be nervous because you'd be there to take care of me."

"She said that?" I'm ridiculously moved.

"Uh-huh."

"She's right. I will take care of you, and there's absolutely nothing to be nervous about."

"After having my kids, this is the most exciting thing I've ever done."

"I'm glad you're excited. I am, too."

"I'm sure it's exciting—and scary—to know that people will see the film for the first time tonight."

"It is, but that's not the main reason I'm excited."

"It's not?"

I shake my head. "My date for the evening is way more exciting than the film. In fact, this is the first time I've ever taken a real date to one of these things."

"Stop. I am not more exciting than the film you've spent years working on, and I can't believe you've never brought a date."

"You are far more exciting than the film, and I usually don't want the bother of having to tend to a date when I'm working, so I usually go with an actress or model who also doesn't want the bother of romantic entanglements at a work thing. But tonight..." I nuzzle her neck. "Tonight, I've never been so happy to be *thoroughly* entangled, and I can't *wait* to tend to my date after the work is finished."

"I can't wait either," she says, sounding breathless. "What're we doing later?"

"That's for me to know and you to find out."

Her hand moves over my inner thigh to cup my erection. "Will it involve some of this?"

"If that's what you want."

"It is. I want it."

I groan from the blast of lust that burns through me. I love how she says whatever she thinks, that I never have to wonder what's on her mind or what she wants. "Keep it up, and I'll be hard all night."

"I want to keep it up," she says, rubbing me shamelessly. "Will this do it?"

I grab her hand, not because I want her to stop, but because I don't want to come in my pants like a schoolboy getting lucky for the first time.

"You're no fun," she says with an adorable pout.

Scowling playfully, I say, "I'll show you fun. Later."

"That's a long time from now," she says with a sigh.

"Believe me, I know." I've been thinking about our private after-party from the time I left her bed this morning. She's almost all I thought about on a day when I had many other pressing matters I was supposed to be focused on. "By the way, you're doing a number on my concentration."

"Am I?"

I love this coy, playful side of her. "You know you are, and I may need to punish you for it when I get you alone."

Her cheeks flush and her eyes go big with surprise and what might be curiosity. "How will you punish me?"

"There're so many ways." Thinking about them doesn't help to quell the throbbing ache in my groin.

"Give me an example."

"I could spank your sweet ass until it's hot pink."

She swallows hard. "And that would count as a punishment?"

Holy fuck. Is she saying she'd *like* it too much to consider it punishment? "All depends on how it's administered."

"How would you administer it?"

"It hurts a little more with a paddle than with a bare hand."

When she squirms in the seat next to me, I rest a hand on her inner thigh and drag it upward, encountering a flash of heat at her core.

"Does it turn you on to talk about this?"

"Incredibly. I've been reading up on it, and I want to try everything."

Jesus. I'm not going to survive this woman. The thought of her reading up on BDSM kills me.

"I'm not saying I'll like it all, but I want to at least try."

"We need to change the subject. Immediately."

"Why?" she asks, her brows knitting adorably.

"Because I don't feel like walking around all night with wet pants."

"Oh," she says on a long exhale followed by a giggle.

"It's not funny."

"It really is."

"Mocking your Dom will earn you another punishment."

She curls her hands around my arm and lays her head on my shoulder. "Okay."

I'm dying a slow painful death from desire, and her sweet capitulation only makes the ache that much worse.

The premiere is filled with celebrities, paparazzi and flashes exploding in our faces as we walk the red carpet in the broiling late-afternoon heat. I'm actually *walking a red carpet* in Hollywood, on the arm of the man I love. This is like a dream I'm going to wake up from any minute now. I try to take it all in, so I can tell the kids about it tomorrow.

We're at Grauman's Chinese Theatre, made famous by the celebrity handprints pressed into the sidewalk. Kristian points to a grouping of handprints to the left of the carpet. "Those are ours."

It's overwhelming and exciting at the same time. I'm about to say something to him about the Quantum handprints when the world seems to tilt, and I'm hit with a head rush. For a brief, sickening moment, I fear I'm going to pass out.

Because he's holding me so closely, Kristian immediately realizes something is wrong. He tightens the arm he has around me and gets me out of the warm sunshine and into the cool relief of the theater. He eases me onto a bench and sits next to me. "What is it?"

"I don't know. I was fine, and then I wasn't. This is better. Sorry about that."

"Don't apologize. Do you want to leave?"

"No!" That's the last thing I want to do. "I just need a minute." It's been months since I had one of the episodes that had frequently come over me during my treatment, leaving me dizzy and nauseated and sometimes disoriented. I've been pushing the limits lately and not getting enough sleep while I prepared for the move and then settled into my new home—and then spending my nights making love with a sexy man rather than sleeping.

Sleep is the furthest thing from my mind when I'm with him. I suppose it was only a matter of time before it caught up to me. The pervasive fatigue that followed me through treatment has lifted somewhat recently, but this episode is a reminder that I'm still recovering. I need to be careful or risk a setback. That's the last thing I need with everything in my life going so well.

"What can I do?" he asks, his concern palpable.

"Nothing. I'm okay. I just needed to sit for a minute."

"Are you sure? We don't have to stay."

"Yes, we do. This is your big night. I don't want to miss it."

Kristian waves down a theater employee. "Would it be possible to get a bottle of water, please?"

"Of course, sir."

"I'm okay," I tell him again, touched by his concern.

The employee returns with the water, and Kristian thanks him. He opens it and hands it to me. "Drink up."

"Yes, Sir."

His eyes blaze with heat, but before he can comment, Flynn, Natalie, Hayden, Addie and Marlowe join us. Natalie immediately senses something is up.

"Aileen was feeling woozy," Kristian says before she can ask. "Might've been the heat."

"Are you better now?" Natalie asks.

"Much."

"They're opening the doors," Flynn says.

"We'll be right in," Kristian replies.

While the others head inside, Kristian stops me from getting up with his hand on my arm. "Take one more minute. Finish the water."

I hate that I've given him reason for concern about my health on such an important night for him—and for us. He'll want to coddle me later rather than dominate me, and that makes me sad.

We're the last two to enter the theater, and we're shown to seats on the center aisle, next to his Quantum partners and their dates.

"You look gorgeous," Marlowe says when I sit next to her.

Oh my God! *Marlowe Sloane* thinks I look gorgeous! "Thank you, so do you." Wearing a black gown with her signature red hair corralled into an elaborate updo and jewels dangling from her earlobes, tonight she's every bit the glamorous movie star the world has come to know. I feel honored to know the other side of her, the casual, funny, fiercely loyal woman who more than holds her own with her male business partners.

"Are you feeling okay?" she asks.

"I'm fine, thanks." It occurs to me that I'll always be the "sick" girl in this group, the one who has cancer, because I was in the thick of treatment when I met them. It's nice that they care so much, but I hope that in time the word *cancer* isn't so closely associated with me.

My thoughts are interrupted by Hayden, who stands before the gathering to introduce the film. He talks about the story in *Insidious* within the context of the opioid epidemic sweeping the country. "This story appealed to my Quantum partners and me because it's the story of our generation. While preparing for the film, we spent time with families that have been touched by this epidemic, and many of them are here with us tonight. We thank them for sharing their stories with us, and we dedicate this film to the loved ones they've lost to addiction. In honor of *Insidious*, my partners and I will make a one-million-dollar donation to several Los Angeles-area treatment facilities on the frontlines of this new war on drugs."

The announcement is met with thunderous applause.

"And now," Hayden concludes, "I'm proud to present *Insidious*."

He walks off the stage, and the house lights go dark.

Next to me, I hear Kristian take a deep breath and release it. I reach for his hand and give it a squeeze.

The film opens with a scene on the streets of LA in which a man is looking to score heroin. It takes a full minute to recognize the drug addict as Flynn. I suppress a gasp. He looks so different! It's astounding. The film captivates me. It's gritty and visceral and spares no punches as it follows Flynn's character from rock bottom through rehab and the effort to put his life back together. Marlowe is fantastic as his take-no-prisoners therapist, and I can definitely see why they're both getting early Oscar buzz.

The closing credits roll, and the theater explodes with a standing ovation, shouts and cheers.

Flynn, Marlowe and the rest of the cast join Hayden onstage for a curtain call.

I'm overwhelmed with emotion after watching the film, the same way I was after seeing *Camouflage*. It's no wonder Flynn is considered one of his generation's greatest actors. Marlowe is his female counterpart. And they're both *my* friends.

I glance to my left and see Natalie wiping away tears as she claps for her husband and the rest of the brilliant cast. How thrilling it must be to play even a small role in such a production, and I begin to understand Kristian a little better as I watch him applaud his colleagues.

"Congratulations," I say to him when the noise dies down to the point where he'll be able to hear me. "It's incredible."

"I'm glad you think so."

"*Everyone* will think so. It's going to be a huge hit."

He hugs me and kisses me right there in front of everyone. "I was hoping you'd like it."

"I *loved* it. I can't wait to see it again. And I loved seeing your name as executive producer."

"That never gets old, no matter how many films we do. To see my name attached to something so amazing..."

"You should be very proud."

"I am, thank you."

I love his humility, his sense of wonder, the excitement that dances in his blue eyes as he watches his partners, the people who have been his family, soak up the adulation of an appreciative crowd.

We're escorted by security personnel to the after-party, which is held on the roof of a nearby restaurant. Waiters pass out flutes of champagne and delicious bite-size appetizers as we hobnob with Hollywood royalty. I can't believe some of the faces I recognize in the crowd. After their big win with *Camouflage* last year, everyone wants a piece of the Quantum partners, or so it seems to me.

Kristian is engaged in an intense conversation with a studio executive he introduced me to, so I signal to him that I'm going to talk to Natalie.

He nods, but I can tell he wishes I'd stay close to him, and I feel his gaze on me as I cross the crowded room to where Nat is sitting in a half-circle booth with Addie, Ellie, Sebastian, Leah and Emmett. They move over to make room for me, and I squeeze in on the end next to Nat.

I'm there about ten seconds when another flute of champagne appears in front of me.

"How're you feeling?" Nat asks. The room is loud with voices and background music. The others are engaged in conversation, so no one can hear us.

"Totally fine. Nothing to worry about. How about you?" I raise a brow that makes her giggle, remembering the news she shared earlier.

"Never better," she says, winking.

I lower my voice even further. "It was mean to do that to me when I couldn't freak out."

"Maybe so, but your reaction was priceless."

I squeeze her arm. "I'm *so* happy for you guys."

"Thanks. We're rather thrilled ourselves."

"Have you told anyone else?"

"Not yet. We were waiting until after tonight. Everyone has been so busy and stressed out getting ready."

"I'm honored to be in the know."

"I needed to tell someone."

"Thanks for picking me."

"Now you have to tell me something no one else knows. You and Kristian? Getting busy, yes?"

"Perhaps," I say with a coy smile.

She nudges me. "Knock it off and spill the deets."

I find him in the crowd, laughing and talking with two other men. It's like he has a spotlight over his head, because he's the only one I see in a crowd of people. "I'm in love with him."

"Oh, Aileen... That's so amazing."

I tear my gaze off him to look at her. "I think I have been since your wedding."

"If you ask me, the feeling is entirely mutual. He keeps looking at you, even while he's talking to other people. Flynn says he's been totally different at the office this week—distracted and leaving early and generally not at all himself."

"Is it wrong to say I love to hear that he's as messed up as I am?"

"Not wrong at all. I'm so excited about this!"

"Could I ask you something super personal? And if it's too personal, you don't have to tell me."

"Of course."

My gaze lands once again on Kristian, because if he's in the room, I want to look at him. "When you and Flynn were first together, how did you deal with..."

"The BDSM?"

"Yes," I say, relieved that she spared me from having to say it. If I'm squeamish about talking about it, maybe I shouldn't be so eager to try it.

"It took some time for him to come clean with me about his needs in that regard, but after he did, we hashed it all out. He insisted on a contract that spells out what I will and will not do. We came up with a safe word, and we gave it a try."

"You have an actual contract? With your husband?"

"Yes, most Doms will insist on a contract so there're no surprises in a scene. Practitioners of the lifestyle are very big on communication—before, during and after. If Kristian is anything like Flynn, you'll talk more about your sex life with him than you ever have. Not that I had anything to compare it to, but from what I'm told, most people outside the lifestyle don't have frank conversations about what they're going to do in the bedroom the way we do."

As a big fan of open communication in all aspects of my life, I find this refreshing. But the thought of discussing, in detail, what's going to happen in bed with Kristian, makes me feel warm all over, particularly between my legs, where an insistent throb has my full attention. I can't wait to be alone with him.

"How long do these parties usually last?" I ask.

"A couple of hours, but I wouldn't be surprised if your man claims you much sooner than that, seeing as how he went to so much trouble to get you alone for the night."

"He keeps telling me he doesn't need the kink when he's with me. That it's already *more* with me."

"Hmm."

"What does that mean? Hmm?"

"I'm certainly no expert, but from what I've come to know about

Flynn and the others, I find it surprising that he's suddenly not interested."

"So do I. I think it's because I was sick, and he's afraid to push me too far. How do I tell him I *want* him to push me? I want to experience everything with him. I don't want him to feel like he has to turn off this part of himself that's been so important to him because he's with me now. You know what I mean?"

"I do, and you need to keep telling him that you want it so he won't be afraid to go there with you. Flynn and I had a lot of similar challenges after what I went through in the past. His inclination was to treat me like I was a delicate flower. I showed him I'm a lot tougher than that, and we got through it. You will, too."

"What if..." I bite my lip, trying to find the courage to express my greatest fear in actual words. If I say it out loud, then it becomes real.

"What, honey?"

"What if I can't take it? What if it's too much for me, and I can't be what he needs?"

"If he cares about you as much as I think he does, he'll adjust what he needs to what you can handle. He'd never want you to be afraid of him. I'm sure of that."

Her assurances make me feel a little more confident, but I'm still full of uncertainty about whether I can be the woman he needs. And if I can't be? What happens then?

CHAPTER 20

Kristian

I want out of here. I've spoken to all the honchos from the studio, absorbed their rave reviews of the film, done the glad-handing I need to on behalf of Quantum, and now I want to be alone with my woman.

My woman.

Two words that have never filtered through my mind in one sentence until now. Until her. She's huddled with Nat at one of the tables. God only knows what the two of them are talking about, but I have my suspicions.

I'm glad Natalie filled her in about the BDSM. She saved us a lot of time by cutting to the chase and telling Aileen. Best of all? Aileen didn't run from me in horror when she found out I like it kinky and rough. In fact, I quickly discovered that she can more than hold her own in the bedroom, despite sometimes seeming fragile in other settings.

She'd hate to hear me describe her that way, but after her near-fainting episode earlier, I'm even more reluctant to push the envelope with her in bed. But *God*, I want to. I want to make her mine in every possible way.

Desire beats through me like an extra pulse that belongs only to her. I can't stop looking at her or thinking about her or *wanting* her.

The studio head is telling me they're devoting an extra four million to marketing the film in the wake of sensational early reviews. This is big news. I ought to be elated, but I'm annoyed that he won't stop talking. He's keeping me from her.

I can't take the wanting any longer. "Thanks for the great news, Jerry." I shake his hand, noting his somewhat stunned expression. No one shuts down Jerry Lautenberg. "Could I call you on Monday to discuss it further?"

"Of course," he says, flustered—and possibly peeved.

I don't care. "Great. Thanks again for being here tonight. Means a lot to us."

"Congratulations on another outstanding film."

"Thank you very much. I'll talk to you on Monday." I shake his hand again and make my escape, keeping my head down and my gaze averted so no one will stop me from reaching my destination. People call out to me, but I ignore them. I reach the table where she's sitting with Natalie and the others. She's on the end, so I lean in to speak directly into her ear. "Let's go." I hold out my hand to help her up.

"Have a good night, you guys," Natalie says with a meaningful smirk. She knows exactly what's on my mind.

Aileen's hand slides into mine, and that's all it takes to calm the uneasiness of being separated from her, even minimally, for the last hour. It occurs to me that I'm becoming slightly obsessed with her, but I make no apologies for wanting to be with her all the time. I've waited my whole life to belong to someone, and now that I do, I want to wallow in the contentment I find only with her.

We leave without saying goodbye to anyone. If anything comes up in my absence, one of my partners can handle it. I'm officially off duty.

Gordon Yates, our director of security in LA, stands by the elevator. "Shall I request your car?" he asks.

"Yes, please. Thanks, Gordon."

"No problem." He speaks into a microphone attached to his earpiece as he summons the elevator for us. It takes less than a minute for the elevator to arrive, but that feels like too long. The logistics of the escape are making me crazier than I already am.

In the elevator, Aileen turns to me and rests her hands on my chest. "Why are you so tense?"

"Because I had to spend an entire hour in the same room with you without being able to touch you or talk to you."

She smiles up at me. "You were working."

"I was dying for you the whole time."

"Well, now you have me."

I put my arms around her and hold her as close to me as I can get her, my hard cock making its presence known between us. "I'm obsessed with you."

"I seem to have the same problem where you're concerned. I couldn't stop looking at you when you were talking to people."

"I saw you looking my way, and that made being separated from you even worse."

"This is crazy," she says with a nervous laugh.

"If this is crazy, sign me up. I want to be crazy every day for the rest of my life."

"Kristian," she says on a sigh.

"Too much too soon?"

"No, not at all. You just said what I was thinking."

Before I can respond to that momentous statement, the doors open. We're greeted by another member of Gordon's team, who escorts us from the venue to the curb where our car awaits. The sidewalk crawls with photographers waiting for Flynn, Marlowe, Hayden and the other celebrities, so I keep Aileen tucked in close to me, hoping to shield her. While the invasion of privacy goes with the territory in my world, it's new to her, and I don't want her frightened by their aggressiveness.

The second we're tucked into the cool interior of the car, I tell the driver to take us to the Quantum building, raise the barrier to close us off from view and lift her onto my lap so I can kiss her the way I've been dying to for hours now. As always, she's worth the wait, responding with ardor and desperation that more than matches mine.

Traffic is heavy, even on a Saturday night, so we have time, or so I tell myself as I break the kiss, breathing hard from the desire that pounds through me.

"Have you checked on the kids?"

"Yes, Cece says everything is fine."

"Good." I kiss her neck and then her lips. "I want you right now."

"Here?"

"Right here." When I had this tuxedo made, I insisted on one button and a zipper. None of the latches and flaps tuxedo pants usually have. As I free my cock from my pants, I never imagined that request would come in so handy. With my free hand, I push her dress up her smooth, silky legs and tug at the scrap of fabric that covers her pussy, feeling it rip.

Her face flushes with heat. "Kristian..." She glances over her shoulder to the dark glass that separates us from the driver. "We can't."

"We absolutely can." She's light as a feather, so I lift her and position her so she's straddling my lap, her heat pressing against the tip of my cock, which aches for her. I lower her onto me slowly when I'd much rather plunge. But that would hurt her, and I never want to hurt her.

Her fingers dig into my shoulders.

Reaching under the dress that's bunched at her waist, I grasp her ass cheeks and tug them open.

Her head falls forward, her forehead propped against mine. "I can't believe we're doing this in a moving car."

"Believe it, baby. It's all your fault that I couldn't wait."

"*How* is it my fault?"

"You're just so fucking sexy and gorgeous. I can't control myself when you're around."

"I can live with that," she says with a sigh.

"I hope so, because you're stuck with me."

"I can live with that, too."

I want to ask her, right here and now, to live with me forever. To make a home with me, to be my person, the one who will always be there for me no matter what. But it's too soon for that, and besides, with her pussy halfway impaled on my cock, I have other things to think about.

"Let me in," I say in a low growl that makes her moan.

"I'm *trying*."

"Relax, sweetheart." I reach down to where we're joined to caress her clit, which is hard and throbbing under my fingers. "The driver won't open the door without my permission. We won't get caught."

The tension leaves her body as her inner muscles relax to allow me in. "*Yes*," I hiss through clenched teeth. "God, *yes*." Nothing—and I do mean *nothing*—has ever felt better than being inside her tight, hot body. I could die right now, and I'd go happier than I've ever been. I grasp her ass and move her up and down on my rigid cock. "Ride me, sweetheart. Move your hips. *Yes*... Just like that." *Fucking hell*... She shifts her hips and takes me right to the edge of release. I bite the inside of my cheek to keep from coming too soon. It's been years since that was a challenge for me.

I need her to come so I can, too. I stroke her clit, and she cries out from a powerful release. The driver definitely heard that, but I'm right behind her, so I can't think about anything but the sweet relief of losing myself in her. I look up at her, panting and red-faced and smiling with satisfaction, and I'm filled with what can only be called euphoria. Not even winning the Oscar could compare to this, and the words are falling out of my mouth before I take even a second to contemplate what I'm saying.

"I love you, Aileen."

She sucks in a sharp deep breath, and the way she looks at me...

I'll never forget it.

"I love you, too."

"You do? Really?" I don't tell her that's the first time in my life anyone has said those words to me. Yes, I know my partners love me, but we don't throw the words around, and I don't remember my mother well enough to know if she ever said it.

"I really do. I think I have since the day I first met you."

On the verge of totally losing my shit, I wrap my arms around her, my head resting against her chest.

She runs her fingers through my hair, the gesture soothing and arousing at the same time. My cock begins to swell again.

"You're insatiable," she says, laughing.

"Only with you." I glance out the window and see we're getting close to the Quantum building, so I lift her up and off me.

"Jeez," she says, gasping. "A little warning next time, huh?"

"Sorry." I flash a grin in her direction because she makes me so damned happy. I've never had someone who belonged only to me before, and I can't begin to process the myriad emotions that come with knowing that she loves me. *Overwhelming* is the best word I can think of to describe it.

"You've made a complete mess of me," she says, squirming in the seat next to me.

I pull some tissues from a box provided by the car service and hand them to her.

She discreetly takes care of business and jams the tissues into a trash bag before righting her dress and running her fingers through her hair. "Will everyone be able to tell I was ravished in the car?"

"So what if they can? We're going to a sex club."

"We are? Right now?"

"Right now. It's the perfect time to go. You won't see anyone you know there with our friends still at the party."

"Oh. Okay."

I glance over at her, trying to get a read on what she's thinking. "Is it? We don't have to do this if you don't want to."

"I want to, but I also want to be alone with you."

My heart swells to the point that I wonder if a heart can burst from feeling *too* much. "We won't stay long." I zip my cock, which is still partially hard, into my pants and tuck in my shirt. By the time the driver comes to the door, we're presentable. I take hold of her hand

and lead her into the building. "Your new office is upstairs." I lay my hand on a palm scanner. "And the club is in the basement. Same setup in New York."

"How do you keep something like this a secret in this town?"

"Everyone who steps foot in the club, yourself included, signs a binding nondisclosure agreement that makes it very clear that we'll ruin them if they breathe a word of what goes on here. In addition to that, we have a one-million-dollar nonrefundable membership initiation fee that tends to keep the riffraff out."

"Wow. I'm trying to imagine what it would be like to have an extra million bucks lying around to spend on something like this."

I don't mention that if I'm lucky enough to convince her to marry me someday, she'll have plenty of millions to do with as she likes. This relationship business may be brand-new to me, but even I know it's too soon for *that* conversation.

"People in the entertainment business appreciate having an exclusive club where they can go and be themselves without fear of being exposed."

"I suppose that would be comforting when you live in a fishbowl."

In the elevator, I turn to her. I slide a finger over her cheek, and she gazes up at me with those big, expressive eyes. In them, I see trust and love and so many other things that rock my world. "If you see anything that disturbs or frightens you, all you have to do is say so. What's your safe word?"

"Destiny."

Best safe word ever. "Use it if you need it." I take her hand and lead her into the reception area, where I'm greeted by Lily, one of the three women we hired to handle guest relations after we opened the club to the public.

"Good evening, Mr. Bowen."

"Hi, Lily. I need an NDA for my guest, please."

"Of course." She leads us into an office where Aileen is given the NDA along with a detailed explanation of the club rules. "If you don't have any questions, you can sign here."

Aileen signs the form.

"Thanks, Lily." I lead Aileen from the office, through the double doors that bear our distinctive Q logo and into the club, which is busy as usual on a Saturday night. Scenes are happening on each of the three main stages, others are being negotiated in the various sitting areas, and servers wearing as little as possible tend to the crowd. The dance floor is full of writhing bodies moving to a sexy hip-hop beat. I keep a tight hold on Aileen's hand as we head to the bar, where one of the backup bartenders is on duty. I believe his name is Marco.

He recognizes me, clears two stools for us and has a Grey Goose and soda with a twist of lemon on the bar for me before I'm seated. Ownership has its perks.

"Evening, Mr. Bowen. What can I get for your guest?"

"Chardonnay, please."

"Coming right up."

"They treat you like a king here," she says.

"They should. I own the joint. What do you think of it?"

"It's a lot to take in all at once." Her gaze moves from the main stage, where a Domme has her female sub bent over a spanking chair as she paddles the sub's ass. The sub is naked except for a pair of six-inch heels.

"What're you thinking watching them?"

"I'm wondering if the paddle hurts."

"It stings more than hurts."

"Is she being pleasured or punished?"

"That's an excellent question. We don't allow punishment on the main floor, so it's all about pleasure out here."

"Where would punishment happen?"

"In the dungeon, which is available for the Quantum principals only, or in one of the private rooms. I'll show you them in a bit."

"And the sub... She likes being paddled?"

"Watch for a minute and see if your question is answered."

Over the next few minutes, the sub orgasms loudly, leaving her inner thighs slick with moisture.

"Wow," Aileen says, her eyes bigger than usual. "She came just from being paddled?"

"Yep, but it's more than the paddling. She allowed someone else to control her pleasure, and that psychological mind game is a huge turn-on for many subs."

Aileen crosses her legs and moves restlessly on her seat.

I put my arm around her and press my lips to her ear. "Does watching turn you on, sweetheart?"

"Mmm. Big-time."

I love her honesty. It's so refreshing—and arousing.

"What's going on over there?" She points to the stage on the left side of the room.

"That's a St. Andrew's Cross."

"I read about them."

"I love that you've researched this."

"It was far more interesting than the research I used to do for the law firm where I worked."

"I'll bet," I say, laughing. "Did it make you hot to read about it?"

"Incredibly hot."

"Aileen…"

She tears her gaze off the sight of the woman on the cross to look at me. "Does it make you happy to hear that?"

"Every single thing about you makes me happy."

CHAPTER 21

Aileen

I lean into him, loving the feel of his arms around me as I watch the action on the stages, intrigued by everything I see.

He loves me. He's sharing both his public and private worlds with me tonight, and I feel so lucky because I know none of what's happening between us comes naturally to him. It's a huge deal for him to open himself to me this way, and his words of love are among the greatest gifts I've ever received. I want to be worthy of them. I want to give him everything he needs, and that's why we're here, so I can learn more about what he needs.

"Talk to me about what you like to do here."

"What I did here is in the past now."

"I'd still like to know."

I feel his deep sigh against my back. "I've done it all. Everything you see happening here, I've done, but it never meant anything. It was a physical thing, akin to working out at a gym, if you can think of it that way. And it was a mental exercise, too. A stress reliever. It doesn't turn me on to watch them," he says, gesturing to the stages, "because I have you now."

"It's okay with me if it turns you on to watch."

"That's good to know, but it doesn't do anything for me. All I want is to show you enough to give you a sense of what it's about and then get the hell out of here so I can be alone with you."

"Give me a tour, and then we'll go."

He takes my hand and is off his stool so quickly, I scramble to keep up. I love that he's every bit as eager to be alone with me. We cross the crowded main room and duck into a hallway that's dark except for three lightbulbs. "Pick one," Kristian says.

"What am I picking?"

"One of three rooms currently in use."

"Oh." I point to the middle one, wild with curiosity about what I might see behind the closed door. I follow Kristian through a doorway to the left of the room I chose. Inside, a woman stands with her arms behind her, while a man dressed in a police uniform circles the table with what looks like a riding crop in his hand. The woman trembles uncontrollably as she watches him with eyes gone wild with fear.

"She's afraid."

"Everything has been agreed to in advance. She can stop it at any time with one word." Standing behind me, he slides an arm around my waist. I can feel his erection against my bottom.

"Do they know we're here?"

"They know it's possible people might watch them."

He presses a button that allows us to hear what they're saying. "You've been a very bad girl, princess," the man says.

"I didn't do it. I swear."

"My sources tell me otherwise." He steps behind her and releases her hands from the cuffs.

She rubs her arms and flexes her hands.

"Our records show you've never been arrested."

"I haven't."

"Then you don't know the drill. I'll need you to remove your clothing."

She stares at him. "I want a female officer."

"I'm sorry. That's not possible. We have no women on duty

tonight, so you're stuck with me. Now, we can do this the easy way or the hard way. It's up to you."

"Wh-what's the hard way?"

"I rip the clothes from your body and do a cavity search without lubricant."

Her throat bulges as she swallows, and her hands tremble violently as she unbuttons her blouse and removes it.

"Hurry up about it," he barks, making me jump.

"Easy, honey," Kristian says, his palm flat against my belly. "It's all for effect."

"It's working."

He holds me tighter. "I love having you here with me."

"I love being here with you."

I'm so close to him, I can feel his every breath as I watch the woman in the room remove her skirt and heels.

"C-can I leave my underwear on?"

"I can't very well perform a cavity search if you're wearing under-wear. *Everything off. Now.*"

Tears roll down her face as she removes her bra and then steps out of her panties. She can't decide what she wants to cover with her hands—her breasts or her pussy. He solves that dilemma for her by telling her to lift her arms and hold them straight out while he runs his hands over her body, examining her.

Tweaking her nipples, he says, "I think someone is enjoying being strip-searched."

"N-no, Sir. I'm not enjoying it."

"Are you *sure* you're not enjoying it?"

"Very sure."

"Get on the table."

"Excuse me?"

"You heard me. Get on the table, lie on your back and spread your legs." As he speaks, he puts on a latex glove.

"Wh-what're you going to do?"

Her stammer and obvious fear make me anxious for her, as if this is happening to me rather than her.

"If I have to say it again, I'm going to spank your ass before I check to make sure you're not sneaking anything into my jail."

She scurries onto the table and gets into the position he requested.

"Spread your legs."

Her feet inch apart.

"Wider."

My anxiety spikes into the red zone, and I shift from one foot to the other.

"Does my baby like what she sees?" Kristian asks, his hand sliding down to cup me intimately.

I wonder if he can feel the heat that radiates from me.

"Mmm... I think she likes it."

"Shhh. I want to hear what they're saying."

His low chuckle makes me smile. I love to make him happy, even if it means stepping way outside my comfort zone to experience something new.

"Are you sneaking anything into my jail?" the man in the room asks.

"No! I wouldn't do that."

"And I'm supposed to take your word for it?" He produces a tube of lubricant that he squirts onto his fingers. "Open up."

"Please... Don't do this."

"This is standard operating procedure for all prisoners. If you don't cooperate with the exam, I'll bring in another officer to hold you down. It's up to you."

"I'll c-cooperate," she says, sobbing now.

I grasp Kristian's hand, needing to hold on to him while I watch the scene unfold before me.

He rubs his hard cock against my bottom, making my legs weak under me. All my senses are engaged. I've never been more aroused in my life than I am with him hot and sexy behind me as I watch the man in the room slide his fingers into her pussy, probing deep and then thrusting them in again.

She raises her hips off the table.

"Stay still," he says, dragging out the "exam" as long as he can before withdrawing his fingers. "Turn over."

"Wh-why?"

"Your pussy's not the only hiding place."

"You've got to be kidding me."

"Do I look like I'm kidding? Turn over now, or this is going to get ugly for you."

She mutters something under her breath that I can't hear, but she does as she's told and turns onto her belly.

He spanks her ass. Hard. "That's for talking back."

Her body shakes with sobs. "I'm sorry."

"Save it for someone who cares." He probes between her cheeks, and her entire body goes rigid with shock.

"Oh my God," I whisper.

"Do you need your safe word?" Kristian asks.

"No, but I think she does."

"She can stop it at any time."

He penetrates her with two fingers, and she screams so loudly, I pull back from the window, feeling almost assaulted by her screams.

Kristian tightens his arms around me. "I've got you, sweetheart. She's not in any danger. I promise."

Watching the man fuck her ass with his fingers, I shake almost as hard as she does, again like it's happening to me. The aching throb between my legs intensifies to the point that I wonder if I can come simply from watching someone else's scene. My breathing is choppy and erratic, my face feels hot, and my nipples are so hard, they hurt.

The man in the room produces a large object that he holds up for her to see.

"Wh-what's that?"

"A plug so you can't sneak anything into your tightest hiding place while we're processing you."

"Where would I get something to hide in there?"

"You'd be surprised how clever our prisoners can be."

"I-I don't want that."

"Too bad. You don't have a choice."

She's crying so hard that her body jerks.

He spanks her other ass cheek. "Knock it off and hold still." After lubing up the plug, which looks huge to me, he presses it against her ass.

She screams even louder than she did with his fingers.

My knees buckle under me, and only Kristian's arms around me keep me from falling.

"That's it," he says gruffly. "Let's go."

"No! I want to see how it ends."

Judging by the tension I feel coming from him, he's not sure he should let me stay, but he doesn't make a move to leave.

The Dom draws out the insertion of the plug to the point that the sub is a drooling, snotty mess by the time it's fully seated in her. With his hands on her hips, he drags her to the end of the table. "One more mandatory examination," he says, withdrawing his huge cock and stroking it before aiming it at her pussy and pushing into her.

She comes the second he enters her, screaming the whole time he's fucking her.

"Did I say you could come?" he asks. "Answer me!"

"N-no, Sir. I'm sorry. I couldn't help it."

"You've earned a prison punishment."

"What's that?"

"You'll find out." He's ruthless as he fucks her, pumping into her over and over, tugging on the plug and making her come at least two more times before he gives in to his own release.

After he comes, he transforms into a caring Dom, removing the plug and cleaning her up before taking her into his arms to comfort and soothe her. "You were so amazing, baby," he says. "I'm so proud of you."

She's still whimpering, but there's an unmistakable glow about her. Three screaming orgasms would probably give anyone a glow, but it's clear that she loved what he did. "I want that," I say, riveted by the man's tenderness in the aftermath.

"What do you want?"

"What they did. I want to do that."

"How much of it?" Kristian asks in a terse tone that has me immediately on edge as I realize my words are akin to throwing gas on the fire, as he said earlier.

"All of it."

"Let's go."

Kristian

I bring Aileen with me when I go to the locked supply closet to pack a bag. Unlike my partners, I don't keep a BDSM room at home, because I don't usually bring women to my place. I make use of the Quantum club and others, such as Black Vice, which is owned by our friend Devon Black. Besides, we aren't going to my place. I've made other plans for us because I wanted tonight to be special for her.

When I've gathered what we need to re-create the scene we just witnessed, I lead her to the elevator, wanting to get her alone as fast as I possibly can after the way she reacted to the scene. Hearing her say she wants to do what they did has me harder than I've ever been in my life. Settled in the back of the Bentley, I'm almost afraid to touch her. I hope I can make it to the hotel I chose for our night together without losing my shit.

"I want you to remember something," she says after a long, tense silence.

"What's that?"

"You promised to treat me like you would any other woman."

I put my arm around her and bring her in close to me, nuzzling her neck and drowning in her distinctive scent. I want that to be the last thing I smell before I leave this life. "I'm afraid I can't keep that promise."

"Why not? You know how important it is to me that you don't treat me like I'm fragile."

"I don't think you're fragile. You may be one of the strongest people I know."

"Then why can't you keep your promise?"

"Because you're the single most important person in the entire world to me, and I will never treat you the way I would anyone else. You, my love, will be treated like a queen for the rest of your life. I hope you're prepared for that."

"The rest of my life?" she asks softly, sounding awed.

"If that's what you want." When have five words ever packed more of a punch than those do? Never that I can recall. I wait breathlessly, feeling as if my entire life and any chance I have to be truly happy is on the line.

"I moved here for you. I think it's safe to assume you're what I want."

"And you'd be okay with being stuck with me for like, well... forever?" So much for it being too soon to talk about such things. Her honesty is infectious, and it's forced me to raise my own bar. I feel like the little boy I once was, hoping that one of my many foster families might decide to keep me. None of them ever did, and I survived that. However, if she were to decide not to keep me...

Her hand on my face compels me to look at her. "There's nothing I want more than to be stuck with you forever."

They are, quite simply, the best words anyone has ever said to me. They're even better than *I love you*, and those three were pretty great, too.

I regret my plan to take her to a hotel, because my place is closer and my need for her urgent. But I wanted tonight to be special, so I reserved the best suite in the famous Beverly Wilshire Hotel.

"Where're we going?"

"Somewhere special." Recalling the late dinner I ordered, I want to groan at the thought of further delays. But anticipation makes the desire that much sharper, although if my desire for her gets much sharper, I might not survive. "Check in with Cece. You're going to be busy when we get to where we're going."

Her cheeks flush a warm, rosy shade that makes me wonder whether her other cheeks would be the same color after a spanking.

I'm in agony from wanting to find out.

Aileen is on the phone with Cece, but she senses my disquiet and places her hand on my leg in a gesture that immediately calms everything but the ache in my cock. That's going to take far more than a hand to the leg.

We finally arrive at the hotel, and I'm grateful for the suit coat that hides my huge erection from the doormen. Lori picked up the key for me earlier, so we head right for the elevator.

"What about our bags?"

I carry only the small black bag I brought from the club. "They'll be delivered to the room."

"Can we slow down so I can look at this beautiful hotel?"

"You can do that tomorrow." Slowing down is not on the agenda. All I can hear is her sexy voice saying, *I want to do what they did.*

"You're in a big rush."

"Fuck, yes, I am. The woman of my dreams wants me to dominate her. You bet your ass I'm in a rush." I angle her into the back corner of the car and press my hard cock against her pussy. I can feel her heat through our clothes. "I ordered dinner for us, but unless you're starving, that might have to wait until after."

"I'm too nervous to eat."

That stops me cold. "You're *nervous*? About being with me?" The thought of that kills me.

"I just hope..." She looks up at me with her heart in her eyes. "I want to be everything you need. I hope I can handle it."

"Sweetheart... You already are everything I'll ever need and then some. If we never do any of what we saw tonight, I'll still love you and need you and want you as much as ever. I swear to God. Nothing is riding on this, so please don't be afraid. I'd never want to scare you or make you nervous."

She visibly relaxes. "I'll try not to be nervous."

"Will you promise me that if you're ever truly scared or nervous about being with me in any way that you'll say so?"

"I promise."

"And you're *sure* you want everything you saw at the club?"

She swallows hard, but her gaze never wavers. "I'm sure."

"Remind me of that safe word again."

"Destiny."

"And you know when to use it?"

"If I want to stop what we're doing."

"If you need a break or a breather, use the word yellow. The word red also stops everything. Understood?"

Still looking up at me with those beautiful bottomless eyes filled with love for me, she nods.

"Excellent, because you, my love, are under arrest."

CHAPTER 22

Aileen

He moves so quickly, I don't see it coming. My hands are shackled behind my back in velvet-lined cuffs, and my sweet, tender lover morphs before my eyes into a harsh, determined police officer with a perp in custody.

"What did I do?" I ask.

"You know what you did." He produces a key card from his shirt pocket and opens the door to a gorgeous suite.

I barely get a chance to look at it as he marches me through the foyer and sitting area to the bedroom. He shuts and locks the door behind us. The sound of that lock engaging and the rush of adrenaline through my system make my heart beat fast and hard.

He comes up behind me, his lips close to my ear. "You have the right to remain silent. Anything you say or do can be used against you as a basis for punishment. You have the right to call me Sir—and only Sir—until I say otherwise. You have the right to do what you're told when you're told or face the consequences. You do *not* have the right to come, unless I give you permission. Do you understand your rights in this matter?"

I swallow hard. "Yes, Sir."

"I'm going to release the cuffs and unzip your dress. You're to remove all your clothing."

"Why?"

"Because I told you to."

"I want a female officer."

"None are available. You're stuck with me." He releases the cuffs and slowly lowers my zipper, letting his fingers glide along my spine as the zipper goes down my back.

I explode in goose bumps and shiver violently.

"I have several other prisoners to process tonight, so the longer you make me wait, the worse the punishment will be."

I'm all thumbs as I try to quickly remove my dress. It clears my hips, leaving me in only a thong.

"You forgot to wear a bra," he says, his blue eyes on fire as he stares hungrily at my bare breasts. "That's another violation."

"Where's it written that going braless is against the law?"

He raises a brow. "Are you questioning me, sub?"

"No. Sir."

"Remove the rest of your clothing, and hurry up about it."

I kick off the heels and step out of the thong. Because I can't leave that exquisite dress in a heap on the floor, I pick it up and drape it over the bed. Then I stand before him completely nude. Despite his fierce countenance, his eyes give away his true feelings. In them I see love and desire and joy, and it's the joy that most affects me. I've never seen that in him before. Knowing I gave him that makes me want to weep.

"I'll need to examine your body to make sure you're not trying to sneak contraband into my jail."

"I'm not sneaking anything in, Sir."

"I'm afraid your word isn't good enough." He steps closer to me, so close I can feel the heat of his body and smell his cologne. I want to lean in to get closer to him, but I remain still, waiting to see what he'll do next."

"Open your mouth."

I do as he asks, and he fully examines the interior of my mouth before running his hands down my arms and over my breasts, belly, back and legs. The feel of his hands on my skin has me shaking with desire, but I try not to move.

"On the bed, legs spread."

It's the strangest thing. I know exactly what's going to happen. I know we're role-playing. I know I'm not really in trouble, but I'm gripped with the same anxiety I might have if this were really happening. I begin to feel somewhat detached from myself as I get on the bed and spread my legs a few inches apart. It's like I'm watching this the way I did at the club, rather than actively participating.

Kristian snaps on a latex glove and squeezes a dollop of lube on his fingers. "The only way this hurts is if you fight me. Do you understand?"

"Yes, Sir." My thighs tremble violently as he pushes them farther apart. "Hold still."

I bite my lip to keep from screaming when he pushes his fingers into me. After what feels like hours of foreplay, I'm right on the brink of orgasm—and he knows it.

His fingers are ruthless as they move inside me. Then he curls them forward, pressing against my G-spot, and it takes everything I have not to give in to the burning need to come. I'm proud of my ability to battle through it, to hold out for his order, but God, it isn't easy.

"Nothing in your pussy." He reaches for the lube again. "Turn over."

"We don't really need to look any further, do we?"

"Turn. *Over*."

Every muscle in my body is made of pudding as I turn facedown on the bed, anxiety and anticipation at war inside me. I said I wanted this, but now that we're doing it, I'm not so sure.

"What's your safe word?" he asks in the same tone he's been using as the aggressive cop.

"Destiny, Sir."

"Do you need it?"

I squeeze my eyes closed and force air into my lungs. "No, Sir."

"Very well, we'll continue our cavity search." His fingers furrow between my cheeks. "Relax, or this will hurt."

I have a feeling it'll hurt whether I relax or not.

"Push back to let me in." His fingers feel huge as they press against my back entrance. Until him, no one had ever touched me there, and now I'm taking two fingers, aware that the plug will be much bigger than his fingers. It hurts. *God*, it hurts. I'm on the verge of using the word *yellow* when my body suddenly yields to let him in, and the pain becomes something akin to pleasure.

His fingers sink into me, taking me right back to the edge of release.

"Have you ever had a cock here?"

I can't believe he expects met to speak while he's doing that to me. "No, Sir."

"Mine will be the first."

"That wouldn't be appropriate."

With his free hand, he spanks my right cheek. "Don't you tell me what's appropriate and what isn't. I'm in charge here."

"I can't let you do that to me. My boyfriend will kill you."

"Your boyfriend won't touch me if he knows what's good for him."

"Please..." A sob erupts from my chest, taking me by surprise. "Please don't."

"Your ass was made for my cock."

"No."

He spanks my other cheek, and I come so hard, I see stars. Holy crap... Afterward, my throat is raw and sore from screaming.

"Someone is in even *bigger* trouble."

"No, please, Sir. I'm sorry. I didn't mean to come."

"If you take my cock in your ass, I won't punish you for coming without permission."

"I... I can't. My boyfriend... I'm saving that for him."

"He's not here, and I am." He pushes his fingers in deep again, and I rub shamelessly against the bed cover.

"If you come again, you'll get a cock in your ass *and* a flogging."

I can tell how much he's enjoying this. I can hear it in every word he says, even though the words are said in a harsh tone he's never used with me before. Knowing I can stop everything with one word allows me to let go and fully lose myself in the moment.

"What's it going to be, little sub? My cock or the flogger?"

"Your cock. Please give me your cock, Sir." I can't believe I'm agreeing to this. Rex used to beg me to let him fuck my ass, and I wouldn't hear of it. But with Kristian... everything is different. He'll make it as good for me as it'll be for him.

He removes his fingers, and I hear rustling behind me, the crinkle of a condom wrapper and the squirt of lube. "Do you need your safe word?"

"No, Sir." I am strong and determined and deeply in love with this man. He can have anything he wants from me, even this.

Then he presses that gigantic cock against my back entrance, and I'm no longer strong or determined. I'm panicked. I can't possibly do this.

"Relax, sweetheart." My sweet Kristian is back. He caresses my bottom with a gentle touch. "We'll go nice and slow. A little at a time. Relax and push back against me."

I follow his directions, and sure enough, that helps. I wouldn't call it comfortable, but it's not unbearable either. Until he gives me more and makes me scream from the pain that overtakes my entire body before becoming a hot ball of need at my core.

We move together. He pushes in as I move back. Little by little, he works his way in until I feel his balls against my pussy. I can't believe I did it. I actually did it. But before I can take a victory lap, he starts pulling back out, and then he's back in again. I lose my mind. That's the only way to describe it. I have no idea who I am or what I'm doing or what is happening to me. I'm one giant nerve ending, radiating from my ass to my fingertips to the top of my head and soles of my feet.

He reaches around me to my clit, pinching it between his fingers as he growls, "Come."

I explode into ten million pieces. All I can do is *feel* as he pounds into me, one orgasm rolling into a second and then a third.

His arms band around me as he drives into me one last time, growling when he comes harder than he has yet with me.

I can't move or think or speak. It's all I can do to continue breathing. My muscles contract around his cock, which is still rock hard inside me.

Then he rolls my clit between his fingers, and another wave rocks through me.

I'm wrecked, demolished, destroyed. And I'm reborn. I'm his, completely and utterly his in every possible way.

"Jesus," he mutters after a long silence. "That was…"

"Insane."

"Yes. Are you okay? You… I… Holy *fuck*, Aileen."

I love that he's as undone as I am by what we did.

"Tell me you're not hurt?"

"I'm not hurt." Although I will be sore. Of that I have no doubt.

"You didn't stop me."

"You noticed that, huh?"

"Yeah." His chin tucks into my shoulder. "Nothing has ever felt as good as this does."

"No?" Hearing him say that makes me rather euphoric.

"Never." He kisses the curve of my neck and my shoulder. "You can't ever leave me, Aileen. You'd ruin me."

I squeeze his arm. "I'm not going anywhere."

CHAPTER 23

Aileen

I start my job as the Quantum receptionist on Monday morning after dropping the kids at an all-day soccer camp on the way to work. I'm coming off the best weekend of my life. Spending an entire night completely alone with Kristian was total bliss. He made it even better with breakfast in bed and a relaxing couples massage at the hotel before we went home to spend the day at the beach with the kids.

At five o'clock this morning, he kissed me awake.

"I'm going before the kids wake up," he said.

I grasped his hand to keep him from leaving. "I don't want this weekend to be over yet."

"It's the first of a lifetime's worth of weekends we'll have together."

A sense of foreboding came over me as he said that, and I wanted to beg him not to go. I still don't know why I was so afraid. I only know I didn't want to let him leave.

"I love you." He said those words to me repeatedly throughout the weekend, as if now that he was allowed to say them, he didn't want to stop. That was fine with me.

"I love you, too. Thank you for the best weekend of my life."

"It was for me, too." He kissed me, and I wound my arms around his neck.

He broke the kiss with a groan. "Let me go, you evil witch. I've got a business to run."

I let him go, but the foreboding stayed with me in the four hours between when he left and when I reported for my first day of work at the office.

Addie greets me with a smile and a hug and a ream of paperwork that I complete while hoping to catch a glimpse of the man I love. She walks me through the paperwork, which includes an application for health insurance for myself and my children.

"Your plan has already been activated," Addie tells me. "Kristian took care of that last week, so this is just a formality." She leans in and lowers her voice. "He told the HR people to do whatever it took and pay whatever it cost to get you on the plan *immediately*."

My eyes fill, and I blink frantically, not wanting to break down in front of Addie. Crying at work is not my thing, but the tears won't be contained no matter how hard I try.

Addie hands me a tissue.

I mop up the flood of tears. "Sorry."

"Please don't be. We're all so happy for you and Kris. We've never seen him like this before."

"Like what?" I ask, because I have to know.

"For one thing, he smiles all the time. We've never seen so much of those elusive dimples of his. For another, he takes time off—real time off. No one heard from him all weekend. That's *highly* unusual. He doesn't say much about his life before he became part of Quantum, but we suspect it was difficult. If anyone deserves to be happy, it's him—and you."

"Thank you." I dab at new tears. "Ugh, you're making a mess of me."

She smiles. "You could never be a mess."

"Why're you crying?"

The sound of Kristian's voice startles me. I look up to find him standing in the doorway to the conference room.

"Addie, give us a minute, please," he says.

"Of course." She gathers the paperwork I've already signed and leaves the room.

Kristian closes the door and comes over to where I'm seated at the big table. "What's wrong?"

He's wearing a light blue dress shirt that does startling things for his beautiful eyes, and he's showered and shaved since I last saw him. As much as I love the stubble he had all weekend, I like the clean-shaven look, too. "Nothing is wrong."

"Then why were you crying?"

"Addie told me how you ordered them to add me and the kids to the health insurance."

"I told you I was going to do that."

"I know."

"You still haven't explained the tears." He takes my hand, helps me up and then sits in my chair, bringing me down on his lap. With the brush of his fingers on my face, he wipes away my tears.

As always, his nearness makes my entire system go haywire in a wild mix of emotion, desire and need.

"Aileen..."

"I've never had anyone who wanted to take care of me and the kids the way you do. Hearing that you demanded your staff take care of me that way..." I flatten my hand over my heart. "It hit me right here, and that's why I was crying."

"I *do* want to take care of you—all of you."

"That makes me feel very lucky."

"You have no idea how it makes me feel."

"Tell me. How do you feel?"

"Amazed. I can't believe something like this is even possible. Of course, I've seen it happen to my friends, but it's a whole other thing to have it happen to me."

I rest my head on his shoulder and breathe in the rich, citrusy scent of his cologne. I want to drown in that scent.

"I'm supposed to be working," I say after a long moment of contented silence.

"So am I."

"You should probably let me go before the whole office is talking about us being in here alone together."

Rather than let me go, though, he tightens his arms around me. "Let them talk."

Kristian

I have no idea where Aileen is, and as one hour becomes two and two become three without a reply to my texts, I'm frantic to hear from her. She left the office after lunch on her second day without telling me where she was going, and now, as the clock creeps toward five o'clock without a word from her, I'm starting to panic. Did something happen to her or one of the kids? She's not used to driving in crazy LA traffic yet. What if she was in an accident?

Before the speculation can give me a heart attack, I get up and go look for Addie in her office. She's not there, so I check Hayden's office.

"Where's Addie?" I ask him.

"Why do you want to know?"

"I can't get ahold of Aileen, and I wanted to ask Addie if she's heard from her."

"Addie went to Calabasas with Natalie for a site visit at the estate where the carnival will be held."

"Will you call her for me?"

"Okay..." He picks up his cell phone and makes the call. "Hey, babe. Kristian is here and looking for Aileen. Do you know where she is?" He listens for a minute, and his furrowing brows take five years off my life.

Something is wrong. I can feel it in my bones.

"Okay, I'll tell him. Are you almost done there?" He listens for another interminable minute, during which I want to rip the phone from his hand and ask Addie myself where Aileen is. Somehow I manage to control myself until he tells her he loves her and he'll see her at home in an hour. "Aileen had an appointment this afternoon with her new oncologist."

The floor seems to disappear beneath my feet at the reminder that she's still battling an illness that could take her from me. Why didn't she tell me about the appointment? Is something wrong? Has she had symptoms? My brain is spinning like a top, and Hayden comes around the desk to push me into a chair.

"Sit your ass down before you pass out."

I drop my head into my hands.

"What the hell, Kris? What's wrong?"

"I... I'm so crazy about her. If something ever happened to her..."

Hayden sits next to me, his hand on my shoulder. "I'm sure it's a routine thing. Didn't she say her New York doctor set her up with someone out here? She's probably just touching base with the new guy."

"Why wouldn't she tell me?"

"Because she didn't want you to do exactly what you're doing now?"

"I would've gone with her."

"Maybe she didn't want you to."

"*Why* wouldn't she want me to?" I honestly don't know the answer to that question.

"Only she can know that, but it could be that she wants to keep what's happening with you separate from that."

"*Why?*" I'm so out of my league in this situation. I want to hunt her down at the doctor's office and force her to tell me every detail of her appointment. But my better judgment tells me that might not be the best idea I've ever had.

Hayden starts to laugh, and it's all I can do not to punch him. "What the hell is so freaking funny?"

"You are. You're a hot mess."

"Kind of like you were when Addie wouldn't give you the time of day?"

"Something like that," he says, smiling as he sits back in his chair.

"If it makes you feel any better, Aileen seems as crazy about you as you are about her. You've got nothing to worry about where she's concerned, Kris."

"Except for the dreadful disease she's already battled once coming back to take her from me."

"You're getting pretty far down the road from what's probably a routine doctor's appointment."

"Maybe so, but tell me how you'd feel if Addie had cancer and went to an appointment with an oncologist without telling you about it."

"I'd probably feel exactly the same way you do."

His agreement only makes me more anxious than I was before, if that's even possible. "I've got to get out of here."

"Where're you going?"

"To her place to wait for her."

"Don't be a bull in a china shop over the appointment, Kris. Let her tell you about it."

"I will." I leave his office, go into mine to grab my keys, and I'm on my way to her house within minutes. Traffic is hideous, and it takes me close to an hour to get there. Several more calls to her go unanswered, inching my anxiety firmly into the nuclear zone. I pull up to her house and breathe a sigh of relief when I see her car in the driveway. At least she wasn't in an accident.

I rush up the stairs and through the front door without knocking. Logan is on the sofa watching TV. He looks up at me, seeming confused by the way I came busting into the house.

"Hey, buddy. Where's your mom?"

"In the kitchen."

"Thanks." I cross the threshold to the kitchen and stop short at the sight of her at the stove, tending to a boiling pot.

She sees me there and smiles at me over her shoulder. "Hey. Where'd you come from?"

Normally, I text her to tell her I'm on my way. I didn't do that today, and she's wondering why.

"Where's your phone?" I ask, even though I can see the shape of it in the back pocket of those drool-worthy cutoff denim shorts that make me want to drop to my knees and bite her sweet ass.

She withdraws it from her back pocket and holds it up. "Right here?"

"Why haven't you answered it all afternoon? I called you. I texted you, and when you didn't reply, I asked Hayden to ask Addie where you were. She said you had a doctor's appointment you didn't tell me about." So much for not being a bull in a china shop...

She glances at the phone and then at me. "I don't have any calls or texts from you."

"Give it to me." I take it from her, look at the settings and see that it's set to airplane mode. "Who put it in airplane mode?"

"Oh no! Maddie was fooling with it in the car earlier. She must've done it by accident."

I switch it out of airplane mode, and the phone goes crazy dinging with texts and voice mails—all of them from me.

She slides her arms around my waist. "I'm so sorry."

I can't seem to bring my arms to move, to return the embrace.

"You were worried."

"That's a tame word for what I was, especially after I heard you'd been at an oncology appointment without telling me."

"I'm sorry, Kristian. I feel terrible for worrying you."

"What did the doctor say?"

"Nothing yet. I had all the usual blood work and scans. I won't hear anything for a few days."

"*Days?*" How am I supposed to survive *days* of uncertainty?

She shrugs as if it's no big deal. "That's how it goes."

I want to shake her. How the hell can she be so nonchalant about such a big thing?

"Are you hungry?"

"No, I am not hungry! I don't want to talk about *anything* other than whether you are okay, and there's *no fucking way* we're waiting *days* to find out if you are."

She smiles up at me, her expression sweet and angelic. "You have to relax. I feel fine, and there's no reason to believe there's anything to worry about."

Every muscle in my body is rigid with tension. "Don't tell me to relax."

"Kristian, honey..." She flattens her palms over my chest and slides them up around my neck. "This is my life now. Every three months, I have a complete workup, and then I wait days to hear that everything is okay. You can't lose your mind every time."

I notice the bandages covering gauze in the crook of each of her elbows where blood was taken, and an ache explodes in my chest at the visible proof of her ongoing illness.

"I can't handle this," I whisper.

"What can't you handle?"

"Worrying about you this way. I can't take it."

"Yes, you can."

"No, I don't think I can." To have waited my whole life to find her only to have to worry about losing her... I can't do it. I break free of her embrace and go out to the deck to get some air. I hear her tell Logan that dinner will be ready soon before the screen door slides shut when she joins me on the deck. Her arms come around me from behind. I want to resist her, but I don't know how. My emotions are like a category-five hurricane swirling inside me.

"I'm sorry you couldn't reach me and that you were worried. I'm sorry that my illness is a lot for you to handle."

Her words snap me out of whatever state I've slipped into. I turn to her, hauling her in close to me, mindless of anything but the craving need I have for her. "I don't give a flying fuck about your illness being a lot for *me* to handle. I care about *you*, and I need you to be okay. I need you healthy, and there is nothing I wouldn't do to make that happen."

"Shhh," she says, her fingers combing through my hair in that soothing gesture that makes me want to weep from the sweetness she gives me without knowing she's the first person to ever give me that. "It's still new to you. It'll take time for you to figure out how to cope with it. I promise that, over time, it'll become less frightening."

"No, it won't."

"Yes, it will."

"I'll never become less frightened about losing you, especially if you sneak off to appointments without telling me or taking me with you."

She pulls back to look up at me. "You want to go with me?"

"Hell, yes, I want to go with you. I'd much rather do that than sit on my ass wondering what the hell is happening to you."

"I'll take you with me next time. I promise."

Hearing that, I relax. A little.

"I'm sorry you were so upset when you couldn't reach me."

"Don't let Maddie play with your phone anymore. I'll buy her one of her own to play with."

"You absolutely will not."

"Yes, I will."

"No, you won't."

I kiss her to end the argument, but the second her lips connect with mine, I whimper from the sweet relief of being back in her arms.

She kisses me with the same desperation I feel, and little by little, the tension starts to leave my body.

I cling to her, needing her more with every passing second. Surely it's not healthy or sane to need someone the way I need her. I only end the kiss when the need for air trumps my need for her.

Her lips move over my neck. "I love you so much, Kristian. I'm crazy in love with you. You have to believe me when I tell you it's going to be okay."

I soak up her reassurances, but I won't be able to breathe normally again until we get those fucking test results.

EVERY MINUTE OF THE NEXT FEW DAYS FEELS LIKE A YEAR. I CAN'T GET anything done at work, and at night, I make love to her until we're both completely exhausted. If I love her enough, maybe I can keep anything bad from happening to her. I can't eat or sleep or do anything other than worry about her and those fucking test results. It's the twenty-first century, for fuck's sake. How long does it take to check some blood and review some freaking scans?

If we don't hear something soon, I'm not going to be responsible for my actions.

A knock on the door precedes Lori's entrance to my office. "Um, there's an LAPD officer here to see you. A Sergeant Markel? He said you'd know what it's about."

As if I've been struck by lightning, I can't move or breathe. "Kristian?"

A lump the size of Canada has taken up residence in my throat. I swallow hard. If there were any way to escape without talking to him, I'd do it, but there isn't. "Show him in."

"Is everything okay?"

"Show him in, Lori."

Thankfully, she doesn't ask any more questions. I force air into my lungs as I wait. The original Officer Markel retired a decade ago, so this would be the son who followed his father onto the force. My mind races, wondering what the hell he wants after all this time.

He comes into the office, and I'm struck by the startling resemblance to his father, who looked just like his son does now when I first met him. My body goes through the rote movements of standing, shaking his hand and muttering a greeting. His father pursued my mother's killer with relentless determination, until mandatory retirement forced him to turn the case over to his son, who's been far less diligent. I haven't heard a word from him in five years.

"I'm sorry to drop by unannounced." He sits on the edge of a visitor chair. "But we've had a development in your mother's case."

The words are like a nuclear bomb detonating in the middle of my life. I can only stare at him, wondering what he'll say and how it'll change everything. "What kind of development?"

"We got the guy, Kristian."

For the second time this week, I feel like a trapdoor has opened beneath me, sending me reeling into free fall.

"You..."

"We got him."

"How?" It's been thirty-three years. Why now?

"Have you heard of law enforcement use of familial DNA to solve cold cases?" Before I can reply, he continues. "We ran the DNA from your mother's autopsy and found a familial match to someone in the system. We've spent the last month tracking down that person's male family members and testing them until we found a match." Standing, he places eight head shots on my desk, four in each row. "Do you recognize the man who killed your mother in any of these photos?"

I'd know those cold, black eyes anywhere, as well as the scar that slashes through his left eyebrow. I was three years old when I watched from the closet as he killed my mother, but I've never forgotten his face. I point to him.

Markel nods. "That's him. Jorge Muñoz. Does that name mean anything to you?"

I shake my head. I never knew any of their names. "What happens now?"

"He's been arrested and will be charged today in Superior Court. I need to warn you... This is going to be a big story. We've tied him to the unsolved murders of six other prostitutes."

What he means but doesn't say is that the whole sordid tale will be made public.

"I tried to keep your name out of it, but as a material witness—"

I have no idea how that sentence ends, because I get up and walk away. I ignore the shout from Lori and the others who try to stop me with questions or routine business things I don't give a shit about. I rush past the reception desk where Aileen is working and ignore her when she calls my name. Pushing open the door, I take the stairs because I'm not willing to wait for the elevator.

I need to get the fuck out of there before the shit hits the fan and ruins my life all over again.

CHAPTER 24

Aileen

What the hell just happened? Where did he go, and why did he take the stairs? He never takes the stairs.

Lori comes running after him. "Where is he?"

"He went down the stairs."

"What? He never takes the stairs."

"What happened?"

The police officer who came to the desk asking to speak with Kristian joins us and hears my question. "We caught his mother's killer."

Lori and I gasp.

"His mother was *killed*?" Lori asks.

"Thirty-three years ago," the cop replies.

"Stop." I don't care that he's a cop. "His personal business is not yours to share."

The cop scowls at me, apparently unused to people questioning his authority. "His personal business is about to be made public. I came here to give him the courtesy of a heads-up."

"Oh my God," I whisper, feeling as if I've been punched in the gut. "Kristian..."

"Go after him," Lori says urgently. "Go to him."

The elevator dings, and Flynn steps into the reception area. Seeing the cop, he says, "What's going on?"

"Thank you for stopping by," Lori says to the officer. "We'll take it from here."

Giving Flynn a starstruck stare, the officer walks to the elevator. The second the doors close and take him away, Lori tells Flynn what happened.

"We have to find him," he says to me. "I'll drive you. Let's go."

Grateful for his offer, I grab my phone and purse and follow him to the elevator.

"Let me know what's going on," Lori calls after us.

I nod to let her know I heard her and get in the elevator with Flynn.

"I never knew his mother was murdered," Flynn says. "Did you?"

I nod. "He witnessed it."

"Oh my God."

"This will ruin him."

"We won't let it."

I cling to his reassurances as we battle midday traffic on the way to Kristian's apartment. It takes forty-five minutes to go a few miles, and by the time we pull into his garage, my nerves are totally frayed. He's not answering calls or texts.

"He isn't here."

I scan the lineup of luxury vehicles, trying to figure out which one is missing. I wish I'd paid closer attention. "How do you know?"

"He had the R8 today. It's not here." He turns his fancy two-seater around and aims for the garage door, which is still open.

"Where else would he go?"

"I don't know." He places a call to Jasper, tells him he's with me and what's happened and asks him where to look for Kristian. Because the call is on speaker, I can hear Jasper's end of the conversation.

"Dear God," Jasper says.

"Where would he be?"

"Try my place in Malibu. He's spent time at the guesthouse there. If he wants to hide out, that'd make a good place."

"We're on our way."

"Let me know, will you?"

"Yeah."

"I can't believe he never told us this."

"Kinda like we couldn't believe you never told us you're a marquess?"

"Touché," Jasper says with a sigh.

"We all have secrets, Jasper."

"I guess so."

"Find Liza," Flynn says, referring to the Quantum publicist I met at the premiere. "Tell her what's going on, and let's figure out how to protect him from the press."

"I'll get right on it."

Flynn ends the call and points the car toward Malibu. Though Kristian's car isn't in the driveway, we do a full search of Jasper and Ellie's home anyway, but there's no sign of him. I've never seen Flynn so flustered as he stands on Jasper's deck, hands on his hips, the picture of frustration.

The breeze off the Pacific makes me shiver, even as the sun beats down on us. "Flynn."

He turns to me.

"Take me to my place."

Without a word, he leads the way through Jasper's house to the driveway, where he holds the door for me and then jumps into the driver's seat.

I can't believe I didn't think to go there first, and I pray that's where he is. The press would never think to look for him at a small bungalow in Venice Beach. But when we pull onto my street, I don't see his car.

I'm deflated. I was so sure he'd be here.

Flynn parks in front of my house. "Let's look anyway."

He follows me inside, where I check every room but see no sign of him. I'm leaving my bedroom when my gaze lands on the closet door, which is cracked open. I touch the door as my heart begins to pound.

I also remember hiding in the closet when she was killed. He never knew I was there.

"Flynn!"

He comes into the bedroom.

"Take me back to Kristian's place."

"Why?"

"I'll tell you on the way."

Kristian

This can't be happening. Everyone will know. They'll pity me. I can't bear it. I hate to be pitied. I hate the way people look at you when they find out something awful happened to you, long before you had any control over anything.

I've put the horror of my mother's murder deep in the past where it belongs, but now... The bandage has been ripped off, everyone will know, and I can't stop it. I can't control it, and that infuriates me.

The LAPD will want the world to know about its detectives closing a thirty-three-year-old cold case, not to mention the other cases tied to the guy who killed my mother. It'll be a huge story. The voracious Hollywood press will go wild when they make the connection to me and Quantum. They'll wallow in every salacious detail of the murdered prostitute who gave birth to one of Hollywood's most influential producers.

At a time when my company should be focused on the long-awaited release of *Insidious*, everyone will be putting out fires with my name on them.

I can't.

I just can't.

So I do what I used to do then when it got to be too much.

I hide in the only place I feel safe.

Aileen

I use the key card Kristian gave me to access his penthouse apartment and run straight to the master bedroom closet, ease the door open and glance inside.

He's not there. I was so sure he would be. I check the other bedrooms while Flynn looks in the study downstairs.

I felt disloyal to Kristian telling Flynn about the closet, but right now the only thing that matters is finding him and wrapping my arms around him to let him know he's not alone. He'll never be alone again.

I meet Flynn in the upstairs hallway.

"Anything?" he asks.

Feeling more desperate by the second, I shake my head. "Wait." The idea comes to me in a flash, and I bolt toward the game room, trying to remember if there's a closet in there.

There is.

I rest my hand on the handle of the closed door, knowing with a certainty I can't explain that he's in there. I glance back at Flynn. "Let me do this alone, okay?"

He nods. "I'll be downstairs."

My mouth is dry, my hands are sweaty, and my heart is set to gallop as I open the door and slip inside, my eyes adjusting to the murky darkness. In the far back corner, I see him. His arms are wrapped around his legs, and his head is down, propped on his knees. He doesn't see me until I put my arms around him.

He startles like a wounded animal that's been cornered.

"Shhh. It's me. I'm here, and I've got you." I hold him tighter than I ever have before, calling on strength I didn't know I had until the man I love needed it.

He tries to get free of me. "I don't want you here."

"I'm here, and I'm not going anywhere."

"Aileen..."

"You can push me away, but I won't go, and neither will the other people who love you. We'll be right here for you the way you would be for us."

"I don't want any of you here."

"Too bad. You're stuck with us."

It doesn't happen right away, but after a long while, his body starts to lose some of the tension that grips his every muscle. He doesn't exactly relax, but he stops trying to push me away. With one hand, I run my fingers through his hair and make circles on his back with the other. I want to know what he's thinking and feeling, but I don't dare ask.

I have no idea how long we're there. Time ceases to exist. When I left the office, I had hours until I needed to pick up the kids from camp. I figure two hours or so have passed since then, so I don't need to worry yet about getting them. I can continue to give Kristian my full attention.

He's leaning against me now, allowing me to comfort him.

I consider that a victory. I kiss his forehead and then tip up his chin to kiss his lips.

At first, he responds with the usual ardor, but then he turns away. "I can't."

"Yes, you can."

He shakes his head. "It's going to be everywhere. Every disgusting detail."

"I won't read a word of it. Anything I hear about it, I'll hear from you—and only you."

He sighs deeply. "Everyone else will devour it."

"The people who love you, the ones who *matter*, won't if you don't want them to."

"There'll be a trial. I'll have to testify. How will you avoid it then?"

"I love you. I love you no matter what."

He snorts with disbelief. "You say that now..."

"I say that forever."

Shaking his head, he rubs his hand over the stubble on his jaw. "You don't even know what happened or the things I did or anything."

"I know *everything* I need to know to be certain I will love you for the rest of my life, no matter what you did."

"I killed someone."

I ache for him. "I assume you had to."

For the first time since I came into the closet, he looks directly at me, his shocked gaze crashing into mine.

"The Kristian Bowen I love wouldn't kill someone unless his own life was at stake. If it was him or you, I'm glad you chose yourself."

"You can't be serious. I tell you I'm a *murderer*, and you act like it's no big deal."

"It's a big deal, Kristian. I'd never say otherwise, but the fact that you're haunted by it means you're not a soulless killer. You were a boy alone in the world. When I asked what you did after your mother was killed, you said you survived. You survived that. You'll survive this, too."

"I was molested, assaulted, attacked, arrested, kicked out of every foster home they put me in. I fucked women for money from the time I was fourteen."

I'm dying inside, but I can't let him know that. "Okay."

"*It's not okay!* I don't want that ugliness to touch you."

"Too late. It already has, and I'm just fine. It doesn't change anything."

"If I asked you to leave me alone, would you?"

"No."

"What if I want you to?"

"What if my test results come back with a recurrence? Would you leave me alone if that happens?"

"That's different."

"No, it's not."

He looks at me fearfully. "Did you hear from the doctor?"

"Not yet." I caress his cheek, wanting to give him all the love and tenderness he's lived so long without. "Tell me about the person you killed."

"No." He tries to pull away, but I don't let him.

"Tell me. I want to know."

"Aileen..."

"*Kristian.*" It's the same tone I use on my children when I want them to know I mean business.

After a deep sigh, he says, "It was over a loaf of bread I found in a dumpster." He speaks in a dull, flat tone I've never heard before. "He pulled a knife on me. I grabbed his arm and plunged the knife into his chest. I took off with the bread and never looked back. I heard later he'd been found dead from a stab wound. I've never told anyone else that I was the one who stabbed him."

"He would've killed you."

"Probably."

"What else were you supposed to do?"

"I could've let him have the bread."

"When was the last time you'd eaten?"

"I don't know. A couple of days."

"So it's probably safe to say you weren't thinking rationally after going days without food."

"I don't recall thinking at all. I just reacted."

"Because you were *starving.* You did what you had to do to *survive.*"

After a long silence, he says, "Years later, I tracked down his mother."

"What did you do for her?"

He looks up at me, stunned. "How do you know I did anything for her?"

"Because I know *you.* What did you do?"

Averting his gaze, he says, "I bought her a house, and I've supported her for twelve years."

"Did you buy her a house before you bought one for yourself?"

"Maybe."

"Does she know who supports her or why?"

He shakes his head.

I take him by the face and force him to look at me. "You're a *good* man, Kristian. An honorable, wonderful, thoughtful, beautiful man, and I love you more than I've ever loved anyone other than my children. There is *nothing* anyone can say about you or your past, no sordid detail or salacious story, that will change the way I love you. I will *always* love you."

His gorgeous blue eyes fill with tears. "I don't deserve you," he whispers.

"Yes." I kiss away his tears. "You do. You absolutely do." I wrap him up in my arms, surrounding him with my love, hoping it will be enough to get him through this. "Come with me, and let's face this head on so we can get past it and move on with the rest of our lives. Hold on to *me*. I'll never let you go."

A full minute passes before he nods.

I stand and offer him my hand along with everything else I have to give.

He takes my hand and stands.

That's when I notice the closet shelves are full of toys. Vintage GI Joe action figures, Legos, Tinkertoys, Rock 'Em Sock 'Em Robots, board games, race cars... "What is all this?"

"I never had toys as a kid, so I kind of collect them."

Now I'm in tears.

"Please don't pity me."

"I don't. I swear I don't." I fight a losing battle with my tears.

He wraps his arms around me and holds me close to him.

"You will never again want for anything," I tell him, fierce in my conviction. "I'll give you *everything*."

"You already have," he whispers.

CHAPTER 25

Aileen

The Quantum team gathers in Kristian's living room, preparing to go to war on his behalf. Emmett Burke, Quantum's chief counsel, is on the phone with the LAPD, negotiating what details of Kristian's story will be released to the media and what will be kept confidential. Liza, the Quantum publicist, works two other phones, fielding the inquiries that have come in since the LAPD announced an arrest in the decades-old cold case murder of Kristian Bowen's mother.

And downstairs, Gordon keeps the paparazzi away from the celebrities he's paid to protect. Natalie picked up my kids at camp and delivered them to Cece, who's watching them at my house.

Everyone is doing what they can to contain the damage, while I do what little I can to comfort Kristian.

He sits beside me on the sofa. We're surrounded by his Quantum partners and their close friends, all of whom came running when they heard we'd found him.

I've never seen this group quieter than they are now. No one knows what to say, so they say nothing.

Emmett and Liza end their calls and join us in the sitting area.

Kristian reaches for my hand. "My earliest memory is being alone in the dark."

No one moves or seems to breathe as we wait to hear what else he will say.

"My mother would leave me, sometimes for an entire day or two. I don't know for how long. I was too young to understand time, but the sun would come and go, and I'd be left in the dark. I wasn't afraid of the dark, though. I could hide in the dark. The dark was my friend. She would bring people home, always men. They would go in her room. I wasn't allowed in there. I remember being hungry and dirty. I remember her face and her brown hair and the smell of cigarette smoke. I would hide in the closet with my blanket until the strangers left."

Next to me, Marlowe is rigid. I slowly let my free hand wander in her direction, and she grasps it, holding on tightly. Across from us, Natalie holds Flynn's hand while Ellie and Addie do the same for Jasper and Hayden. Kristian's Quantum partners are his family. This is hard for them to hear.

"One night, the stranger didn't leave. He dragged my mother out of the bedroom by her hair. She was crying and pleading with him. I vividly remember the sound of her begging him, but I don't recall exactly what she said. He knocked her down onto the floor and got on top of her. I didn't know then what was happening. That took until I was about twelve, the first time a woman did to me what he did to her. I understood then that my mother hadn't wanted it, because she was crying and screaming, and then she didn't move anymore."

A soft sob comes from Marlowe.

Jasper, whose expression is tight with tension, slides an arm around her while keeping his other arm around Ellie.

"When he left her, I saw his face. I was so sure he saw me because I felt like he looked right at me. But he kept going out the door. I went to her and tried to wake her up. I shook her and talked to her, but she never moved."

I can't bear this. Even though I've heard the story before, hearing him tell it to the others is somehow harder than hearing it the first time when it was just us. It doesn't come naturally to him to share his private agony, even with the people who love him. I wish there was something I could do to make it easier on him, but there isn't anything any of us can do but listen. So that's what I do. I listen, and I ache.

"I was alone with her body for four days before one of the neighbors called the cops because of the smell and the child crying."

Hayden gets up and walks over to the window, his shoulders rigid, his head bent.

Addie wipes away tears as she follows him, putting her arms around him.

"I spent a week in the hospital because I was dehydrated and had been bitten by the rats that lived with us."

"Dear God," Emmett says under his breath.

Next to him, Leah lets the tears slide down her cheeks as she stares blankly at the far wall.

"After that came a progression of foster homes, each worse than the one before. At ten, I landed in one I actually liked. The people were nice to me, and their son was the first real friend I ever had. But then their older son came home from college and they needed my room for him, so I was relocated. Again. I lasted a week in the new place before I decided the streets would be better than living with a mean son of a bitch who got his kicks from beating on defenseless kids. I lived on the streets for the next eight years, hustling for money and food and shelter wherever I could. I saw things... I did things..."

He shakes his head, regret pouring off him in waves. "I met Max Godfrey when he was filming a scene in Compton. The greatest stroke of luck of my life—until recently," he says, glancing at me, "was meeting Max. I'll never forget that day. I'd heard about the movie being shot in the neighborhood, and I wanted to see what it was like, so I went there. He caught me stealing food from the craft services table and took me into his trailer, set me up with a proper meal and grilled me about my goals in life."

Flynn grunts out a laugh. "Of course he did."

To him, Kristian says, "Neither of us have ever told you about that day when he offered a hard-luck street kid a job in his company and set me up with an apartment. Then he introduced me to his son, who became one of my closest friends, and the rest, as they say, is history."

"He always says he saw something special in you from the first day he met you," Flynn says. Like everyone else, his eyes are bright with tears after hearing Kristian's story.

"He saved my life. Without him, I would've ended up dead or in jail. I owe him everything." After a long pause, he says, "I lied to you guys when we formed our partnership. I never graduated from high school. I barely have a fifth-grade education."

Hayden whirls around, his expression ferocious. "*Who the fuck cares about that?*" Gesturing to the assembled group, he says, "None of this works without you. I don't give a shit if you fucking flunked kindergarten. You're the heart and soul of Quantum."

"Agreed," Flynn says. "We're nowhere without you."

Kristian bows his head, overwhelmed by the outpouring.

"Liza, what's it going to take to protect him?" Flynn asks.

"We'll have to go to war on the media," she says bluntly.

"Then let's go to war."

KRISTIAN IS COMPLETELY DRAINED AFTER SHARING THE STORY WITH HIS partners and the others. I lead him upstairs to lie down while his partners and friends wage war on his behalf. Emmett is working with the district attorney's office to try to get Kristian treated as a victim, which would keep some of the more salacious details out of the news. Emmett's argument is that because Kristian was a child when his mother was murdered, he should be afforded the same protections any child victim of violent crime would be granted.

But because he's a public figure, it's a stretch to hope that Emmett will succeed, but he's trying nonetheless.

"I can't believe what they're doing for me," he says.

"They love you."

He nods. "It means the world to me that you're here, too."

"Where else would I be with this happening to you?"

In his bed, I cuddle up to him, my arm around his waist, my leg tucked between his.

"This must be what people mean when they refer to someone as their other half."

I smile up at him, and see the look of wonder in his expression. "What do you think of having another half?"

"I think I love it." He caresses my face and then kisses me. "What about the kids?"

"Cece said she can spend the night. She told the kids you aren't feeling well, and I'm taking care of you. They said they hope you feel better."

"We can go to your place if you want to be with them."

"We're fine right here. Try to relax and get some rest."

"I'm too wired to rest."

"What would you rather do?"

He tilts my chin up to receive his kiss. "This. I'd rather do this."

"I'm always happy to do that."

But rather than kiss me, he leans his forehead against mine and releases a deep, shuddering breath. "Thank you."

"For what?"

"Everything. I never could've told the others without your encouragement, without you sitting next to me, holding my hand, offering your support. If this had happened before I had you, I'd be losing my mind without you here to tell me it's going to be all right."

"No, you wouldn't have. You would've done what you always did before. You would've survived."

"But this is so much better," he says, kissing me. "So, so much better." As he kisses me, he removes my dress, only pulling away from the kiss to lift it over my head. He continues to kiss me while removing my bra, breaking the kiss again to slide the panties down my legs. His hungry gaze travels over my body, making me feel beautiful and desired—two things I used to wonder if I'd ever feel again after my illness.

I reach for him, help him out of his shirt and tug at the button to his pants.

When he's naked, he settles on top of me, gazing down at my face and holding my hands over my head. "I love you so much. I've never had anyone who belonged to me the way you do."

"I've never had that either. Not like this."

His lips curve into a small smile, but in his eyes, I still see the wounded little boy. I'm determined to ensure that little boy is never hurt again.

"Make love to me, Kristian."

"There's nothing I'd rather do."

He drives me wild with his lips and teeth, kissing every part of me and refusing to allow me to come until I'm nothing but writhing, desperate need. Then he enters me, triggering the release that's been building from the first kiss.

"Very naughty," he whispers in my ear. "Subs who come without permission get their asses paddled."

"Yes, please."

His eyes go dark, and his cock gets even harder inside me. "You want me to paddle you?"

"I told you I want everything with you."

Gripping my shoulders, he thrusts into me several times before pulling out abruptly, leaving me gasping from the sudden loss. "On your knees."

Everything about him is different, including the tone of his voice. Gone is the wounded little boy. In his place is the commanding Dom who thrives on control. "Hurry up."

Adrenaline speeds through me as I move into the requested position, anticipation and anxiety spiking into a hot throb of need between my legs. This is what Kristian meant by *more*. He hasn't even touched me yet, and I'm about to explode. I hear rustling in another part of the room and start to glance over my shoulder to see what he's doing.

"Head down."

That commanding tone makes me shiver. I drop my forehead to

my hands and wait. And wait some more. He doesn't make a sound. I have no idea where he is or what he's doing.

Until the paddle connects with my ass in a blaze of heat and pain that quickly turns to desire. I immediately want more.

He gives it to me. The paddle rains down on my ass, more times than I can count.

I love it. I want more. "Don't stop."

"*Fuck*, Aileen," he says through gritted teeth, but he doesn't stop.

The next thing I know, I'm in his arms, looking up at him. I blink him into focus. Why does he look so concerned?

"Thank Christ," he mutters. "You totally punched out on me." He caresses my face and runs his hand down my arm. "Are you okay?"

I feel... *divine*. I can't recall the last time I was so relaxed or free of worry. It's like I'm floating on the softest cloud in a sea of absolute contentment.

He gives me a little shake. "Aileen."

"I'm fine. Better than fine."

"You are? Really?"

Nodding, I grasp his hand and link our fingers. "I loved it."

"You came so hard."

"I did?"

"You don't remember?"

"Not really. It's like I was somewhere else or something. I can't explain it." As I regain my senses, I realize my ass and pussy are tingling.

"It's subspace. That's what happens when the endorphins kick in."

"I feel so relaxed."

"I'm glad one of us is relaxed. You kind of scared me with the way you zoned out."

"I'm sorry you were scared."

"I don't know if I can do this stuff with you. I love you so damned much. The thought of hurting you makes me sick."

"You didn't hurt me, and I knew how to stop it. Did you hear me say I loved it?"

"Yeah, but—"

I kiss him. "No buts. I *loved* it. I want more."

He shakes his head in disbelief. "I'm still trying to figure out how I got lucky enough to find you."

"We were both lucky to find each other. Everything is going to be better now."

Tightening his hold on me, he says, "You promise?"

"I promise."

EPILOGUE

Kristian

I've never had a warm, soft place to land before, and now that I do, I want to wallow in it. I want to wallow in *her*. I want to be with her all the time. The best part is, she wants to be with me just as much. We no longer try to hide from the kids the fact that I sleep in her bed. Last night, during a thunderstorm, Maddie crawled into our bed and let me comfort her while Aileen slept through the whole thing.

Holding her little girl in my arms during the storm, I told her that nothing can find her in the dark, not even the thunder or lightning. "The dark," I whispered, "is your friend."

"I used to be scared of the dark," she whispered back.

"There's no need to be. I'm here now. You've got nothing to be afraid of."

She fell asleep in my arms and stayed there all night.

Despite our best efforts, the story about my past exploded in the media, every sordid detail broadcast and printed for the world to see. Rather than being consumed by it, though, I've cruised below the radar, spending time with Aileen, the kids and our friends. I've ignored every report and the scores of interview requests. Liza put out the word that I won't comment on my mother's case now or ever.

I've accepted the heartfelt condolences of business associates, friends, former subs and others who've only just heard about my mother's murder. I thank each person and move on, unwilling to linger on the pain of the past when the present is so sweet.

I'll have to testify at the trial, which I'll gladly do to make sure the man who killed my mother gets what he deserves. For thirty-three years, he lived free and clear after killing my mother and subjecting me to a life I wouldn't wish on anyone, let alone a helpless child. But the trial is months in the future, and for now, I focus on my many blessings rather than dwelling in my painful past.

Today, we're attending the carnival Flynn and Natalie's childhood hunger foundation is hosting at a Calabasas estate. I'm proud to sit on the board of directors of this great organization and have established a scholarship in my mother's name that will be awarded annually to children who grow up in the foster care system. I like to think that if she'd lived, my mother would've found a way out of prostitution and drug abuse. Maybe that never would've happened, but it brings me comfort to think about a better life for both of us.

In the meantime, I'm focused on the better life that I've found with Aileen. Yesterday, she heard from the oncologist that her tests came back normal. He said he'd see her in three months, when we'll go through the whole cycle again. She tells me I'll get used to the waiting, the worrying, the speculating. I doubt I'll ever get used to it, but I'll find a way to handle it because that's what she needs me to do —and there's literally nothing I won't do for her.

On the way to Calabasas, the kids chatter with excitement about the rides, the petting zoo, the face painting and the prizes, one of which is a pony I donated in exchange for Natalie making sure that Maddie is the winner. I donated two more, along with stable fees, so two other kids will get lucky, too. Logan is set to win a drone. In the park last week, he was fascinated by one we saw, and I wanted to get him one of his own.

Since Aileen won't let me spoil them, I have to get creative.

But those aren't the only surprises I have planned for today.

We arrive at the estate where valets are on hand to take care of the

Mercedes G-Wagon I find myself driving more and more often as it has room for a family.

I have a *family*. An *actual* family, not just the one I've cobbled together over the years, but one that belongs exclusively to me. It's my most prized possession.

As we walk toward the tents and rides, Maddie slips her hand into mine. She's feeling shy about the big crowd now that we're finally here. I reach down to pick her up, and when she wraps her arms around my neck, I swear my heart skips a beat.

"I've got you, pumpkin."

She holds on tighter to me.

I love it. I love her.

We encounter our entire gang on the way in. Flynn's sisters and their families are there, along with his parents, who greet us warmly. I use my free arm to hug Stella and Max Godfrey, the closest thing to parents I've ever had.

"Who've you got there, Kris?" Max asks in his big, booming voice.

Maddie snuggles in tighter.

"This package? This is Maddie, and she's excited to ride the ponies today."

"Oh, I *love* ponies," Max says.

Maddie lifts her head off my shoulder to give Max a skeptical look, as if to ask if he's for real. "You're too big for ponies," she says.

Max laughs. "I'm not too big to lead them around for little girls like you." He tugs on a lock of her hair. "Will you let me lead your pony?"

Enchanted by him, Maddie nods.

Max offers a high five. "It's a date."

Maddie smacks her hand against his, and my heart... It's so full of love for them, the man who gave me everything, and the little girl, who, along with her brother, is slowly but surely making a father out of me.

Maddie holds on to me until she sees the rides, and then she's all about the merry-go-round with Logan, who tolerates the ride because he knows she wants to sit on the horses.

Aileen and I wave to them as they go by.

This is what it's like to be a dad, I realize. Having never had one of my own, I hope I can figure it out as I go along. Thankfully, I have men like Max Godfrey in my life to show me how it's supposed to be done.

"You're so great with them," Aileen tells me, as she does most days.

I never have to wonder if she approves of the way I deal with the kids. Her complete support and encouragement of my relationships with them is one of many ways she demonstrates her love for me every day. I can't think about the other ways she demonstrates her love, or I'll be hard as a rock anticipating bedtime, which has become my favorite part of the day.

"They make it easy on me, and I love them as much as I love their mother." I kiss the top of her head. The curly hair that's getting longer tickles my nose.

"I used to hope that someday I'd meet a guy who loved me and my kids, but you're so much better than anything I ever dared to hope for."

"Even when I snore and hog the bed and demand sex three times a day?"

She leans into me, and I wrap my arm around her. "Even then," she says on a long sigh.

This... This is what contentment feels like. That's one of many new emotions, including joy, that I've learned to identify in the last few weeks. I experience them so often these days that they're like new friends, along for the ride that is my wonderful new life.

Natalie comes over to us, bright-eyed and smiling at the successful event she spearheaded as the foundation's director. Everyone is thrilled about their big news. They'll be amazing parents. "Having a good time?" she asks.

"The best time," Aileen says.

We wave at the kids as they go by again.

"Can I steal Aileen for a few minutes?" Natalie asks me.

"If you must." I reluctantly release her.

"Do you mind being on kid duty for a few?" she asks.

"Not at all, and you don't have to ask me. I never mind being on kid duty."

Smiling, she kisses me and takes off with her friend. I love seeing her healthy, tanned and happy. I'm so damned thankful for her continued good health, and I, who never said a prayer in my life until recently, beg God every night to keep her that way because I can't live without her.

The kids come off the merry-go-round, and I take them to get cotton candy. While they enjoy the sweet treat, I ask them if I can talk to them about something.

Logan is immediately wary.

"Nothing bad," I quickly add. "In fact, it's something kind of cool. At least I hope you'll think so."

"What is it?" Maddie asks, her mouth full of sugar that stains her lips pink. She's so damned cute.

Here goes... "I was wondering how you guys would feel about me asking your mom to marry me."

For what feels like forever, neither of them replies.

Maddie glances at Logan, looking for him to take the lead.

"Would you be our dad then?" he asks.

"Only if you want me to." *Please want me to. Please...*

"That'd be cool," he says, taking another bite of his cotton candy, as if he hasn't just changed my life with three little words.

Maddie nods in agreement. "I want you to."

I put my arm around her. "I want that, too. What do you think your mom will say?"

"Duh," Logan says with preteen disdain. "She'll cry and freak out."

"You think so?"

"She's a girl. They freak out over stuff like that."

Snorting with laughter, I bump his shoulder with mine. "You're very wise about women for only being nine."

"I'm almost ten."

I love the way he says that. I can't wait to see what he's like at sixteen or seventeen. Hell, I can't wait to see him at every age and to watch him become a man.

"Don't say anything to your mom, okay? I want to surprise her later."

"Can we come when you surprise her?" Maddie asks.

"Of course you can." I'd already decided they should be part of it. After all, they've been part of us from the beginning, and they always will be. I wouldn't have it any other way.

Maddie's beaming smile tells me she likes my answer.

Aileen finds us a short time later, and we fully enjoy the carnival. The kids are ecstatic when they win the pony and the drone. Their mother, on the other hand, is suspicious.

"I can't believe they both won such *extravagant* prizes," she says while we watch Maddie get to know her new pony, while Logan shows the drone to Flynn's nephews and some other boys.

"I know! It must be their lucky day."

"Or someone arranged for it to be their lucky day."

"Who would've done that?"

"Gee. I wonder."

I should've known she'd figure me out. "What do you think Maddie will name her?"

"We're going to talk about this later."

"Talk about what?"

She elbows me in the gut.

I crack up laughing, sling my arm around her and direct her toward the face painting so we can check on the kids.

THREE HOURS LATER, WE LEAD TWO TIRED, DIRTY, HAPPY KIDS BACK TO the main entrance to the estate and claim the car from the valet stand.

"What was your favorite part?" I ask them once we're on our way to our next destination. I can get away with heading away from home because Aileen hasn't lived here long enough to realize we're going the wrong way.

"Winning Daisy!" Maddie says of the pony.

"The tilt-a-whirl and the drone," Logan says. "When can we fly it?"

I catch his eye in the rearview mirror. "We'll take it to the park when we get home."

"Not tonight," Aileen says. "It'll be too late."

"Oh, come on, Mom! It's summer vacation."

I nudge her leg and send her a pleading look. By now I know better than to contradict her when it comes to things like bedtimes and eating vegetables.

"Thirty minutes tonight, and that's my final offer."

"Fine," Logan huffs.

I look at him in the mirror, raising a brow. "Logan?"

"Thanks, Mom," he says begrudgingly.

She smiles at me.

I wink at her.

We got this.

We're almost to our destination, about a mile from the estate where the carnival was held, when she tunes in to where we are.

"This isn't the way home."

"Isn't it?" The joyful feeling that's become so familiar in recent weeks takes flight once again. I'm so excited to surprise her, I can barely contain myself long enough to drive through the gates, pull up to the house and cut the engine.

"What is this place?" she asks, leaning in for a closer look.

"Come on in, and I'll tell you." Without giving her a chance to reply, I get out of the car and head for the front door to punch in the code I was given yesterday. I hear three car doors close behind me as I step inside and wait for them, taking a series of breaths to calm a sudden outburst of nerves. I've never done anything remotely like this. What if I get it wrong? What if she says no? What if...

Stop. The inner voice inside my head, the same one that once told me I was doing the right thing staying away from Aileen, now speaks up to let me know I'm getting wound up for nothing. She won't say no. She loves me like no one else ever has. I'm safe with her, and this is going to be the best day of our lives.

"Kristian, what're we doing here?"

The kids are uncharacteristically quiet, which I appreciate. They're in on the surprise, so they know to let it play out.

"Let me show you around, and then I'll tell you more."

"*Okay...*"

Maddie giggles at her mother's obvious befuddlement.

Logan, I notice, keeps a close eye on Aileen, looking for any signs of trouble. I hope that in time, he'll stop anticipating disaster around every corner and start acting more like a regular kid again. In the meantime, however, he watches her as I lead them into the huge kitchen that forms the heart of the big, open house. It's eight thousand square feet and has a separate suite for the kids who would each have their own bedroom and bathroom. It's also got a media room that Logan says is "sick," a game room, in-ground pool, pool house, outdoor kitchen and incredible views of the Pacific. On the other side of the pool house is a building that could be converted to a stable for Daisy the pony.

But the best part, at least in my opinion, is the master suite that takes up most of the second floor. It includes a huge bedroom with an adjoining bathroom and a cozy little hideaway where I can see us spending time alone together after the kids are asleep. There's a fireplace and glass walls that look out on the ocean. The master bedroom is what sold me on the place, and I can tell that Aileen loves it as much as I do.

Next to the master bedroom are three smaller bedrooms that we might fill someday with more kids. Hey, a guy can dream. She's shown me that it's safe to dream big.

But before I can see to future dreams, I need to seal the deal on the one I'm currently living.

"What do you think?" I ask her when we've checked out every room, the pool and the backyard. We're downstairs in the family room off the kitchen.

"It's... the most beautiful house I've ever seen. Whose is it?"

I've practiced what I'm going to say for days, and now that the moment is upon me, I use the trick that Flynn once told me he relies upon when memorizing lines. Nail the opening, he said, and the rest will come. Here goes nothing.

Rather than answer her question, I have one for her. "Remember when you said you need to register Logan and Maddie for school?"

"Yes," she says, obviously baffled. "What about it?"

"They have great public and private schools in Calabasas."

She looks at me in total confusion, those expressive eyes bigger than ever. "But we *live* in Venice Beach. That's where they'll go to school."

"Well, I was thinking that maybe we could all get a place together, and this house was on the market..."

She gasps, covers her mouth and takes another look at the foyer, the grand staircase, the formal living room on the left and the study on the right. "Wh-what've you done?"

"I bought this house for us. For all of us." I drop to my knees and hold out my hands to her.

Gasping again, she joins her trembling hands with mine.

I nod to the kids, urging them to come closer, and they stand on either side of her with their arms around her. "Aileen, I love you, and I love Logan and Maddie. I've waited all my life for a family of my own, and now that I have you guys, I want us to be a family in every way if you'll have me. There's nothing I wouldn't do for you or for them, and earlier today, Logan and Maddie told me they'd like for me to be their dad."

Tears roll down her face as she glances at her kids, looking for confirmation. "You guys knew about this?"

Maddie smiles up at her. "We kept the secret."

"You sure did!" She looks to Logan. "Are you okay with this, buddy?"

He nods. "I've always wanted a dad, and Kristian is already my best friend."

I blink back tears and release one of her hands so we can both dab at our eyes.

Before they ruin me completely, I ask the most important question of my life. "Will you please marry me and allow me to adopt your children so we can all live in this house happily ever after together and with any other children we may be blessed to have?"

"Yes," she says without hesitation even as tears continue to slide down her cheeks. "*Yes*, I'll marry you, and yes, you can adopt my children, who love you as much as I do."

"And the house?"

"The house is..."

The three of us wait breathlessly to hear what she will say.

"Perfect. Absolutely perfect."

As I slide a three-carat engagement ring on the finger of the woman I love and stand to hug my fiancée and children, I decide that word sums things up rather nicely.

My life, which was once a complete disaster, is now absolutely *perfect*. And it's all because of her.

∼

Keep reading for a sneak peek of *Outrageous!*

OUTRAGEOUS

QUANTUM SERIES BOOK 7

Chapter One

Leah

I want to lick him. I want to strip him naked and lick every hill and valley of his muscular body. I want to know if all his muscles are as big as the ones on his arms. I want to ride him like a cowgirl. And then I want to ride him like a *reverse* cowgirl.

My obsession with Emmett Burke began on my first day at Quantum Productions, where I work as assistant to mega star Marlowe Sloane, a Quantum partner and overall amazing, badass woman. On day one, Emmett was charged with reviewing the company's nondisclosure agreement with me. Even with Flynn Godfrey's assistant, Addie, sitting with us, I didn't hear a word Emmett said about the NDA because I was so fixated on his obscenely sexy mouth. Right there in the Quantum office, I had visions of all the places I'd like to feel that mouth.

Then he mentioned how I could be sued for discussing Quantum business or the partners outside of work, and that got my attention off his mouth, for a second or two, long enough to sign the NDA. I would never blow the amazing opportunity my friend Natalie secured for me after she fell in love with Flynn the superstar and ran away to Hollywood to marry him. But I sure would love the opportunity to blow Flynn's attorney.

At her wedding, Natalie hooked me up with Marlowe, who hired me on the spot and bought out my contract with the charter school I'd worked for in New York—unhappily, I might add. Teaching wasn't for me. Being the assistant to one of the top movie stars in the world? *Hell to the yes*, that's for me. Marlowe paid for my move to LA, and now that I'm here, doing a job I truly love, I'm the envy of everyone I know.

Telling tales out of school—no pun intended—is *not* going to happen. I'd never do anything to screw up this sweet deal and the amazing opportunity I've been given to have a career I couldn't have dreamed up for myself.

But me and Emmett Burke? That is *so* going to happen. If I can just figure out a way to break through his uptight, always-professional demeanor to find the hot-blooded man under the three-thousand-dollar suits that have to be handmade for him because no off-the-rack suit would fit those biceps.

In the meantime, I spend an inordinate amount of time thinking about licking him and trying to come up with reasons to talk to him. I wish I had the balls to come right out and tell him I want to suck his dick until he explodes down my throat, but something tells me that wouldn't be the best career move I could make.

While Emmett isn't one of the Quantum principals—and let me tell you, the word *principal* in this business is a whole lot different than it was in the school business—he is best friends and chief legal counsel to Flynn, Hayden, Marlowe, Jasper and Kristian, otherwise known as the bosses. That means I need to tread lightly and keep my drooling and licking to a minimum.

But God help that man if I ever get him alone in a bedroom—or any room that isn't an office in the building where we both work. I have to laugh at how ridiculous this obsession has become, because it's truly out of character for me. Before now, before Emmett, my interest in men has been more along lines of wham-bam-thank-you-sir. I've never actually given a shit about any of them. But this one... This one is different, and I knew it right away. Every time I've been with him since that first day, and I'm "with him" just about every day between work and play—these people love to party—I only want him more than I did the day before. It's insanity. I willingly admit that, but I have no desire to make it stop. No, my desire is entirely focused on making it *start*.

Sometimes, when I'm home alone at night with my trusty rabbit, I allow my wildest fantasies to take flight. I picture myself with Emmett in every conceivable position, as well as a few that haven't been invented yet. I've begun to anticipate rabbit time a little too eagerly, which is worrisome. I've never been the kind of girl to run from a challenge, but I suspect Emmett thinks I'm too young and immature for him.

There's really no one I can talk to about my "dilemma," since my closest friends here also work for Quantum or are married or engaged to the partners. Of course, they're the ones whose opinions I most want because they know him better than I ever will at this frustrating rate.

I'm going to have three whole days with him when we head up to Napa at the end of this coming week for Hayden and Addie's wedding. I've been counting the days with plans to implement Operation Nail Emmett Burke while we're there. I figure I only need to get Marlowe and Sebastian out of the way, because other than Emmett and me, they're the only ones who aren't in relationships. With lovebirds circling all around us, I expect the four of us to end up on our own quite a bit and will fully exploit any opportunities that present themselves without humiliating myself in front of Marlowe.

Fine line that'll be...

I've made up my mind that the weekend in Napa is *go* time. Enough fantasizing about what I'd do if I had a night with him. It's time to make those fantasies a reality. The thought of being naked and horizontal with him makes me wish I'd thought to bring my rabbit to work.

I'm supposed to be planning Marlowe's trip to Paris the week after Napa, but so far, I've only managed to accomplish making a list of things that have to be done. My obsession with Emmett is interfering with my dream job, and I can't let that happen. It's time to buckle down and plow through my to-do list so I can present Marlowe with a full itinerary when she returns from lunch with her agent.

I'm working on booking first-class plane tickets when the extension on my desk rings with a call from Addie's number. I take the call on speaker. "What's up, buttercup?" I *adore* Addie and aim to be just like her when I grow up into a world-class Hollywood assistant. She's endlessly generous with advice and counsel as I continue to get comfortable with my new job, and she's madly in love with Hayden Roth, the sexy, surly Academy-Award-winning director who is the heart and soul of Quantum.

"Can you come to the conference room for a quick meeting?"

"Yep. What do I need to bring?"

"Your laptop. Five minutes?"

"I'll be there." I'd do anything Addie asked of me. She's been instrumental in helping me to make the transition from fourth grade teacher in New York to assistant to a movie star in Hollywood. Sometimes I still can't believe I actually made that transition, but all I have to do is look out the window at the palm trees that line the Quantum parking lot to realize I'm not in the Big Apple anymore, Toto.

Don't get me wrong. I *loved* New York. I hated being a teacher, though. I have mad, crazy respect for people who can spend their days in rooms full of kids. I am not one of those people. I thought I was until I actually had to do it every day and realizing I had made a grave error in my life plan was jarring, to say the least. I worked with some truly amazing teachers, and their passion for the job helped me to see that I lacked what it took to give the kids the dedication they deserved.

I'd already decided I was leaving the job at the end of the school year when Natalie came up with the brilliant idea for Marlowe to hire me. Now that I've made the move, there's nothing I wouldn't do for the people here at Quantum, which is one reason I try to keep my massive crush on Emmett under control at work. I don't want to cause any trouble or embarrassment for Natalie, who went out on a limb to get me this amazing job, or Marlowe, who took a chance on a total newb for an assistant.

I gather up my laptop, a notebook and my phone and head into the conference room for the meeting. Who do you think is the only other person in the hallway? Yep, you guessed it. The object of my obsession, and oh my, he looks particularly lickable today in a navy pin-stripe suit with an ice blue tie and a white dress shirt that shows off a deep year-round tan that comes from surfing.

How do I know that? What don't I know about him? I'm obsessed, remember? Right now, I require all my wits to conduct an actual conversation with the man of my dreams.

"Emmett." Excellent opening salvo. I love the way his name sounds as it rolls off my tongue. Did someone say tongue? *No licking at work, Leah.*

"Leah."

Sigh. He said my name. "How are you today?"

"Fine, you?"

"Very, *very* good." Does he notice the suggestive way I say that or how my new two-hundred-dollar bra from La Perla makes my small boobs look a little more spectacular than they actually are? Never let it be said that I don't know how to properly invest my much larger LA salary.

"No legal dilemmas today?" he asks, his lips forming an expression that might be amusement. Dare I hope?

"Not yet, but you'll be the first to know if that should change."

"Oh goody," he says, his sarcasm making him even more attractive to me.

I absolutely *adore* sarcastic people. I *wrote the book* on sarcasm, and a sarcastic sense of humor is right at the top of my list of attractive qualities. With Emmett, sarcasm is number five on my list after sexy lips, sexy ass, sexy biceps and sexy, cut abs. You can see how sarcasm might take a distant fifth place to those things.

Ask him out after work.

I'm not sure where that thought comes from, but the words are falling from my mouth before I can decide if I should say them. "Do you want to get a drink after work? I'm buying to thank you for the legal advice."

"Oh, um, I can't, but thanks anyway." He moves past without so much as brushing against me. I mourn the missed opportunity for body contact. "Got to get back to it. Talk to you later."

"Bye." Okay, so that didn't go as well as it could have, but I didn't give him much advance notice. And he said he *couldn't*, not that he didn't *want* to. I take this as a positive sign and continue on my way to the conference room where Addie is waiting for me along with Ellie Godfrey's assistant, Dax, Kristian's assistant, Lori, and Aileen, our receptionist-slash-administrative assistant who also happens to be engaged to Kristian.

I take a seat across from Aileen, who offers a warm, welcoming smile. She's the sweetest person, always happy and willing to lend a hand where needed. We all love her, but no one more so than Kristian, who is positively *gone* over her—and her kids. The love circulating in the air around here has given me hope that it might happen for me someday. Hopefully, long after I get to take a spin or two around the bedroom a hot-as-fuck lawyer who doesn't realize yet that I'm exactly what he needs to lighten up a bit.

"Thanks for coming in you guys," Addie says.

I immediately notice that the always-unflappable Addie seems seriously flapped.

"What's wrong?" Dax asks.

"I'm freaking out," Addie confesses. "I told Hayden I didn't want a wedding planner overseeing our big day, and I've seen to everything myself, but I keep waking up in the middle of the night in a cold sweat and riddled with anxiety that I've missed something critical, like food or booze or *something*. I was hoping you guys could go over everything and double check me."

The most organized human being on the planet—hell, in the *universe*—wants my help? I'm in.

She hands out packets that contain detailed plans for the wedding that will take place at the Napa Valley winery owned by the Quantum partners. Pushing aside all thoughts of Emmett and licking, I focus exclusively on the information on the page, reading every word as the others do the same.

While we read, Addie paces.

Food, check. Booze, check. Flowers, check. Tent, check. Arbor built from grapevines for the ceremony, check. Tables and chairs and linens and centerpieces, check, check, check and check. Lodging for the entire Quantum group, check, including room assignments that I don't look at too closely, but I will, later. You can bet on that.

"Music," I say, breaking the long silence. "Where's the music?"

Addie stops pacing to stare at me. "It's in there."

"Where?"

She comes over to me, leans over my shoulder and sifts through the papers twice before letting out a shriek. *"I forgot the fucking music?"*

My first impulse is to try to calm her, but she's already around the bend from freaked out and is heading toward nuclear meltdown. The others realize it, too, and immediately spring into action.

"Who do we know?" Lori asks.

"Um, everyone?" Aileen says, her tone calm and controlled, which is what we need. "Who do you want, Addie? We are rather well-connected around here."

Addie is like a deer in high beams. "I, um, I don't even know who to ask."

"Let us take care of it," I say, as the others nod in agreement. "Tell us what kind of music you want, we'll figure it out for you and get someone great."

"It's *next* weekend."

"It's *Hayden Roth*," I remind her, as if she needs a reminder of who she's marrying or that he's the most celebrated director of his generation. I'm counting on the fact that just about anyone would *kill* to play at his wedding.

"Um, I'm almost afraid to ask," Aileen says, "but you do have a dress, right?"

"Yes, Tenley has taken care of that," she says, referring to her maid of honor, a top stylist to the stars.

"Oh phew," Aileen says, smiling. "Hayden already owns a tux and so do his groomsmen, so you're good there. What about your brides-maids? What are they wearing?"

Addie's eyes bug again, and I realize it's going to be a *long* day.

Emmett

She's driving me crazy. Does she think I don't notice her staring at me or how she has a different legal question every day, none of which have anything to do with her job as Marlowe's assistant? Two days ago, she wanted lease advice for a "friend" in New York with a landlord from hell. I'm an entertainment and corporate lawyer. What the hell do I know about leases in New York? Of course, she knows what my specialty is, but that doesn't stop her from finding a reason to ask me some stupid legal question every day.

It doesn't help that I want to toss her across my desk and fuck the sass right out of her. Maybe if I do that, she'll leave me alone.

But that can't and *won't* happen for many reasons, not the least of which is the ten-year age difference between us. We celebrated her *twenty-fourth* birthday with a cake in the office last week, and I swear she looked right at me as she licked frosting off her finger, completely oblivious to the fact that we were in the fucking office surrounded by our fucking coworkers, including the partners that fucking *employ me* to keep them out of the kind of trouble I want to get into with her.

She's *twenty-four*. I keep telling myself that puts her firmly off limits. She's young, naïve, inexperienced, vanilla and thoroughly out of her league with the likes of me.

Her best salvo yet came yesterday when she brought in the company handbook and asked for a clarification on the fraternization policy. Does she think I can't see right through her game? She came around my desk and leaned over me to point out the area that had her confused: *Employees must seek the written approval of their supervisor before embarking on a romantic relationship with a fellow employee, and no employee shall date or otherwise fraternize with an employee under their direct supervision.*

"Does that mean I need Marlowe's approval before I date someone from the office?"

"Yes," I'd said through gritted teeth, trying to ignore the press of her breast into my shoulder. "That's what it means. And your potential date needs to do the same. Now can I get back to work?" Who the hell is she thinking about dating anyway? And why the fuck do I care? Whoever it is, I pity the fool. She'd be a handful for the most patient of men.

"Is there a form or something we have to fill out before we embark on our relationship?"

"An email will suffice," I told her, my patience nonexistent where she's concerned. I had fourteen million things to see to on behalf of the five people who pay me a king's ransom to oversee their legal matters, and all I wanted to do was strip Marlowe's assistant naked and have my wicked way with her right there on my desk.

That's not how I roll. I'm a consummate professional. I value my job and friendships with my employers, both of which are the most important things in my life.

In this era of enhanced scrutiny on workplace behavior, I have no time or tolerance for a twenty-four-year-old troublemaker who wants to walk on the wild side. She can find someone else to go wild with.

Except... I no sooner have that thought that I'm filled with unreasonable rage at the idea of any other man's hands on her sweet, lithe body. When I first met her, I wasn't immediately attracted. No, that special treat came later, when I saw her in a bikini at Flynn's house and realized she was hiding a smoking body under conservative work clothes that don't begin to do her justice. Since then, I've made an effort to keep my mind—and my eyes—from wandering in directions they shouldn't go.

But when she was leaning over me, pressing a small but plump breast to my shoulder as she pointed out "inconsistencies" in the policy I drafted myself, it was damned *hard* to ignore her.

She's baiting me intentionally. I get it. She's set her sights on me because I'm one of two guys in our group who's still single after the love bug set off an epidemic of happily ever afters among our friends. Sebastian would squash her like a proverbial bug, so she probably sees me as the "safer" alternative to big, dark, broody Sebastian.

Little does she know that I have a wild side of my own, and if I ever let it loose on her, she'd run screaming for her young life. Part of me would enjoy that. A lot. But it's not going to happen.

Yesterday it was the fraternization policy. Today it was an invite for after-dinner drinks. What will tomorrow bring? As much as I wish she'd go away and leave me alone, I find myself wondering what she's got planned for me next.

Outrageous is available in print from *Amazon.com* and other online retailers, or you can purchase a signed copy from Marie's store at *marieforce.com/store*

ALSO BY MARIE FORCE

Contemporary Romances Available from Marie Force

The Quantum Series

Book 1: Virtuous *(Flynn & Natalie)*

Book 2: Valorous *(Flynn & Natalie)*

Book 3: Victorious *(Flynn & Natalie)*

Book 4: Rapturous *(Addie & Hayden)*

Book 5: Ravenous *(Jasper & Ellie)*

Book 6: Delirious *(Kristian & Aileen)*

Book 7: Outrageous *(Emmett & Leah)*

Book 8: Famous *(Marlowe & Sebastian)*

The Gansett Island Series

Book 1: Maid for Love *(Mac & Maddie)*

Book 2: Fool for Love *(Joe & Janey)*

Book 3: Ready for Love *(Luke & Sydney)*

Book 4: Falling for Love *(Grant & Stephanie)*

Book 5: Hoping for Love *(Evan & Grace)*

Book 6: Season for Love *(Owen & Laura)*

Book 7: Longing for Love *(Blaine & Tiffany)*

Book 8: Waiting for Love *(Adam & Abby)*

Book 9: Time for Love *(David & Daisy)*

Book 10: Meant for Love *(Jenny & Alex)*

Book 10.5: Chance for Love, *A Gansett Island Novella (Jared & Lizzie)*

Book 11: Gansett After Dark *(Owen & Laura)*

Book 12: Kisses After Dark *(Shane & Katie)*

Book 13: Love After Dark *(Paul & Hope)*

Book 14: Celebration After Dark *(Big Mac & Linda)*

Book 15: Desire After Dark *(Slim & Erin)*

Book 16: Light After Dark *(Mallory & Quinn)*

Book 17: Victoria & Shannon (Episode 1)

Book 18: Kevin & Chelsea (Episode 2)

A Gansett Island Christmas Novella

Book 19: Mine After Dark *(Riley & Nikki)*

Book 20: Yours After Dark *(Finn & Chloe)*

Book 21: Trouble After Dark *(Deacon & Julia)*

Book 22: Rescue After Dark *(Mason & Jordan)*

Book 23: Blackout After Dark *(Full Cast)*

Book 24: Temptation After Dark *(Gigi & Cooper)*

The Green Mountain Series

Book 1: All You Need Is Love *(Will & Cameron)*

Book 2: I Want to Hold Your Hand *(Nolan & Hannah)*

Book 3: I Saw Her Standing There *(Colton & Lucy)*

Book 4: And I Love Her *(Hunter & Megan)*

Novella: You'll Be Mine *(Will & Cam's Wedding)*

Book 5: It's Only Love *(Gavin & Ella)*

Book 6: Ain't She Sweet *(Tyler & Charlotte)*

The Butler, Vermont Series

(Continuation of Green Mountain)

Book 1: Every Little Thing *(Grayson & Emma)*

Book 2: Can't Buy Me Love *(Mary & Patrick)*

Book 3: Here Comes the Sun *(Wade & Mia)*

Book 4: Till There Was You *(Lucas & Dani)*

Book 5: All My Loving *(Landon & Amanda)*

Book 6: Let It Be *(Lincoln & Molly)*

Book 7: Come Together *(Noah & Brianna)*

The Treading Water Series

Book 1: Treading Water

Book 2: Marking Time

Book 3: Starting Over

Book 4: Coming Home

Book 5: Finding Forever

The Miami Nights Series

Book 1: How Much I Feel *(Carmen & Jason)*

Book 2: How Much I Care *(Maria & Austin)*

Book 3: How Much I Love *(Dee's story)*

Single Titles

Five Years Gone

One Year Home

Sex Machine

Sex God

Georgia on My Mind

True North

The Fall

The Wreck

Love at First Flight

Everyone Loves a Hero

Line of Scrimmage

Romantic Suspense Novels Available from Marie Force

The Fatal Series

One Night With You, *A Fatal Series Prequel Novella*

Book 1: Fatal Affair

Book 2: Fatal Justice

Book 3: Fatal Consequences

Book 3.5: Fatal Destiny, *the Wedding Novella*

Book 4: Fatal Flaw

Book 5: Fatal Deception

Book 6: Fatal Mistake

Book 7: Fatal Jeopardy

Book 8: Fatal Scandal

Book 9: Fatal Frenzy

Book 10: Fatal Identity

Book 11: Fatal Threat

Book 12: Fatal Chaos

Book 13: Fatal Invasion

Book 14: Fatal Reckoning

Book 15: Fatal Accusation

Book 16: Fatal Fraud

The First Family Series

Book 1: State of Affairs

Historical Romance Available from Marie Force

The Gilded Series

Book 1: Duchess by Deception

Book 2: Deceived by Desire

ABOUT THE AUTHOR

Marie Force is the *New York Times* best-
selling author of contemporary romance,
romantic suspense and erotic romance. Her
series include Gansett Island, Fatal, Treading
Water, Butler Vermont, Quantum and Miami
Nights.

Her books have sold more than 10
million copies worldwide, have been translated into more than a
dozen languages and have appeared on the *New York Times* bestseller
more than 30 times. She is also a *USA Today* and *Wall Street Journal*
bestseller, as well as a Speigel bestseller in Germany.

Her goals in life are simple—to finish raising two happy, healthy,
productive young adults, to keep writing books for as long as she
possibly can and to never be on a flight that makes the news.

Join Marie's mailing list on her website at marieforce.com for
news about new books and upcoming appearances in your area.
Follow her on Facebook at www.Facebook.com/MarieForceAuthor
and on Instagram at www.instagram.com/marieforceauthor/. Contact
Marie at marie@marieforce.com.

CPSIA information can be obtained
at www.ICGtesting.com
Printed in the USA
LVHW070720110623
749447LV00021B/213

9 781946 136237